HOMER'S
DAUGHTER

HOMER'S DAUGHTER

ROBERT GRAVES

Academy
Chicago

© 1955 by Robert Graves

Academy Chicago edition 1982
425 N. Michigan Ave.
Chicago, IL 60611

Library of Congress Cataloging in Publication Data
Graves, Robert, 1895–
  Homer's daughter.
  Reprint. Originally published: 1st ed. Garden City, N.Y.:
Doubleday, 1955.
  Summary: Nausicaa, a Sicilian princess of the eighth century B.C., looks
back on the events of her life and tells how she came to write the epic poem
known as the *Odyssey*.
  1. Nausicaa—Fiction. 2. Sicily—History—To 800—Fiction. 3. Homer
in fiction, drama, poetry, etc. [1. Nausicaa—Fiction. 2. Sicility—History—
To 800—Fiction. 3.Homer in Fiction, drama, poetry, etc.] i. Title.
PR6013.R35H6 1982 823'.912 [Fic] 82-16383
ISBN 0-89733-058-7
ISBN 0-89733-059-5 (pbk.)

To Selwyn Jepson, of course

HISTORICAL NOTE

THE SONS OF HOMER, a guild of travelling minstrels who claimed descent from the famous blind poet and
owned a large repertory of heroic sagas, were in classical
times based on the sacred island of Delos. They went from
city to city throughout Greece, Asia Minor, Sicily, Italy
and North Africa, enjoying protection and hospitality every-
where. Their sagas were ascribed to Homer himself, though
it was an open secret that many of them were of recent
composition. Since the most ancient and famous of the whole
collection was the *Iliad*, which concerned the Siege of Troy,
the Sons of Homer enlarged the Trojan cycle with new sagas
explaining what had happened before and afterwards. For
instance, they composed a number of tragic "Returns," tell-

ing how the Greek survivors of the ten-year war sailed home, but were either wrecked on the voyage or driven far out of their course, and returned only to find their wives unfaithful and their thrones usurped.

The *Odyssey*, though invariably ascribed to Homer, was composed at least a hundred and fifty years later than the *Iliad* and the atmosphere is altogether different: sweeter, more humorous, more civilized. The *Iliad* is a poem about and for men, the *Odyssey* (despite its male hero) is a poem about and for women. Whoever wrote it had read the greater part of the Homeric sagas which are still extant in whole or part, except the very latest, and seems to have worked from an original *Return of Odysseus*. But the saga has been recast, only the prologue and a few score lines being preserved more or less as they stood. The original Odysseus, it seems, found his wife Penelope living riotously with fifty lovers, all of whom he killed on his return to Ithaca, and after sending her home to her father in disgrace, was himself accidentally transfixed with a sting-ray spear by his long-lost son Telemachus, who had landed unannounced and did not recognize him. Odysseus's "many cities," mentioned in the prologue, have been reduced to two and the rest replaced by ungeographical islands borrowed from an entirely different story —an allegorical myth of one Ulysses, famous for his frequent cunning evasions of death. But once the saga element and the allegorical element have been isolated, what remains of the *Odyssey* is intimate domestic description of Greek provincial life in the far west about the year 750 B.C. The central character is Princess Nausicaa, daughter of King

Alcinous and Queen Arete of Phaeacia—another ungeographical place.

Apollodorus, the leading classical authority on Greek myths, records a tradition that the real scene of the poem was the Sicilian seaboard, and in 1896 Samuel Butler, the author of *Erewhon,* came independently to the same conclusion. He suggested that the poem, as we now have it, was composed at Drepanum, the modern Trapani, in Western Sicily, and that the authoress was the girl self-portrayed as Nausicaa. None of his classical contemporaries, for whom Homer was necessarily both blind and bearded, deigned to pay Butler's theory the least attention; and since he had, as we now know, dated the poem some three hundred years too early and not explained how a Sicilian princess could have passed off her saga as Homer's, his two books on the subject are generally dismissed as a good-humoured joke.

Nevertheless, while working on an explanatory dictionary of Greek myths, I found Butler's arguments for a Western Sicilian setting and for a female authorship irrefutable. I could not rest until I had written this novel. It re-creates, from internal and external evidence, the circumstances which induced Nausicaa to write the *Odyssey,* and suggest how, as an honorary Daughter of Homer, she managed to get it included in the official canon. Here is the story of a high-spirited and religious-minded Sicilian girl who saves her father's throne from usurpation, herself from a distasteful marriage, and her two younger brothers from butchery by boldly making things happen, instead of sitting still and hoping for the best.

CONTENTS

HOMER'S
DAUGHTER

PROLOGUE

WHEN MY CHILDHOOD HAD SLIPPED BY, and the days no longer seemed eternal but had shrunk to twelve hours or less, I began to think seriously about death. It was my grandmother's funeral procession, in which half the women of Drepanum marched, lamenting like curlews, that made me conscious of my own mortality. Soon I should marry, bear children, grow stout, old and ugly—or thin, old and ugly—and presently die. Leaving what behind? Nothing. Expecting what? Worse than nothing: everlasting half darkness, where the ghosts of my ancestors and ancestresses wander about an unfeatured plain, gibbering like bats; skilled in all the lore of past and future, yet forbidden to profit from it; still endowed with such human passions as jealousy, lust, hatred and greed, but powerless to consummate them. How long is a day when one is dead?

A few nights later my grandmother appeared to me in a vision. Three times I sprang towards her and tried to hug her, but each time she stepped aside. I was deeply hurt and asked: "Grandmother, why will you not stay still when I try to kiss you?"

"Darling," she answered, "all mortals are like this when they are dead. Sinews no longer constrain their flesh and bones, which perish in the cruel flame of the pyre; and the soul flits away like a dream. Do not think I love you less; but I have no substance."

Our priests assure us that certain heroes and heroines, children of the Gods, enjoy an enviable immortality in the Islands of the Blessed; a fancy which the tellers themselves do not believe. Of this I am certain: that no true life exists beyond the life we know, namely the life beneath the sun, moon and stars. The dead are dead, even though we pour libations of blood for their ghosts to drink, hoping to give them an illusion of temporary rebirth. And yet——

And yet there are the songs of Homer. Homer died two hundred years ago, or more, and we still speak of him as though he were living. We say that Homer records, not that he recorded, such and such an event. He lives far more truly even than do Agamemnon and Achilles, Ajax and Cassandra, Helen and Clytaemnestra, and the others of whom he wrote in his epic of the Trojan War. They are mere shadows, given substance by his songs; which alone retain the force of life, the power to soothe or stir or draw tears. Homer is now, and will be when all my contemporaries are dead and forgotten: I have

even heard it prophesied, impiously, that he will outlast
Father Zeus himself, though not the Fates.

Brooding on these things at the age of fifteen, I grew melancholy and reproached the Gods for not making me immortal; and envied Homer. This was odd, certainly, in a girl,
and our housekeeper Eurycleia often shook her head at me
when I mooned about the Palace with a set, downcast face,
instead of enjoying myself like others of my age. I never
answered her, but thought: "And you, dear Eurycleia, have
nothing left in store for you but ten or twenty years at the
most, during which your strength will gradually decline and
your rheumatic pains increase, and then what? How long is
a day when you are dead?"

This preoccupation of mine with death excuses, or at least
explains, the most unusual decision I have recently taken: of
securing for myself a posthumous life under the mantle of
Homer. May the Blessed Gods, who see all, and whom I never
neglected to honour, grant me success in this endeavour, and
conceal the fraud. Phemius the bard has sworn an unbreakable oath to put my epic poem in circulation: thus paying
the debt he incurred on that bloody afternoon when, at the risk
of my own life, I saved him from the two-edged sword.

As for my condition and lineage: I am a princess of the
Elymans, a mixed race living on and about Eryx, the great,
bee-haunted mountain which dominates the westernmost
corner of three-sided Sicily and takes its name from the
heather upon which countless bees pasture. We Elymans pride
ourselves on being the remotest nation of the civilized world;
though this is, indeed, to disregard certain flourishing Greek
colonies planted in Spain, and Mauretania since we first

made the boast—not to mention the Phoenicians, who, though non-Greek and addicted to barbarous human sacrifice, have some claim to be called civilized, and are established at Carthage, Utica and elsewhere on the African coast. I must now give a brief account of our origins. My father claims direct male descent from the hero Aegestus. Aegestus was born in Sicily, a son of the River God Crimissus and the exiled Trojan noblewoman Aegesta, but is said to have sailed to Troy at King Priam's request when King Agamemnon of Mycenae besieged the city. Troy, however, was fated to fall, and Aegestus had been fortunate to escape death among the Achaean spears. Roused from sleep by his kinsman Aeneas the Dardanian, as soon as the enemy, breaking into Troy, began to massacre the drowsy inhabitants, he led a party of Trojans out through the Scaean Gate and away to Abydus; Abydus being a fortress on the Hellespont where (so they say), mindful of a prophetic warning given by his mother, he kept three well-provisioned ships moored in readiness. Aeneas also escaped. Cutting his way through the Achaean forces to Mount Ida, he made preparations there for embarking his Dardanian subjects in a fleet beached at Percote, and presently followed in Aegestus's wake.

A fresh gale carried Aegestus south-westward across the Aegean Sea, past Cythera, Aphrodite's island; and westward across the Sicanian Sea, until he sighted Etna, the ever-burning mountain, which rises on the opposite side of Sicily from us. Here he landed and drew water for his fleet before steering south to round Cape Pelorus. Five days later, the Aegadean Islands rose into view, and he thankfully beached his ships in the landlocked bay of Rheithrum, under the shadow of

Mount Eryx, where he had been born. A blue halcyon bird skimmed past the ships' sterns, and at this sign of favour from the Goddess Thetis, who calms the sea, Aegestus burned them in her honour; but first he prudently unloaded all the cargo, cordage, sails, metal, and other objects which might be of use to him ashore. It was to commemorate this sacrifice, offered some four hundred years ago, that my parents named me Nausicaa, which means "Burning of Ships".

No other Greek-speaking colonists had as yet settled in Western Sicily. The entire island, except for a few Cretan colonies, was then inhabited by Sicans, an Iberian race, many of whom had befriended Aegestus and his mother in their strong city of Eryx, which nestles on the mountain's knees. Aegestus approached their King, his foster-father, with noble gifts of cauldrons, tripods, and bronze weapons fetched from Troy, interceding for the Trojan refugees; and though, being a naturally morose and self-sufficient race, the Sicans of Eryx did not disguise their suspicions, the King at last persuaded his council to let Aegestus build himself a city nearly at the top of the mountain. Aegestus named it Hypereia, or "Upper Town"; and bought from the Sicans a large stock of sheep, goats, cattle and hogs. Soon Aeneas arrived with six more ships, on his way to Latium, and proved his friendship by helping Aegestus to complete the city walls. He also founded the Temple of Aphrodite on the summit—an erotic institution in favour of which I have little to say; though Aeneas's act was a pious one, Aphrodite being his mother. At first the people of Hypereia lived on neighbourly terms with those of Eryx, who showed them all the riches of the mountain and, in return, were taught the finer mysteries of smithcraft and carpentry, besides the art of harpooning tunny and sword-fish from a platform set halfway up the ship's mast. The two nations being united in their devotion to the Sican Mountain Goddess Elyme—whom our people identified with Aphrodite, though she bore a far closer resemblance to the Goddess Alphito of Arcadia—we are now known as Elymans.

Some seven generations later, another element, the Pho-caean, was added to the Elyman nation thus formed; and by then the proud Achaean cities of the Peloponnese, in which the destruction of Troy had been planned, lay ruined. Bar-barous Dorians, the so-called Sons of Hercules, wielding iron weapons, and with iron hearts, had swept through the Isthmus of Corinth, burned citadel after citadel, and driven the Achae-ans from their rich pastures and cornfields into the mountain-ous regions of the North; there they still survive, dwindled and inglorious. The elder inhabitants of Greece, however—Pelasgians, Ionians and Aeolians—as many as loved liberty and possessed ships, hastily gathered together their treasures and set sail to find new homes overseas, especially on the coast of Asia Minor, where they had often before gone trad-ing. Among these emigrants were Phocians from Mount Par-nassus, descendants of Philoctetes the archer, whose arrows accounted for Prince Paris at Troy; but two Athenian noble-men led them. Their new city of Phocaea, built on the main-land behind Chios, became famous for its fifty-oared mer-chant-galleys which ventured across the length and breadth of the Mediterranean: as far westward as the Pillars of Her-cules, and as far northward as the mouth of the Po. Geryon, King of Tartessus in Southern Spain, having taken a liking to certain honest Phocaean traders, invited these to settle in

his country, and promised to build them a city. They agreed
with joy, and sailed home to fetch their wives, children,
household goods and sacred images; expecting to find the city
walls already raised to receive them when they landed in the
following summer.

Yet the Blessed Gods disposed otherwise. The colonists sailing in convoy, their prows wreathed in myrtle, were blown off
course by a north-easterly gale and cast ashore among the
lotus-eating Nasamonians of Libya. Though they saved five
of their seven ships, these proved so unseaworthy that, taking
advantage of a brisk south wind, they steered for Sicily, the
nearest land where it would be possible to refit. Mount Eryx
was reached in safety, with every hold deep in water, and they
beached the flotilla at Rheithrum, not having lost a man,
though their provisions were spoilt. Believing that the God
Poseidon had designed them to settle hereabouts rather than
in Tartessus—the myrtle on their prows forbade their return
—they came as suppliants to the King of Hypereia, who
magnanimously forgave them the wrongs which their ancestors had done to the Trojans. It is said, nevertheless, that
the captain and crew of one ship attempted to sail back to
Asia Minor, but they had gone no farther than a mile and a
half before Poseidon transformed the ship into a rock; and
there she still rides for all the world to see. They call her the
"Rock of Evil Counsel", and also add that Poseidon threatened
to topple down the summit of Eryx on the heads of any other
would-be deserters.

Now, the Hypereians had built a hamlet on the northern
foothills of Eryx and named it Aegesta, after their ancestress;
as they also named its two streams Simoïs and Scamander,

after the Trojan rivers mentioned by Homer. Here, with the permission of the King of Eryx, they had set up a hero shrine for the ghost of Anchises the Dardanian, Aeneas's father, who was said to have died during the building of Hypereia. The Phocaeans using Sican labour and adopting the Sican style, soon enlarged this village to a city, over which a prince of Hypereia was appointed to rule. But the wild Sicans, resentful of this new encroachment on their grazing and hunting grounds, did not hesitate to ambush and kill the newcomers; and Eurymedon, the Sican King of Eryx, refused to intervene, declaring that he had never consented to the Phocaean occupation of Aegesta. He even lent his compatriots secret help; and this naturally precipitated a quarrel between the cities of Eryx and Hypereia. Armed clashes led to a full-scale war, in which Eurymedon was soundly defeated. The Hypereians seized Eryx, proclaiming their own King "Father of the Elyman League"—Eryx, Hypereia, and Aegesta—and ordered the city councils to foster intermarriage between the three races. Our blood is therefore mixed, yet our ruling tongue is Ionian Greek, touched a little with Aeolian; and though remotely placed, we are far better people in every way than the Dorians of the Peloponnese, who camp sluttishly among the blackened ruins of the beautiful cities celebrated in Homer's songs.

This land of ours is good and its seas full of fish—especially tunny, the firm flesh of which has always been our staple food; but if we are entitled to one complaint, it is that the greater part of the Sican nation has obstinately refused to join our Elyman League. The Sicans are wild, tall, sturdy, uncouth, tattooed, unhospitable, prolific folk, who respect neither travellers nor suppliants, and live like beasts in mountain caves, each family apart, with its flocks. They acknowledge no king, and no deity except the Goddess Elyme, worshipped as a fertile, prescient sow, and no law but their own inclination; moreover, they brew no liquor, use neither iron nor bronze weapons, never venture out to sea, keep no markets, and will not even shrink at certain seasons from the taste of human flesh. With these abominable savages—I am ashamed to call them our cousins—we are neither at peace nor at war; wise travellers, however, pass through their land only in well-armed companies, sending hounds ahead to raise the alarm should an ambush have been laid in any forest or narrow defile.

At least we had the good fortune to live out of the way of the Sicel invasion, which took place shortly before the arrival of the Phocaeans. The Sicels are Illyrians, of an entirely different stock from the Sicans, who crossed the Strait of Messina on rafts and, being busy and numerous, soon possessed themselves of Central and Southern Sicily, swallowing up the settlements planted there by Cretans and Achaeans. But all war bands exploring in our direction were driven off with heavy loss—they are not so sturdily built as the Sicans, nor such formidable fighters—and ever since, by tacit agreement, the Sicels have kept within their own boundaries, leaving us alone. Their commerce is mainly with the Greeks of Euboea and Corinth. A few small Phoenician trading posts on promontories or small islands off the north coast have caused us no trouble so far; for, as my father says, "Trade begets trade." And now Greek colonies are being planted to the east of us, and on the toe of Italy; which pleases us well.

To come down to more recent times: my great-grandfather, King Nausithous, son of Eurymedon's daughter, called a council of all the Elymans to deliberate on a vision which had been granted him in a dream. He saw an eagle swoop from the top of Eryx and skim the sea, in company with a flock of white-winged sea mews, some of them on his right hand, some on his left. This vision the soothsayers interpreted as a divine command to quit Hypereia and henceforth make his living from the sea, on a spit of land between two harbours. Leaving behind a strong force to guard his cattlemen, shepherds and swineherds against the depredations of Sican bandits, Nausithous led down the greater part of the Hypereians to a sickle-shaped peninsula two miles south of Rheithrum, where he built the town of Drepanum. According to a local tradition it was here that the ancient God Cronus threw into the sea the adamantine sickle with which he had castrated his father Uranus; and old men sometimes whisper darkly: "One day it will be fetched up in a net; Apollo is fated to use it against his father Zeus."

Drepanum was a splendid site for Nausithous's new town. The neck of the peninsula could be protected by a wall from Sican raids, and of the two harbours specified by the oracle, one sheltered ships against north-westerly gales, the other against south-easterly ones. Since, therefore, the Phocaeans of Aegesta, whom Nausithous invited to join him in this enterprise, had not forgotten their sea skill, he was soon sending fifty-oared ships on long voyages in every direction. The chief Elyman exports, then as now, were wine, cheeses, honey, fleeces, sun-dried tunny and swordfish, and other food products; as well as folding bedsteads of cypress wood, in the manufacture of which we excel, embroidered clothes of the finest wool, and salt from our salt pans. These goods were exchanged for Cyprian copper, Spanish tin, Chalybean iron, Cretan wine, Corinthian painted ware, African sponges and ivory, and many other luxuries. Our two sandy harbours proved of great advantage, since if ever the weather shows signs of changing, ships can be rowed from one to the other, and hauled up beyond reach of the waves. In short, we have grown rich and prosperous, and are welcomed by all nations with whom we trade as honest men and no pirates. Rheithrum, however, is now rarely used as a harbour, not being defensible against raids, and has of late been silting up; but we sacrifice there annually to Aphrodite and Poseidon, and graze our cattle on the neighbouring plain.

My father, King Alpheides, married the daughter of an ally, the Lord of Hiera, largest of the Aegadean Islands. She bore him four sons and one daughter, myself. At the point where this story begins, Laodamas, my eldest brother, was already married to Ctimene of Bucinna, another island of the Aegadean group; Halius, the second, driven from home by my father's displeasure, had gone to live among the Sicels of Minoa; Clytoneus, the third, had shaved his first manly hair and taken arms. I was three years older than Clytoneus, and unmarried—but by choice, not from lack of suitors, though I may as well confess that I am neither tall nor particularly beautiful. My fourth brother, Telegonus, the child of our mother's middle age, still lived in the women's quarters, rolling nuts or riding a dappled hobbyhorse, and being threatened with King Echetus, the bogeyman, if he did not behave. In the poem which I have now completed my parents appear as King

Alcinous and Queen Arete of Drepane—the royal couple who welcomed Jason and Medea in the *Song of the Golden Fleece*. I chose these names partly because "Alcinous" means "Strong-minded", and my father prides himself most on his strong-mindedness; partly because Arete (if you shorten the second *e*) means "Staunchness", which is my mother's ruling virtue; and partly because, at the crisis of my drama, I was forced to play Medea's part. So much, then, for that.

CHAPTER
ONE
THE AMBER
NECKLACE

ONE LUCKLESS EVENING, three years ago, when my brother Laodamas had been married for only a short time, the southern wind we call sirocco began to blow, and a great cloud brooded heavily on the shoulders of Mount Eryx. The effect was, as usual, to wither the plants in the garden, put my hair out of curl and make everyone touchy and quarrelsome: my sister-in-law Ctimene not the least. That night, as soon as she found herself alone with Laodamas in their stifling bedroom, which was on the upper storey overlooking the banqueting court, she began to reproach him for his idleness and lack of enterprise. Ctimene enlarged on the great value of her dowry, and asked him whether he were not ashamed to spend his days hunting or fishing, instead of winning wealth by bold adventures overseas.

Laodamas laughed, and answered lightly that she had only herself to blame: it was her fresh beauty that kept him at home. "Once I tire of your delectable body, Wife, I shall certainly sail away—as far as any ship can take me, to the Land of Colchis and the Stables of the Sun, if need be—but that time is not come."

Ctimene said crossly: "Yes, you do not seem destined to tire of my embraces for a long while yet, the way you pester me with your nightly attentions. But at the first streak of dawn, off you go, eager only for your hounds, your boar spear, and your bow. I never see you again until nightfall, when you eat like a wolf, drink like a porpoise, play a foxy game or two of chess, and lurch along to bed once more to smother me with your hot, bearish caresses."

"You would not think much of me if I failed in my husbandly duty."

"A husband's duty is not performed only between linen sheets."

It was as when a long-armed boxer manages to keep his small, hard-hitting opponent at a distance with left-handed jabs, until at last he slips under the tall fellow's guard and pummels him below the heart. Laodamas grew rattled, but showed that he, too, was no novice at in-fighting. "Do you expect me to lounge around the house all day," he asked, "telling you stories while you spin, skeining the wool, and running errands for you? I intend to remain at Drepanum until you have obliged me by becoming pregnant—if, indeed, you are not barren, like your aunt and your elder sister—but while I am still here it is certainly a manlier pastime to hunt wild goats or wild boars than to kill the hours between break-

fast and supper as most young men of my age and rank do:
namely to drink, dice, dance, gossip in the market place,
fish with line, hook and float from the quay, and play quoits
in the courtyard. Or perhaps you would prefer me to spin and
weave myself, as Hercules did in Lydia, when Queen Om-
phale bewitched him?"

"I want a necklace," said Ctimene suddenly. "I want a
beautiful necklace of Hyperborean amber, with nubbly gold
beads between the lumps, and a golden clasp shaped like two
serpents with interlocking tails."

"Oh, you do? And where is such a treasure to be had?"

"Eurymachus's mother already owns one, and Captain
Dymas has promised another to his daughter Procne, Nau-
sicaa's friend, when he returns from his next voyage to Sandy
Pylus."

"Do you perhaps wish me to ambush his ship as she sails
home past Motya and steal the necklace for you—in the
Bucinnan style?"

"I refuse to understand your joke against my island—if
it is supposed to be a joke. No, do not dare kiss me! The wind
is cruel and I have a headache. Go away, and sleep elsewhere.
Dawn, I hope, will find you in a more reasonable frame of
mind."

"I may not kiss my wife good night, is this what you mean?
Take care that I do not send you back to your father, dowry
and all!"

"Dowry and all? That will not be easy. Of the two hundred
copper ingots and twenty bales of linen salvaged from the
Sidonian ship which my father found drifting, crewless, off
Bucinna . . ."

"Drifting, do you say? He murdered the entire crew in traditional Bucinnan style; as is well known in every market place of Sicily."

". . . of copper ingots and bales of linen, I repeat, you invested nearly half in a Libyan trading venture. They were to be bartered for herb Benjamin, gold dust and ostrich eggs; but I doubt whether you will see them again."

"Women can never believe that once a ship has raised anchor and spread her sails she will ever make port."

"I am not questioning the seaworthiness of the ship, but only the integrity of her captain, whom you were a fool to trust on the advice of your friend Eurymachus. It would not be the first time that a Libyan defaulted, and if anyone tells me that Eurymachus demanded a commission for his part in the fraud, I shall believe him."

"Look, this argument can be doing your headache very little good," said Laodamas. "Let me fetch you a bowl of water and a soft cloth to bathe your temples. The sirocco is killing us all."

What he intended for kindness she took as irony. After lying silent and inert until he brought the silver bowl to her bedside, she sat up suddenly, seized it from him, and deluged him with water.

"To cool down your hot thighs, Priapus!" she screamed.

Laodamas did not lose his temper and take her by the throat, as many a more impetuous man would have done. I never knew him to lay violent hands on a woman, not even to chastise a saucy slave girl. He merely cast Ctimene a baleful look and said: "Very well, then: you shall have your necklace, never fear, and may it bring less sorrow on our house than did the necklace of Theban Eriphyle in the Homeric song!"

He walked over to a nail-studded wooden chest, unlocked it, and took out a number of personal possessions—a gold cup, a helmet with an ostrich-feather plume, a buckle of silver and lapis lazuli, a new pair of scarlet shoes, three undershirts, a jewel-hilted dagger in an ivory sheath carved with lions pursuing a royal stag, and a fine whetstone from Seriphos. He pulled the helmet on his head, spread a thick cloak of striped wool on the floor and laid the treasures in it. Then he locked the chest, replaced the key on the nail above the bed head, caught up the bundle, and fumbled at the latch.

"Where are you taking those things? I demand to know. Put them back at once! I have something to tell you."

Laodamas paid no attention, but walked out, bundle on shoulder.

"To the crows with you, then, madman!" screamed Ctimene.

This conversation took place about midnight. My bedroom was next door, and my hearing being unusually acute when I have a touch of fever, as I had then, every word reached me. Slipping hurriedly into my shift, I ran after Laodamas and caught him by the sleeve. "Where are you going, Brother?" I asked.

He looked at me dully. He had been drinking sweet dark wine that evening, and though his gait was steady, I could see that he was by no means himself.

"I am going to the crows, little Sister," he answered sadly. "Ctimene has consigned me to their care."

"Please, pay no attention to what your wife may have said tonight," I begged him. "A sirocco is blowing; and at this time of the month she is never at her best."

"She demands a necklace of amber with nubbly gold beads,

and a clasp of interlocking golden snakes. It has to be pale
Hyperborean amber; our own darker variety does not content
her, though it has a lovely play of purple which occurs in no
other. I mean to fetch her what she wants: in proof that I am
neither idle nor a coward."

"From where? From the crows?"

"Or the jackdaws . . . I cannot let her abuse me again as
she has done. All the maids must have been listening, and
soon the story will travel around the city. When it reaches
Eurymachus and his friends, they will call me a fool for not
taking a strap to her."

"No strap ever cured either a shrew or a sick woman."

"I agree; though if I loved Ctimene in a different way I
might think otherwise. It is to keep my hands from violence
that I am leaving her."

"For how long?"

"Until I can bring her the necklace. Two or three months'
separation may do us both a deal of good."

"I heard you mention the necklace of Eryphyle, which
was a word of ill omen. Unless you offer a sacrifice to the
Goddess of our Hearth, and another to Aphrodite, the safety
of our whole household will be endangered. Do not go off
with your wrong foot thrust forward. Stop, and replace those
things in the chest."

"And ask Ctimene's pardon, I suppose? No, I cannot turn
back now. Some god is urging me on. Good night, Sister! We
shall meet when we shall meet."

The story of Eryphyle is part of the famous Theban cycle
which the Sons of Homer recite. This hateful woman was married to King Amphiaraus the Argive but, for the sake of

Aphrodite's necklace, which made its wearer irresistibly beautiful, she sent him to his death at Thebes.

Laodamas clumped slowly downstairs, and I heard him growling at the porter to unbar the front gate. Presently I leaned out of my window and saw him in the moonlight on his way towards the quay, where a big Rhodian ship was tied up. I thought of rousing my father, but knowing that he had fallen into a deep, refreshing sleep, after three days of fever, dared not disturb him with what might prove a matter of little importance. Ctimene herself treated it as such. Laodamas, she told herself, would not retract his insulting remarks about her father, nor listen when she tried to apologize for having lost her temper. So she turned her face to the wall with a good conscience, and was soon fast asleep.

I lay awake in the moonlight until I heard a distant burst of singing, as if a crowd of men had come pouring out of some storehouse or other; and, in the chorus of drunken laughter which followed, I recognized Eurymachus's high-pitched cackle.

"All is well," I thought wearily. "Eurymachus is still about. How I dislike him; but he will at least prevent my brother from behaving rashly or stupidly."

CHAPTER

TWO

THE PALACE

WHEN, NEXT MORNING, we found that the Rhodian ship had disappeared, taking advantage of a sudden change of wind, and that Laodamas was also missing, I hurriedly visited the Temple of Poseidon, where Eurymachus would soon be offering the monthly sacrifice of a red bull, to ask him what he knew of the matter.

"Nothing at all, my dear Princess. Why should I?" he answered stolidly, leaning on the sacrificial axe, and looking straight into my eyes, as if to disconcert me.

"Why? Because you were on the quay with Laodamas last night; please do not attempt to deny it. I heard your cackle of laughter when the Rhodians sang that obscene song about their ancestor Hermes and the slippery goatskin."

"That must have been just before I said good night."

"Why did you not look after him with decent care? He was drunk and unhappy. Your duty as his comrade demanded it."

"He showed me little tenderness and, as the saying is, two are needed to make a comradeship, but only one to dissolve it. The failure of that Libyan adventure seems to have turned his wits. Last night he wildly accused me of conspiring with the captain to steal Ctimene's copper and linen and then pretend that the ship had been wrecked off the Syrtes. When I reminded him of our old friendship, and hinted that he must be bewitched to talk such extravagant nonsense, he grew unbearably abusive. So, rather than encourage him to use his fists and have his nose flattened—I am by far the better boxer even when he is sober—I turned on my heel and retired to bed, pleased with my own moderation. It came as a surprise this morning to find the Rhodian purple-sellers gone. Do you think that Laodamas joined them?"

Eurymachus could never be frank with me. I thought at the time: "Because he is one of my suitors, and the one whom my father would most like me to marry (always supposing that he offers an adequate bride price), he does not care to reveal his faults to me prematurely." Yet I have always hated a man who, trying to hide crooked intentions behind a honeyed smile, is vain enough to believe that I cannot see through him.

"If he has sailed," I answered severely, "my father will not think the better of you."

"No, perhaps not—until I have explained what happened, in the same words that I have used to you. Then doubtless I shall find him more ready to believe me." As he spoke, one of our house-born slaves brought a message from my father himself, announcing that the fever had passed, and that he would be greatly obliged if Eurymachus could confer with him, as soon as the sacrifice was over, about the two night watchmen.

"Which watchmen?" I asked the slave.

"The dawn watch on the quay," he answered. "Their relief has just reported them lying in a drugged sleep behind the sail shed. Two sails and three coils of the best Byblian cordage are missing."

"There now, Eurymachus," I said. "What do you make of that?"

I studied his face, but he had made it a blank. "Surely a most unusual piece of news?" I pressed him. "Rhodians have a reputation for strict commercial honesty, and I cannot see why one of their big ships should jeopardize it merely for the sake of two sails and a coil or two of cordage."

He answered glibly: "There is something in what you say, lovely Nausicaa. Perhaps they needed the gear at once and could not wait for an audience with the port authority; so helped themselves, drugged the guards to prevent them from raising the alarm, and went off."

"In that case they would have left adequate payment behind in the form of metal or wine."

"Not if Laodamas went with them and undertook, in payment for his fare, to settle the debt on his return. Here comes the red bullock with the fillet on his head. Excuse my haste. Slave, tell the King that I rejoice to hear of the improvement in his health, and that I will discuss the affair of the watchmen as soon as this sacrifice is over and I have inspected the entrails."

"I wish you well of your interview," I flung at his insolent back.

Laodamas's departure did not, at first, seem a very serious matter, though the omens taken from the entrails of that bullock were most menacing—the beast looked healthy enough, but had advanced intestinal decay. The port authority agreed, in debate, that the Rhodian captain, who had visited Drepanum three years before as mate of another ship belonging to the same merchant, was an honest and capable seaman; payment for the sails and cordage would doubtless be made one day, nor had the watchers necessarily been drugged by the captain, or by any member of his crew. It might well be that an Elyman comrade had played a joke on them. Laodamas would find himself in safe hands and, this being April, should have returned by July at the latest, bringing Ctimene her promised amber necklace.

My father, though angry that his eldest son had gone off suddenly without a good-bye or waiting for the fever to pass —the banishment of my brother Halius five years before still rankled in his heart—contented himself with telling Ctimene that it should be a lesson to her never again to tease a good man beyond endurance. Ctimene pleaded that the fault lay with Laodamas, who had made fun of her headache, insulted the noble people of Bucinna, and kept her awake by talking drunkenly when she wanted no more than to fall asleep, pillowing her head on his breast.

This version of the quarrel, though dishonestly one-sided, I did not care to contradict. And Phytalus, my mother's old father, who had resigned the lordship of Hiera in favour of a son-in-law and come to potter about our estate as honorary steward, held that Ctimene was right to condemn Laodamas's idleness. "The only excuse for hunting in a civilized country," he grumbled, "is to prevent wild beasts from ravaging the cornfields or vineyards; the provision of flesh being incidental. But our cornfields are so well fenced, and game so scarce in this neighbourhood, that Laodamas has been obliged to scour distant forests, seldom bringing home so much as a hare. It is not as though hunter's meat were desperately needed at the Palace; do we ever lack for fat hogs or tasty steers? If the boy needs adventure, on the other hand, let him go slave-raiding in Italian Daunia or Sardinia, as I did at his age."

My mother never opens her mouth to comment on a situation that is still obscure; and since it was not yet certain that Laodamas had boarded the Rhodian ship, she remained silent. But Clytoneus offered a prayer to Father Zeus for his brother's safe return, and then asked Ctimene's permission to exercise Argus and Laelaps, Laodamas's hounds, which she granted with a sour smile. "He must surely have sailed," Clytoneus told her, "because if he had gone out hunting somewhere in the hills, he would never have left his hounds behind."

The mystery deepened a month later, when a ship's captain reported having spoken the Rhodian ship off Scyra, her last port of call. Laodamas, however, was not aboard; or at least the Rhodians said nothing of him. Possibly they had put him ashore at Acragas, where Aphrodite has a famous shrine, or at some other intervening port. Then Eurymachus's mother suddenly recalled that at dawn on the day in question, while the Rhodian ship was still moored in Drepanum Harbour, she had noticed a twenty-oared galley, Phoenician by the build and rig, lying just inside the southern bay. Perhaps Laodamas

had rowed out to her and bargained for a passage? Then
another woman, Ctimene's maid Melantho, who had been
sleeping on the roof, also claimed to have seen the ship, with a
dinghy in tow. But when pressed to explain why she had not
mentioned so important a sight before, all that she would say,
over and over again, was: "I did not want to cause trouble;
silence is golden." The news provoked a fresh crop of un-
profitable speculations, yet nobody grew seriously concerned
about Laodamas until the weather broke, at the end of
October, and our ships, beached for the winter, were given
their annual coat of tar.

I had to bear the brunt of Ctimene's passionate grief and
self-pity. We were thrown together by household business,
and she pretended that she could not unbosom herself to the
maids without either being accused of having treated Laodamas harshly, which would not be fair, or blaming him, which
would be indecent. She said that I alone knew the circumstances; and, besides, she was justified in making me the re-
pository of her secret grief because Laodamas's disappearance had been largely my fault. "Indeed!" I cried, opening
my eyes wide and jerking up my head. "How do you make
that out, Sister-in-law?"

"If you had stayed quietly in your room, he would have
nursed a hope that our conversation had been drowned by the
rattling of doors and shutters under the sirocco; it was your
officious sympathy that sent him away. And if you had then
roused one of the porters, and told him to shadow your
brother, and report his movements to your uncle Mentor, or
someone else responsible, I should not now be crying out my
eyes in hopeless longing for him."

Though murmuring gently: "Yes, we were all to blame," I knew very well that the maids sleeping in the corridor near the bedroom door had not only overheard as much of the dispute that night as I, but been afterwards taken fully into her confidence. However, for Laodamas's sake I bore with Ctimene. She was not altogether a bad woman, I decided; ill-health plagued her, and on the rare occasion when I fell sick myself, did I not behave just as irrationally? Ctimene's perpetual complaints made me even less eager for marriage than before, and I kept out of the house as much as I decently could, carrying my needlework into the garden, where Ctimene seldom followed, because she had a horror of spiders; and surrounded myself with a protective screen of women whenever I was obliged by the weather to stay indoors.

Here let me describe our Palace. For the purposes of my epic poem I have furnished it far more splendidly than is really the case: giving it a bronze threshold, golden doors, silver doorpost, and golden hounds to stand guard on either side; also bronze walls with a frieze of lapis lazuli; and golden statues of boys with hollowed hands into which torches cut from resinous pine heart were thrust, and so forth. But this embellishment costs nothing; neither does it cost anything to portray myself as tall, beautiful and gentle-voiced, nor to enlarge our household staff from twenty to fifty women. Yet, on the whole, I have respected the truth because, not being a born liar, I find wanton invention confusing; though I do exaggerate at times, like everyone else, and must adapt, disguise, shift, diminish and enlarge incidents to square them with the epic tradition. I have, indeed, kept as closely as possible to my own experience and, whenever obliged by the set theme to describe events and places beyond my experience, have either passed over them lightly, or given a description, instead, of what I know well. For instance, about Ithaca, Zacynthus, Same, and the other islands of that group, which are the main scene of my epic: never having visited these, nor been able to get a precise account of their position or aspect, I make do with the Aegadean Islands, which are a good deal smaller, but thoroughly familiar to me. Ithaca is really Hiera, which though invisible from Drepanum, because Bucinna—I call it Same—blocks the view, looks very noble from the top of Mount Eryx, lying far out on the western horizon. I call Aegusa "Zacynthus"; and as for the rest of the islands mentioned in the *Iliad*—Neritum, Crocylea and Aegilips—I have omitted them because there are only four Aegadeans and I need the fourth one, Motya, low-lying and rich in corn, to represent Dulichium. It cannot matter much. Those who listen to my poem and find that it does not fit their own geographical knowledge will respect the fame of Homer and believe either that an earthquake must have altered the configuration of Ithaca, Same and the other islands since his days, or that their names are changed.

As I was saying, our Palace is more or less as I have described it in my epic, though the front door of the main building is really of oak studded with bronze, and the doorposts are of dressed stone, and the threshold of ash wood. We have only one boy torchholder, of cypress wood, covered with rather badly rubbed gold leaf; and the door dogs are of red Egyptian marble; and the walls are panelled in olive with a vermilion frieze. Our Palace lies north and south, and consists of three parts. The main building has an upper storey protected by a ridged roof, and gutters made of tiles which carry off the winter rains into a well at one corner of the banqueting court; the water roaring down to fill the deep, stone-lined well makes a glorious noise when the summer drought first breaks. My father's throne chamber and the other living rooms are on the ground floor, our bedrooms lie above, and the front door opens into the banqueting court. At the back of the throne chamber, underneath the kitchen, is a large, cool cellar, which we use as our storeroom. My mother keeps the keys to its massive door on a ring attached to her girdle; but Eurycleia, the housekeeper, has a duplicate.

The banqueting court is surrounded by paved and covered cloisters, the wide central area being of rammed earth. Here we entertain guests, seating them on stools or settles at trestle tables. A door leads into the outer court, or court of sacrifice, which is likewise cloistered and dominated by the great altar sacred to Zeus and the other Olympians. On the western side of this court, my father has built a round vaulted chamber for his private retreat; while on the eastern side the main gateway, with a guest room above, leads into the street and is commanded by a tall watch tower rising between the two courts. Near the vaulted chamber, a door in the wall opens on a narrow passage running the whole length of the Palace, with a side entrance to the banqueting hall, and another to the servants' hall of the main building; and a couple of doors opening into the orchard. Ours is the most fertile orchard in Sicily, of several acres, rising in slow terraces and protected by a thorn hedge. The fruit are pear, mulberry, cherry, quince, sorb apple, arbutus, pomegranate, and several varieties of grape and fig, ripening at different times. Of course, there is no all-the-year-round vintage season, as I pretend in my poem, and as my uncle Mentor used to claim when he was in his cups. We also have a melon patch, a hazel grove, and a garden of potherbs and salads: cabbage, turnip, radish, carrot, beet, mallow, charlock, fennel, onion, leek, broccoli, arum, parsnip, celery, rocket, chicory, basil, marjoram, mint, endive, fennel and asparagus. (I see that I have mentioned fennel twice; but it is a very useful vegetable.) Two springs rise at the head of the orchard, one of which serves for irrigation. The other passes under the court of sacrifice and issues close to the main gateway; this is the chief source of drinking water for the townsfolk, who come in crowds all day long with pitchers and buckets. Behind the house stand stables and styes; and behind these an acre or so of olive yard.

The island of Hiera is more or less ours, though nominally ruled by my mother's clan; we raise horses there, and a fine breed of red cattle. We also graze large herds of hogs and oxen on Eryx, with numerous flocks of sheep; and countless bees from our apiaries use the same pastures. We bring the skips down to Drepanum in the winter to keep the bees warm. So what with the produce of earth and sea, our house slaves eat better than does many a king's son in the barren islands of the Aegean Sea. (There the staple food is roast asphodel root and mallows, for lack of wheat or barley, and fish in season; and figs; and a modicum of olive oil; and goat flesh.) No wonder that enemies envy our good fortune; and no wonder that when misfortune visited us because of Ctimene's untimely demand for an amber necklace, my father's rebellious subjects proved to have little loyalty or love for our house, and came swarming like ants to eat us up.

My father has the reputation of being close-fisted, which is unjust. Certainly the Gods cannot complain that he stints them of sacrifice; or his household that they go ill fed or underclad. He is industrious and energetic, condemns waste, regards poverty as the Gods' punishment of improvidence; and scorns the man who presents splendid gifts to strangers for display, rather than in the hope of eventual return. It was he who first introduced the cultivation of flax into Western Sicily, and set up a small linen factory near the main gateway. We pride ourselves on the fineness of the web—if one pulls a piece of our linen sheeting tight and tilts it at an angle, one can roll drops of oil all the way down; they do not penetrate the linen. My father abhors idleness in man or woman, always finds plenty of work for the slaves, even when it rains, and believes that early marriages are an incentive to industry.

This brings me to the subject of my suitors. No sooner was I sixteen years old than my father announced in the Elyman Council—which is organized on the twelve-clan system—that he would now accept offers for my hand, but that the honour of an alliance with the royal house could be bought only at a substantial price. In answer, Aegyptius, one of the Phocaean councillors, remarked that, as a general rule, an Elyman bride carries a dowry to the bridegroom's family, which guarantees her respectful treatment, and that this dowry is of far greater value than any complimentary presents which a suitor might think fit to bestow, without prejudice, on the bride's father. Doubtless, he said, the suggested innovation, reversing the rôles of bride and bridegroom, was justified in this case by the advantages at which my father hinted. But would it not, if popularly followed, tend to place young women of quality

on a level with common concubines, bought at so many head
of cattle or the equivalent in stamped copper, and thus de-
prive them of any rights or privileges except the title of wife?

A Sican councillor named Antiphus then observed that
my sister-in-law, Ctimene, had brought a dowry with her, and
so had my mother. Might it not be more consistent and generous, he asked, if the King extended this custom to the case
under discussion?

My father replied that he found neither inconsistency nor
lack of generosity in his proposal. Marriage customs change,
he said, and not so very long ago a man was unable to dis-
pose of his daughter at all; this being the prerogative of her
maternal uncle—a prerogative still insisted upon by the
Sicans of the Aegadean Islands. Dowries were inconvenient
relics of this outmoded system, and had no place in our
patriarchal economy. No, no, any young man of good family
who aspired to marry me, rather than the daughter of a poorer
and less influential house, would find it advantageous both to
disburse considerable treasure for that purpose and to treat
me with the utmost respect when I became his wife.

"Would my lord the King enlarge on these advantages?"
asked tall, sneering Prince Antinous. "Nausicaa is not an
heiress in her own right; besides, she has four brothers,
among at least three of whom you will, I daresay, divide your
property?"

"I refuse to commit myself on that head," cried my father,
stamping his foot. "The advantages of marrying Princess
Nausicaa, though indirect, are likely to be solid."

Eupeithes, Antinous's father, brought the debate to a close
by suggesting that when I was a year older, a span taller, and

of a more rounded figure, the beauty which I already promised would doubtless bring me suitors by the score, each
competing with the others in the bestowal of rich gifts. Until
then, discussion of my future seemed to him somewhat pre-
mature.

My father was angered by the mixed reception of his announcement, and I felt like a skinny fish, brought to market,
for which nobody cares to bid. The cry goes up: "Throw it
back into the sea and let it grow fatter!" Some of my girl
friends teased me cruelly the next day. One asked me to name
my marriage price; if it was a reasonable one, she said, her
parents might well be persuaded to buy me as a wife for their
cowman. I could see that my mother regretted that the question had ever been aired in public, though she was too loyal
to admit this. At all events, she undertook that I should be
consulted before a husband was finally chosen for me and
have the right to refuse any candidate if I could justify my
dislike of the match. Meanwhile she would weave me a bridal
robe of sea purple, which I might embroider with needlework
pictures in gold and crimson as a proof that I was my father's
obedient daughter. She duly provided the robe, and I busied
myself very unbusily on the pictures; and for every three that
I completed, I would secretly unpick at least one when nobody
was looking.

Drepanum presently learned what my father had meant
by "indirect advantages". When Eurymachus came forward
at the end of the year and asked permission to court me, he
was awarded the vacant junior priesthood of Poseidon, which
carried rich perquisites, and promised, at our marriage, the
monopoly of a sea ferry between the islands. Antinous,

Mulius, and Ctesippus, three other suitors who then entered
the field, were given or promised similar favours. None of
them professed to be in love with me, and all seemed a little
afraid of my tart tongue, which I did not spare them when
out of my father's hearing. I certainly had no liking, or even
respect, for any of the four.

"It is, however, better not to feel too passionately attached
to your husband," my mother told me. "A husband should
never know exactly where he stands with his wife, though
hopefully relying on her faithfulness to the marriage bed;
I realized, for instance, when your father bought Eurymedusa
of Apeira, that he must be under a strong temptation to make
her his concubine, because the slavers asked an excessively
high price—twenty cow shekels instead of four—and he paid
it almost without bargaining; yet not daring to risk my annoyance, he restricted himself to an occasional fatherly pat
on the girl's cheek or shoulders. No, child, whoever falls
in love with her own husband is ruined. That was what went
wrong between Ctimene and Laodamas, as you may have
guessed: she lost her heart to him and grew jealous of the
wild goats and boars which he hunted all day. He has never
loved her—the marriage was arranged by your father—but
is far too well mannered to confess this. So she grew exasper-
ated; first with herself and then with him. If only it could be
the other way about: if only his passion were stronger than
hers!"

CHAPTER
THREE
THE DEPARTURE
OF ODYSSEUS

THE WINTER PASSED, olives were harvested and pressed, ewes lambed, she-goats kidded, the cheese-making season began, swallows, quails and cuckoos flew across from Libya, the Love Goddess ascended her mountain, bees thronged our fruit trees, young men put out in boats to harpoon tunny and swordfish, blankets were no longer needed on our beds, and the first merchant ships called. We confidently expected Laodamas, or a reassuring message from him, or at least some sort of news; but for a month or more not a word came, though every port in Sicily had heard of our anxiety. Then a merchant of Italian Hyria arrived, hoping to sell us carved stone vases and Daedalic jewellery, the art of making which still flourished in his city, a former colony of Crete. He was a great haggis of a man, but wore clothes embroidered with flowers in the Cnossan style, and a little kiss curl on his forehead, which set my maids giggling. Immediately upon coming ashore he asked to be taken to the Palace, where he greeted my father with suppressed excitement, and after dinner—since it is considered bad manners for host and guest to exchange anything but compliments until that is over—spoke as follows:

"Here is good news for you, my lord King, about your lost son, Prince Laodamas. I met him last autumn among the Thesprotians of Epeirus, and found him in perfect health, blessed be the Gods! It appears that the Phoenician ship in which he sailed from Drepanum ran aground off rocky Corcyra in a gale; yet he managed to escape black death. Yes, the keel had broken adrift, and kept him afloat, clinging tightly to it, until the whitecapped waves subsided and he could paddle ashore with his hands. The King of Corcyra entertained your son royally, exclaiming that he was clearly a favourite of the Goddess Thetis; and soon discovered that they had an ancestor in common—Zacynthus, an early Trojan king, great-grandfather of the Princess Aegesta. He not only heaped treasures on Laodamas, but gave him a letter of introduction to another distant kinsman, King Pheidon of the Thesprotians, who proved hardly less generous. Your son has, in consequence, amassed a great store of gold and silver, amber, armour, ivory toys, goblets, cauldrons, and tripods: enough, one might say, to enrich his descendants until the tenth generation. When we met, he had just consulted Zeus's dove oracle at the Oaks of Dodona. I stood him several drinks, and he recommended me to you, my lord, and promised that

I should find a ready market for my wares among your dis-
criminating Elyman subjects. He hopes to be back here about
the season of the first figs, though not earlier, because the
oracle warned him—who can guess why?—against hurrying
home. No, my lord, he had failed to save even his clothes
from the wreck: he was wearing only a loincloth, and a
coral amulet around his neck, when the hospitable people
of Corcyra found him half dead on the beach, his long hair
crusted with salt."

You can imagine what relief this news afforded my father,
who clapped his hands like a child. Clytoneus buried his head
in a wine cup and drank until he was tipsy. I was hastily
summoned and charged with carrying the glad news to
Ctimene, who by now had almost given up eating and drinking. She spent most of her time in bed, overcome by frequent
fits of hysterical sobbing. Seldom have I taken a message
more readily or been more rapturously thanked—or had so
little confidence in its truth. Nothing seemed too good for
the Hyrian merchant: my father summoned an all-Elyman
Council and announced that on the following night a feast
of homage to our benefactor would be held in the banqueting
court. Each of the twelve tribes must send several representatives. A dozen sheep, eight boars, and two bullocks would
be sacrificed, there would be no stint of wine and bread, and
Demodocus, the most famous poet in Sicily, a blind Son of
Blind Homer, had consented to sing of the Trojan War.

At least a hundred men attended the feast, all wearing
their ceremonial robes. Glad hymns to Zeus arose while the
animals were being slaughtered, flayed and roasted in the
court of sacrifice. Demodocus, who is toothless as well as

blind, sat in a silver-studded chair, backed against one of the
cloister pillars, his seven-stringed oryx-horn lyre hanging
from a peg within easy reach. Near by, on an inlaid table,
Pontonous the butler had set a cup of wine to refresh him in
his pauses between fyttes, and a basket of bread. In a half
circle around the old man, at a decent distance, were ranged
a score of beechwood trestle tables, waxed and polished, each
supporting a great dish of well-scrubbed copper, on which
lay steaming joints of mutton, pork and beef. Once again it
occurred to me: how disgustingly men eat, hacking off strips
of meat with daggers, and cramming them into their mouths
until the juice runs down wrists and chins! A few used bread
to wipe themselves clean; the remainder did not trouble. Pontonous kept the wine flowing, his sharp eye noting any cup or
goblet set down empty. They were our best goblets. We are
always afraid that when a banquet is over someone will have
thoughtlessly carried off one of them, though all are stamped
or engraved with the palace sign (which is a hound rending a
fawn) and therefore easy to trace. Some are of silver, some
of gold, some carved out of alabaster or liparite, three or four
of Egyptian ware.

The Hyrian merchant, who claimed descent from King
Minos's brother Sarpedon, was given the portion of honour,
an unbroken length of beef chine, and a draught of our best
dark wine in a rock-crystal goblet. Having downed a pint or
two of this superlative drink, moderately tempered with
water, he beat his breast, rapped his forehead, and exclaimed
that he had forgotten to deliver several messages of affection
from Laodamas to his wife, parents, and brothers, and to the
principal citizens of Drepanum. He delivered these amid a

respectful hush, and though the phrases were uncharacteristic of Laodamas, they gave pleasure. He also told us that Laodamas meant to sail home from Sandy Pylus in Elis.

Word now came to us women that our own feast was ready, so we trooped to the dining room downstairs. Men take pride in eating hugely on all occasions; and by way of politeness, at a dinner party, they bolt their food as though dying of hunger. We women make do with only half the food and drink, and are no less robust. Personally, I hate to see a well-born girl, however ravenous she may be, spilling wine or gravy on her dress; and if I catch one of my maids with her snout in the trough, as the saying goes, I send her to grind corn in our heaviest quern when the next mealtime is announced.

After the men had acknowledged themselves defeated by the plenty set before them, slaves went around carrying towels, sponges, and basins of warm water, into which a little vinegar had been poured, to wash the guests' hands; while others cleared the tables and took out the broken meats to an expectant crowd assembled in the court of sacrifice. Demodocus then struck up, and his song was the *Departure of Odysseus for Troy*, which he chose by way of honouring the Phocaeans, because Odysseus's grandfather Autolycus, their ancestor, is said to have lived on Phocian Parnassus, where stands Delphi, Apollo's prophetic seat. After invoking the Muses, whom Apollo had led down from the cold northern wilderness and entertained in his lofty Delphic halls, Demodocus described the arrival at Sparta of Queen Helen's suitors.

This was his story, and he had brought along two women tumblers who performed acrobatic feats in time to the music, and illustrated dramatic episodes with wordless mime.

When Helen, Leda's beautiful daughter, grew to woman-hood, all the princes of Greece came with rich gifts to the palace of her foster father King Tyndareus, or sent their kinsmen to represent them. Argive Diomedes, fresh from his victory at Thebes, was there with the Aeacids Ajax and Teucer; Idomeneus, King of Crete; Achilles's cousin Patroclus; Menestheus the Athenian; and many others. Odysseus of Ithaca, Autolycus's grandson, came too, but empty-handed, knowing that he had not the least chance of success—for even though Castor and Pollux, Helen's brothers, wanted her to marry Menestheus of Athens, she would, of course, be given to Prince Menelaus, the richest of the Achaeans, repre-sented here by Tyndareus's powerful son-in-law Agamemnon.

King Tyndareus sent no suitor away but, on the other hand, accepted none of the proffered gifts; fearing that his partiality for any one prince might set the others at odds. Odysseus asked him one day: "If I tell you how to avoid a quarrel will you, in return, help me to marry your niece Penelope, the daughter of my lord Icarius?" "It is a bargain," cried Tyndareus.

"Then," continued Odysseus, "my advice is: insist that all Helen's suitors swear to defend her chosen husband against whoever resents his good fortune." Tyndareus agreed that this was a prudent course. After sacrificing a horse, and jointing it, he made the suitors stand on its bloody pieces and repeat the oath which Odysseus had formulated; the joints were then buried at a place still called "The Horse's Tomb".

It is not known whether Tyndareus himself chose Helen's husband, or whether she declared her own preference by crowning him with a wreath. At all events, she married

Menelaus, who became King of Sparta after the death of Tyndareus and the deification of the Dioscuri. Yet their marriage was doomed to failure: years before, while sacrificing to the Gods, Tyndareus had stupidly overlooked Aphrodite, who took her revenge by swearing that all three of his daughters—Clytaemnestra, Timandra and Helen—should become notorious for their adulteries.

Why, Demodocus asked, had Zeus and his aunt Themis the Titaness planned the Trojan War? Was it to make Helen famous for having embroiled Europe and Asia? Or to exalt the race of demi-gods, and at the same time to thin out the populous tribes which were oppressing the surface of Mother Earth? Alas, their reason must always remain obscure, but the decision had already been taken when Eris threw down a golden apple inscribed "For the Fairest!" at the wedding of Peleus and Thetis. Almighty Zeus refused to arbitrate in the ensuing dispute between Hera, Athene and Aphrodite, each of whom claimed it as her own, and let Hermes lead the Goddesses to Mount Ida, where Priam's long-lost son Paris would act as arbiter.

Paris was herding his cattle on Mount Gargarus, the highest peak of Ida, when Hermes appeared before him, accompanied by Hera, Athene and Aphrodite. Hermes delivered the golden apple of discord and Zeus's message, which ran: "Paris, since you are as handsome as you are wise in affairs of the heart, Zeus commands you to judge which of these Goddesses is the fairest, and to award her this golden prize."

Paris accepted the apple doubtfully. "How can a simple cattleman like myself become an arbiter of divine beauty?" he cried. "I shall divide this fruit equally between all three."

"No, no, you cannot disobey Almighty Zeus!" Hermes exclaimed. "Nor am I authorized to give you advice. Use your native intelligence!"

"So be it," sighed Paris. "But first I beg the losers not to grow vexed with me. I am only a human being, liable to make the stupidest mistakes."

The Goddesses all agreed to abide by his verdict.

"Am I to judge them just as they are?" Paris asked Hermes. "Or should they be naked?"

"The rules of the contest are for you to decide," Hermes answered with a wary smile.

"In that case, will they please disrobe?"

Hermes told the Goddesses to do so, and politely turned his back.

Aphrodite was soon ready, but Athene insisted that she should remove the famous magic girdle, which gave her an unfair advantage by making everyone fall in love with the wearer. "Very well," said Aphrodite spitefully. "I will, on condition that you remove your helmet—you look hideous without it."

"If I am permitted," announced Paris, clapping his hands for order, "I shall judge the competitors one at a time, and thus avoid distractive arguments. Come here, Divine Hera! Will you other two Goddesses be kind enough to leave us for a while?"

"Examine me conscientiously," said Hera, turning slowly around, and displaying her magnificent figure, "and remember that if you judge me the fairest, I will make you lord of all Asia, and the richest man alive."

"I am not to be bribed, my lady . . . Ah yes, thank you.

Now I have seen all that I need to see. Come, Divine Athene!"

"Here I am," said Athene, striding purposefully forward; but, being no less modest than virginal, hid as much of her body as she could behind the Aegis. "Listen, Paris," she said, "if you are prudent enough to award me the prize, I will make you victorious in all your battles, besides being the handsomest and wisest man in the world."

"I am a humble herdsman, not a soldier," said Paris, a little annoyed by the interposition of the Aegis. "You know very well that peace reigns throughout Lydia and Phrygia, and that King Priam's sovereignty is unchallenged. But I promise to consider fairly your claim to the apple. Now you may put on your clothes and helmet again. Is Aphrodite ready?"

Aphrodite sidled up to Paris, who blushed because she came so close that they were almost touching. She smelt of nard and roses.

"Look carefully, please, pass nothing over . . . By the way, as soon as I saw you, I said to Hermes: 'Upon my word, there goes the handsomest man in Phrygia! Why does he waste himself here in the wilderness herding stupid cattle?' Well, why do you, Paris? Why not move into a city and lead a civilized life? What have you to lose by marrying some-one like Helen of Sparta, who is almost as beautiful as I, and no less passionate? I am convinced that, once you two have met, she will abandon her home, her family, everything, to become your mistress. Surely, you have heard of Helen?"

"Never until now, my lady. I should be most grateful if you would describe her."

"Helen is fair and of a delicate complexion, having been

hatched from a swan's egg. She can claim Zeus for a father, loves hunting and wrestling, caused one war while she was still a child—and when she came of age, all the princes of Greece were her suitors. At present she is wife to Menelaus, brother of the High King Agamemnon; but that makes no odds—you can have her if you like."

"How is that possible, if she is already married?"

"Heavens! How innocent you are! Have you never heard that it is my divine duty to arrange affairs of this sort? I suggest now that you tour Greece, taking my son Eros as your guide. Once you reach Sparta, he will oblige Helen to fall head over heels in love with you."

"Would you swear to that?" Paris asked excitedly.

Aphrodite took a solemn oath by the River Styx, and Paris, without a second thought, awarded her the golden apple.

By this judgement he incurred the unappeasable resentment of both Hera and Athene, who went off arm-in-arm to plot the destruction of Troy; while Aphrodite, a naughty smile on her matchless face, stood wondering how best to keep her promise.

"Elymans of Mount Eryx," cried Demodocus, "no goddess in the universe is so powerful as our Aphrodite!"

I disliked this extremely partial statement. The competition was only for the fairest, not for the wisest or the strongest; and Homer relates that when once Aphrodite presumed to fight on the Trojan plain she had to flee, wounded, from a mere mortal.

Demodocus replaced his lyre on the peg and began mumbling bread and sipping wine. My father coughed consequentially. "A very pretty story," he said, "and beautifully told, revered Demodocus. The Gods, who deprived you of both your eyes and all thirty-two of your teeth, have given you instead a splendid voice and an inexhaustible memory. But, confess, is this the whole truth? I cannot easily believe that the elopement of Priam's forty-eighth or forty-ninth son with a Spartan queen occasioned the Trojan War, which involved nearly every city in Greece and Asia Minor, and must have caused at least a hundred thousand casualties, one way or another. It was not even as if Paris attempted to seize the throne of Sparta. Tell me: what value in cattle or metal would you put on a wife who, after nine years of wedlock, had failed to bear Menelaus a son, and belonged to a notoriously adulterous family? His loss of conjugal rights could have been settled for ten or twenty pounds of gold at the outside."

"I repeat the story as it has come down to us from our ancestor, the divine Homer," said Demodocus shortly.

"Women, of course," my father persisted, "can cause serious local feuds, especially when they are heiresses, marriage to whom involves a transfer of property; but I cannot believe, either, that Helen's suitors would have committed themselves to an overseas war on behalf of Menelaus, whose choice as a bridegroom seemed a foregone conclusion, or that Paris's father and brothers would have agreed to defend Troy for ten years against them, rather than hand her back."

"All civil wars are dynastic wars, my lord King; all overseas wars are trade wars," agreed the portly Hyrian. "And Troy, which had been jointly founded by our Cretan ancestors, certain local Phrygians, and a force of Aeacids from Eastern Greece, was in its time the most important city of Asia.

Troy commanded the Hellespont, and therefore controlled the rich trade of the Black Sea and beyond; gold, silver, iron, cinnabar, ship's timber, linen, hemp, dried fish, oil and Chinese jade. A great annual fair was held on the plain of the Scamander, to which the merchants of the world resorted; they all brought gifts to the King of Troy, who, in return, protected them while the fair was in progress, and supplied food and drinking water. The Trojan kings, however, being of Phrygian stock, would allow neither Greeks nor Cretans to trade directly with the Black Sea nations. A generation previously, Priam's father Laomedon had tried to prevent the Minyan ship *Argo* from sailing to fetch the Golden Fleece laid up in a temple at Colchis, but she slipped through; and the Sons of Homer themselves tell how Hercules, who was a member of her crew, afterwards disembarked in Phrygia and, gathering a few allies, took Troy by storm and punished Laomedon for his greed and obstinacy."

"Exactly," cried my father. "The story is as plain as the polished knob on that door! Those Cretans and Greek Aeacids as co-builders of Troy, which was designed to safeguard their trading interests in the Black Sea, found the entrance to the Hellespont barred: King Priam had erected strong forts at Sestus and Abydus to control the narrows. After protesting to him without success, they asked their Achaean allies to help them take sanctions, and promised, if the expedition proved successful, to share the spoils of the city with them. Agamemnon, High King of Mycenae, agreed to lead the expedition and persuaded Odysseus to join it, because Odysseus was King of the Ionian Islands, the home of my ancestor Zacynthus, one of the Cretan founders of Troy. So, at a conference

held in the temple of the Spartan Goddess Helle, they sacrificed a horse to her and took oaths on the jointed pieces. They
swore to free the straits honoured with her name—I refer to
the Hellespont—for Greek navigation. I cannot think that
any man of experience will challenge my argument. Pray
now, Demodocus, continue your song, when you have well
rinsed your gums and throat."

Demodocus replied: "King Alpheides, since you despise my
tale of Paris's visit to the Spartan court, and his subsequent
exploits in Phoenicia, I beg leave to omit this fytte tonight,
and pass on to the less vexed account of Odysseus's departure
for Troy."

"No, no! Pray do not omit a line of the cycle," cried my
father, "merely on my account. I hold, of course, that the
tale of Paris's behaviour at Sparta is neither particularly in-
structive nor particularly elevating: how he courted her with
loud sighs and amorous glances, frequently setting his lips to
that part of the goblet's rim from which she had drunk. Men
and women should never dine together except on family occasions, do you not agree? And how he scrawled 'I love Helen!'
in wine spilled on the table top; and how Aphrodite blinded
Menelaus's eyes to this shameless performance. What a tale
to sing in the hearing of impressionable young women! It
is not even as though Paris's crimes were punished. He enjoyed Helen for ten years—until, in fact, her beauty had
faded, as it must when a woman reaches the forties—then
gained deathless fame by killing Achilles, the greatest champion alive; and, dying gloriously in battle, was buried with
heroic honours. No, no! Use your reason, my lords and gentle-
men. Let me record my studied opinion that Helen never went
to Troy at all."

My father is a simple-minded, practical man, and my mother has always found it impossible to argue with him in one of his provocative moods. I should have liked to walk into the banqueting court and say: "Father, this is not the time to use the word 'reason'. Please understand that a Homeric song is sung to the lyre, and therefore intended for entertainment, no more and no less. Moral or historical instruction is quite another matter, given by priests and old councillors to young men who gather around them in the evening after the day's sport. On such occasions the lyre is left unstrung; no religious hush is observed; the young men rationally question and are rationally answered. Surely the Sons of Homer know what is required of them? They have been professional minstrels for a couple of hundred years at least, and few indeed of their stories are unconcerned with the mischief caused by love. That is what their hearers expect: songs of love and songs of battle. A fine entertainment a trade-war epic would make!"

> *Sing, ye countinghouse Muses, of so many talents of copper,*
> *So many horsehide bales, and so many measures of broadcloth:*
> *How the monopoly-mad King Priam defied the Achaeans,*
> *Charging them fifty per cent on goods from the shores of the Euxine.*

But shame held me back, and in any case my reproach would have fallen on deaf ears. An awkward silence ensued, and after a while Demodocus, somewhat crossly, skipped about fifteen hundred lines and began to declaim the *Summons of Odysseus.*

This is what he told us:

King Odysseus of Ithaca married Icarius's daughter Penelope, after winning a suitors' race along the Spartan street called Apheta. Icarius had called out: "One, two, three!" and then clapped his hands sharply, instead of shouting "Go!"— at which all the suitors but Odysseus started, and were at once disqualified. For Odysseus, warned beforehand, held his ground until the word "Go!", whereupon, being the only competitor left, he won the prize without exertion, despite the crookedness of his legs. It is said that Icarius begged Odysseus, in reward for this favour, to stay with him at Sparta and, when he declined, pursued the chariot in which the bridal pair were driving away, entreating them to come back. Odysseus, who had hitherto kept his patience, turned and told Penelope: "Either come to Ithaca of your own free will; or, if you prefer your father, dismount and let me drive on alone!" Penelope's reply was to draw down her veil. Icarius, realizing that Odysseus was within his rights, let her go, and raised an image to Modesty, which is still shown some four miles from the city of Sparta, at the place where this incident happened.

Now, Odysseus had been warned by an oracle: "If you sail to Troy, you will not come home again until the twentieth year, and then alone and destitute." He therefore exchanged his royal robes for filthy rags, and Agamemnon, Menelaus and Palamedes found him wearing a felt cap shaped like a half egg, ploughing with an ass and an ox yoked together, and flinging salt over his shoulder as he went. When he pretended not to recognize his distinguished guests, Palamedes snatched the infant Telemachus from Penelope's arms and set him on the ground before the advancing team, which were about to plough the tenth furrow. Odysseus hastily reined them in to avoid killing his only son and, being then reminded of the oath he had sworn on the bloody pieces of the horse, was obliged to join the expedition.

"I hope that this tale pleases you, my lord King," said Demodocus in peevish tones, when he had been roundly applauded.

"Your voice is delightful," my father answered, "but I cannot refrain from pointing out that this part of the cycle also carries little conviction. If Odysseus wished to feign madness, as an excuse for breaking his promise, which is the only sense that I can make of your story, why did he not act even more irresponsibly? After all, an ox and an ass are often yoked together by impoverished farmers—indeed, I have myself watched a needy Sican ploughing with an ox yoked to his own wife—and felt caps are a very reasonable wear for ploughmen, when the north-easter blows. Now, had I been Odysseus, I should have chosen a pig and a goat as my team, and dressed myself fantastically in owl feathers, a golden tiara, and snake-skin leggings—ha, ha!"

I trembled for shame to hear the venerable Demodocus addressed in this petulant and condescending style.

"And to plough ten straight furrows is hardly a sign of insanity—why did he not drive the team furiously in an ever-widening spiral? That would have been far more convincing, and would have greatly improved your story, which is not so laughable as one would expect from a Son of Homer."

"My lord King," said Demodocus, with a smile that came as close to a sneer as he dared, "have you not taken the wrong pig by the tail? My glorious ancestor, who composed this song, nowhere suggests that Odysseus feigned madness. Odysseus wore the felt hat of a mystagogue to show that he was prophesying, and all his actions were therefore symbolic. Ox and ass stand for Zeus and Cronus, or summer and winter, if you prefer; and each furrow sown with salt for a wasted year. He was demonstrating the futility of the war to which he had been summoned; but Palamedes, having superior prophetic powers, seized the infant Telemachus and halted the plough at the tenth furrow, thus showing that the *decisive battle*, which is the meaning of 'Telemachus', would be fought in the tenth year; as indeed it was."

Applause and laughter greeted my father's discomfiture. He blushed red to the ears, and showed his good sense by cutting Demodocus a large piece of roast pork, with plenty of crackling, which a page carried over in his fingers; and promised him a new gold-headed staff of cornel wood, to guide his steps and add to his distinction. But though he accepted the pork, Demodocus would never again play or sing in our Palace; honour forbade it. Some of the townsfolk even attributed our subsequent misfortunes to his ill will, because Apollo has granted all Sons of Homer the power to curse; yet I cannot think that Demodocus would have cursed us after accepting a gift offered in token of apology. We were left with Phemius, Demodocus's assistant, who had come from Delos a few years before and was still perfecting his repertory at the old man's knees; it was he who taught me to read and write in Chalcidian characters. So far Phemius's eyes remain unclouded; the family affliction overtakes a Son of Homer only when his hair begins to turn grey and when, as they say, the sap has ceased to rise. As for the Hyrian, my father insisted that each of the twelve clans should present him with some object of value—a cauldron, a tripod, a rich robe, or the like; and undertook, when these were collected, to supply a cedarwood chest to stow them in, and a gold goblet to mark his personal gratitude. Being King of the Elymans, he had every right to make these demands from the clan leaders, in payment for the protection he afforded them, and the justice he dispensed; while grudging him his power, they always obeyed, and he encouraged them to recoup their expenses by a general levy on the common people.

The Hyrian sailed away three days later, well content with his visit (though my father somehow forgot the goblet). He had disposed of his vases and Daedalic jewellery in the market place at a substantial profit, and made all the merchants laugh by his farewell speech: "May the Queen of Heaven shower blessings on you, and may you continue to give satisfaction to your wives and daughters!" We never saw him again. My mother and I, it should be said, were the only two people in Drepanum who disbelieved his story, but we said nothing to discourage Ctimene, who soon recovered her appetite and good spirits and went singing about the house. "I wonder how long my necklace will be," she said to my brother Clytoneus. "As long, do you think, as the one which Eurymachus's mother wears?"

"Honoured Sister-in-law," Clytoneus answered angrily, "though he finds one three ells long, the grief and anxiety caused by your demand for such a necklace will rob it of all

beauty for me! If I were you, I should vow it to Apollo, who
consented to guard the hateful necklace of Eriphyle and keep
it from making further mischief among vain women."

"Nothing of the kind," cried Ctimene. "Laodamas would
think me ungrateful."

Pondering on Aphrodite's victory, I decided that hers is
a blind and mischievous power which makes its victims ridiculous and deprives them of all shame. I composed a story
for my own amusement, basing it on a scandalous event in
the early married life of Eurymachus's mother: how one day
the Goddess told her husband, the Smith God Hephaestus,
that she was off to visit her temple at Cyprian Paphos. "Do so,
Wife; and I will take advantage of your absence to visit my
temple at Lemnos," replied Hephaestus. But, knowing that
she was an inveterate liar, he hurried back that same night
and found her in bed with the Thracian War God Ares. Limping to his smithy, he forged two adamantine nets, thinner than
gossamer and quite invisible. One of these he fastened underneath the bed, the other he hung from the beam above, afterwards silently gathering and uniting the edges to make an
unbreakable cage around the drowsy pair. Then in a loud
voice he called his fellow deities to witness this disgraceful
act of adultery, and pressed Zeus for a divorce. Aphrodite,
though she hid her blushes, was secretly pleased that Hermes
and Poseidon had seen how beautiful she looked without
even a shift, and how ready she was to deceive her husband.
Hera and Athene turned away in disgust on hearing the news,
and refused to attend this obscene peep show; but Aphrodite,
putting a bold face on the matter, explained that making
people fall in love, and doing so herself, was the divine task

which she had been allotted by the Fates—who, then, could blame her? Presently Aphrodite's friends, the Graces, bathed and anointed her with fragrant oil, dressed her in soft, semi-transparent linen robes and set a wreath of roses on her head. She was now so irresistibly charming that not only did Hephaestus forgive her on the spot, but Hermes and Poseidon thereafter came calling on alternate days, whenever he was busy at the forge. Meeting Aphrodite in the corridors of Olympus, Athene called her an idle slut; whereupon Aphrodite flounced away in a temper, sat down at Athene's loom and tried her hand at weaving. Athene caught her in the act and, since weaving was the divine task allotted to her by the Fates, asked in exasperation: "What would you think if I worked on the sly at *your* shameful trade? Very well, then, dear colleague, go on weaving! I shall never do another hand's turn at the loom myself. And I hope that it will bore you to the point of misery!"

Then I wondered: "Are such jests against the Olympians permissible?" Only, I decided, when a god or goddess is worshipped in a manner offensive to public decency and good manners: when the adulteries of Aphrodite, the thefts and lies of Hermes, and the bloody-mindedness of Ares are perpetuated in the cults of these deities and quoted by foolish mortals to excuse their own depravity. Homer goes further than I would dare, in his disdain of the Olympians, whom he makes inflict punishments or bestow protection on mankind for mere caprice, rather than requiting them according to their moral deserts, and quarrel scandalously among themselves. Moreover, in the *Iliad*, Zeus sends a dream to gull Agamemnon, who has always behaved piously towards him;

and, prompted by a divine conclave, Athene persuades
Pandarus to commit an act of treachery; and Hera uses an
erotic charm to distract Zeus's attention from the battle before
Troy; and the Olympians laugh cruelly at the Smith God's
lameness, caused by a devoted championship of his mother
Hera against the indecent brutality of his stepfather.

Finding such anecdotes frankly irreligious, I close my ears
and mind when they are declaimed in our Palace. My father
once laughed at me for this and explained that Homer is far
from being irreligious: in the *Iliad,* on the contrary, he has
satirized the new theology of the Dorian barbarians. For these
Sons of Hercules, having dethroned the Great Goddess Rhea
—once acknowledged as the Sovereign of the World—had
awarded her sceptre to the Sky God Zeus; and made him the
head of a divine family composed of deities cultivated by their
subject tribes, namely Hera of Argos, Poseidon of Euboea,
Athene of Athens, Apollo of Phocis, Hermes of Arcadia, and
so on. Homer, explained my father, secretly worshipped this
earlier Goddess and deplored the moral confusion which the
sack of her religious centres had caused, caricaturing the
Dorian chieftains in the shameless, ruthless, treacherous,
lecherous, boastful persons of the Greek leaders.

Historically, my father may be right, as when he criticized
the Homeric version of Helen's flight to Troy. Yet the Zeus,
the Hera, the Poseidon, the Athene and the Apollo whom I
worship in my heart, and whom he honours at the altar of
sacrifice, are noble-minded, just and trustworthy deities. For
me, Hermes is a courteous messenger and conductor of souls,
no thief; Ares fights in defence of good causes only; Aphrodite . . .

Yes, I confess that Aphrodite presents mankind with a difficult problem. I acknowledge her dreadful power, as I acknowledge the power of Hades, King of the Underworld; but ought I not to condemn Helen, Clytaemnestra, and Penelope for defiling their husbands' nuptial couches and becoming a reproach to their sex, rather than smile and say: "They were loyal devotees of Aphrodite, scorning the ties of marriage and home the better to honour her"? The Nasamonians of Libya, the Moesynoechians of Pontus, the Gymnasiae of the Balearic Islands and similarly promiscuous peoples may worship her with moral consistence; no law-abiding Greek can do so.

Nevertheless, I sacrificed a young she-goat to Aphrodite on the following day, burning its thigh bones on juniper billets; and vowed to take an offering up to her temple when I had the opportunity. She resides there between the spring visit of the quails and the vintage season; but, because her mountain top is cold and cloudy during most of the winter, she afterwards flies off, they say, to Libya, riding in a chariot drawn by white doves. Her priestesses and eunuchs then seek their warm college on the plain, bringing with them the image enclosed in a cedarwood chest, the golden honeycomb said to have been Daedalus's own votive offering to Elyme, and the sacred dovecotes; there to live as chastely for the next six months as the attendants of Artemis or Athene. The Goddess's annual ascent of Eryx and her subsequent descent are marked by scenes of wild abandonment to her power, especially among the Sicans. My father has done his best to suppress these revels, which raise vexatious problems of paternity; but without success. Only if some national disaster occurs in winter does the Goddess reascend the mountain, calling back her priestesses, eunuchs, image honeycomb and doves; and is then propitiated with costly sacrifices, while the eunuchs whip one another until the blood flows, howling ecstatically. I hate the whole performance.

CHAPTER

FOUR

MY FATHER'S

DAUGHTER

N OT LONG AFTERWARDS, my father took out a ten-oared galley to inspect our red cattle and the mares with their mule foals on the island of Hiera; but had gone only about half a mile when he sighted a large Rhodian vessel approaching from the west. The sea was calm, and her sailors were pulling a long, even stroke in time with the helmsman's lugubrious chant. My father hailed the captain, and as soon as each of them had satisfied himself that the other was no pirate—one cannot be too careful nowadays—they drew alongside and exchanged gifts and compliments. The Rhodian ship was bound for Sardinia with a mixed cargo, and at Sandy Pylus, her last port of call in Greece, two staid merchants had come aboard to join the trading venture. Overjoyed to meet

these Pylians, my father enquired anxiously for news of
Laodamas. They shook their heads. "If such an important person had visited our city," they declared, "at any time since the
autumn, we should certainly have heard of him." When he
quoted the Hyrian captain's report, they admitted having
met the fellow at Sandy Pylus and formed a very poor opinion
of his character. "As slippery as a cuttlefish," they said, "and
as mendacious as a Lerian slave. His wine was watered; his
vases were flawed; his silver ingots leaden-cored."

This came as a great shock for my father, who abandoned
his visit to Hiera and returning home more depressed in mind
than I had ever known him, found Ctimene back in one of her
old black moods, biting her nails and moaning the popular
song: "Why does my darling delay? Has he no pity on my
loneliness?" over and over again. He retired to his vaulted
chamber, where he had built himself a curious bed, using
a live olive tree as the bedpost, inlaid with gold, silver and
ivory. In theory, the room is a tomb; and once a year at mid-
winter, when the customary Demise of the Crown occurs, he
shaves his head, enters, eats the food of the departed, and
pretends to have been killed. He lies in state under a scarlet
coverlet; while the Boy King, chosen from our own clan,
dances the Ballet of the Months, and assumes the sceptre for
a day. My father now locked the door and, after pacing up
and down, his hands tightened into fists, flung himself miserably on the bed, and closed his eyes. I asked one of my maids
to peep in at the window occasionally, and report his movements; which I regarded as most ill-omened, though I did not
tell her so.

Some hours later, he emerged, went to his study, and sent

for me. "Nausicaa," he said, "what shall I do? You are, at times, the most sensible member of this family (always excepting your dear mother) and I feel that—ahem—some god may have inspired you to advise me."

He then described his meeting with the Pylian merchants, and waited for my comment.

I sighed deeply before I answered. "Father, the news does not surprise me. Your shameless Hyrian guest was lying—as I could have told you at the time. So could my mother, and perhaps she did. Let us dismiss that whole story as a fantasy designed to improve his trade; and think only of Laodamas's possible fate. It now seems certain that the Rhodian captain never took him aboard . . ."

"I do not agree. As Eurymachus points out, the Rhodian would hardly have risked his reputation by going off with our sails and cordage, unless Laodamas had given him permission in my name."

"If he had Laodamas's permission, would there have been any need to drug the guards?"

My father brushed off this question as impatiently as if it were a bluebottle settling on his morning slice of bread-and-honey; nevertheless, he shifted his ground.

"Well, then, what of that Sidonian vessel which the women saw? Laodamas may have rowed out to her."

"In that case, why was no dinghy missing from the quay?"

"He may have swum. He is a strong swimmer."

"Father, please use the reason on which you so justly pride yourself! Could he swim with a cloakful of treasure on his back?"

My father fell silent and I continued: "The first report of

that mysterious Sidonian vessel came a month or two after Laodamas had disappeared."

"Are you suggesting that Eurymachus's mother also lied? Why should she lie? Why should Melantho lie? She is Ctimene's own maid, and devoted to our house."

I shrugged my shoulders. "I wish I knew why, Father. But my heart assures me that they are in collusion."

"What can you be trying to tell me?" he asked fiercely.

I did not blink an eyelid. "That Laodamas never sailed at all," I replied.

"Stop joking, child. Everyone knows that he sailed."

"Everyone knows that Helen eloped to Troy with Paris: or everyone, except you! To be alone in your knowledge does not prove you wrong; as it did not prove Laocoön wrong when he told the incredulous Trojans that the Wooden Horse was full of armed enemies."

That pulled him up short. "Oh, so Laodamas went off overland somewhere? Perhaps to join your rebellious brother Halius among the Sicels? It is possible, but not likely. Why did nobody meet him on the road?"

Again I shrugged. "Let me tell you, Father, what the Goddess Athene has put into my mind: Laodamas never left Drepanum."

He looked searchingly at me, as though he feared for my sanity, and went out, slamming the door. A long piece of plaster fell from behind the doorjamb—shaped like a dagger.

A ship had just made port in the northern harbour: a Taphian thirty-oarer, with a cargo of Chalybean iron ingots, bound for the Temesan copper mines in south-west Italy. Her captain, a cousin of the Taphian king, called at the Palace,

and when he had been entertained in a manner befitting his
rank, my father, as usual, asked him whether he brought
news of Laodamas.

He brought none, but proved liberal with advice. "My lord
King, it is clear that his absence is eating at your heart like
a mouse at one of these splendid Elyman cheeses, and I can
see only one course for you to take. First: despatch a responsible member of your household to Sandy Pylus, where, since
it is the centre of the amber trade, your son will naturally
have gone to buy his necklace. If the Pylians have no news,
mourn him as drowned, return, and build him a cenotaph
worthy of his fame. Afterwards send your peevish daughter-
in-law back to her father's house with the bride price; there
let her marry again. Why keep her here in the Palace, my
lord King, weeping and mourning without cease? A half-blind
man could see that the Lady Ctimene depresses your spirits
and those of your admirable servants."

"Yes," my father agreed, "and she is not even breeding
me grandchildren."

"Well, then," the Taphian continued briskly, "who can go
to Sandy Pylus? Your son Clytoneus? Though young, he is
keen-witted. Or, failing him, what of your capable brother-in-
law, my lord Mentor?"

"I trust nobody but myself," replied my father, "to make
the necessary enquiries. Yet how can I go?"

"Every king believes that his presence is indispensable;
but a short holiday does him good, and his people little harm.
Why not accompany us, when we sail home, in twenty days'
time at the most, from Temesa? I prefer, you see, to take the
longer route back, avoiding the Strait of Messina, which is

both dangerous to navigate and a notorious haunt of pirates.
We could land you at Sandy Pylus within the month. How
would that be?"

My father was goaded into taking a sudden resolution:
he would leave the kingdom under the regency of my uncle
Mentor and sail to Sandy Pylus. Despite my warnings, he
still obstinately believed the first part of the Hyrian merchant's story—which was, I admit, circumstantial enough—
and concluded that Laodamas must have reached Thesprotia
by way of Corcyra. But what happened then? Had he met with
unexpected trouble? Had he been robbed of his wealth by
King Pheidon? Perhaps even sold into slavery?

"If all other sources of information fail," my father told
the Taphian, "I shall visit Delphi and consult the Oracle of
Apollo. Or, maybe, Zeus's at Dodona would be the more
reliable of the two."

Though reposing small faith in the prophetic gifts of the
divine priestesses, he knew well that Delphi and Dodona
were centres of information and gossip for all Greece, and
that he would learn from the sacrificial butchers, or the in-
telligent corps of messengers, whatever was to be known of
Laodamas's whereabouts. He summoned my mother, my
brother Clytoneus, my uncle Mentor, my grandfather Phytalus, and myself to a family council; but not Ctimene.

"Let me tell the truth," he confided to us. "The fact is that
I cannot face the prospect of Ctimene's prolonged anxiety
and grief. She makes the very walls of the Palace weep and
shudder in sympathy. Often I despair of her life; more often
I grow enraged and am tempted to send her back to Bucinna,
with the bride price which she brought—or its equivalent in

sacerdotal and commercial privileges. But this I will not do, for fear of antagonizing Laodamas when he returns—you must notice that I refuse to take your pessimistic view and say *'if* he returns'."

Fifteen days later, the Taphian put in again with his cargo of copper, to which my father now added a valuable consignment of linen, honey, and folding bedsteads, and stepped cheerfully aboard. Almost the whole town sped him on his way, offering generous sacrifices to all the deities who rule the sea or protect travellers. Clytoneus and I climbed halfway up Mount Eryx to watch his sail, bellied out by a stiff westerly breeze, disappear behind the island of Motya, some eight miles to the south. When we regained the Palace, my mother drew me aside, and said: "Child, your father has told me what Athene put into your mouth: namely that we must mourn Laodamas as dead. Nor was it a lying oracle. I myself saw him in a dream three nights ago: he came, dripping blood and sea water, a dagger between his shoulders, and stood piteously before me. Then he pointed to the banqueting court, and cried: 'Let them avenge me, Mother! Let them avenge me with the bow of Philoctetes!' 'How shall I know that you are truly my son Laodamas?' I asked him. He answered: 'Dear Mother, when you wake tomorrow, I shall fly in by one window and out by the other, taking the shape of a white dove.' And so he did. Tell nobody of this, even my brother Mentor, even my son Clytoneus. But be resolute to find his murderers, and let us take exemplary vengeance. You alone of my children have a better head than heart."

"If you really believed in your vision, Mother," I said, not altogether pleased by this reflection on my capacity for

tender feelings, "why did you let my father sail for Sandy
Pylus on a useless errand?"

She grew grave. "He is a self-willed man, and though,
since I first married him, he has come to learn that I always
tell the truth, he hates to admit that I can possibly be better
informed than himself. Besides, he has never visited the main-
land of Greece and this may be his last chance: for he is
already past his prime. I told him of my vision, but because
you had come to much the same conclusion independently,
and because he had not seen the dove with his own eyes, he
accused me of plotting to keep him at home. 'Go, then,' I said,
'and the sooner you return, my lord, the longer we shall all
live.' Daughter, this is the threshold of danger. I can trust you
to do nothing foolish; meanwhile, let Ctimene warm herself
at what embers of hope she still can rake together."

Three days passed, and I became aware of a subtle but
pervasive change in the local atmosphere. Not among the
common people, nor among my few real friends, such as
Captain Dymas's daughter Procne and my cousins from
Hiera; nor among our faithful maids headed by Eurycleia,
who was once my dry nurse and now acts as housekeeper. I
can best describe it as a disdainful reserve noticeable in the
greetings that certain daughters of the nobility gave me, and
an overheartiness in the manner of their brothers and fathers,
as if they knew something that was being kept from me. Every
summer, Elyman children play a hide-and-seek game on the
hills called the Bull's Treasure, which consists in their all
going out to search for a boy, called the Bull, who has hidden
himself in some cleft or cave. Whoever finds him, stays behind
to collect the secret treasure, not proclaiming the discovery

to his companions; but presently first one, then another, also stumbles on the Bull's hiding place, until at last all are in the secret, except for one unfortunate, who goes wandering disconsolately over the deserted hillside, lonely and perplexed. That was how I felt now.

When I am in a bad temper, it amuses me to visit our linen factory, where the sight of women quietly plying the shuttle on the tall looms has a soothing effect on my mind; yet here, too, I found an unfamiliar spirit abroad. Several of the women had left their work and were gathered in a knot near the door, talking in excited whispers, but scurried off to their looms as soon as they saw me rounding the corner, and pretended to be weaving busily. Their shuttles flew backwards and forwards like the fluttering of aspen leaves in the wind.

"Good day, industrious linen workers," I sang out ironically. "I suppose that you have been discussing the man-headed fish drawn up in the mullet nets this morning? I saw the prodigy myself: it had arms instead of fins, and talked Phoenician—at any rate, everyone thought it must be Phoenician because none of us, not even I, could understand a word. There it lay: jabbering and gesturing, gesturing and jabbering until at last it turned blue in the face; so I threatened it with the strap, shouting that I expect both Phoenician fish and Elyman linen workers to keep their mouths shut when I come on the scene. The monster had the sense to obey."

A dead silence followed. All our women are afraid of me, believing that I am often under the influence of some deity or other; a fear, perhaps well grounded, which I exploit by talking this sort of nonsense at them. They are a good-natured set of girls, but the least thing will disturb them, and then their work suffers alike in quality and in quantity; as with the milk supply, when a fox runs through a flock of milch ewes, or a dog breaks loose and chases them.

"Where is Eurymedusa?" I asked. Eurymedusa, the handsome young manageress, dealt out the flax, saw to the comfort of the weavers, was responsible for the condition of the looms, and kept a close eye on the pattern of the web. We always set the looms working together on a single stock pattern—one or other of those in constant demand among the Libyans and Italians—so that Eurymedusa may find it easier to notice mistakes and encourage the laggards. On this occasion she had set up a simple check, with five purple and two scarlet threads occurring after every hundredth white one. My mother nicknames her Eurymedusa of Apeira, meaning the "Incompetent", but though she has been slow to learn her duties she is popular in the factory.

No, there was nothing strange in Eurymedusa's absence: she had merely gone to draw a pitcherful of drinking water, the day being sultry. "Mix it with a little wine, Eurymedusa," I said when she returned, "and dole out a gill to each of these tongue-tied women. Then get Gorgo the gooseherd to tell them one of her old-fashioned Sican stories, and keep their minds off the man-headed Phoenician fish which caused such a fright this morning."

Eurymedusa fetched a wineskin, and did as I ordered. They all drank my health politely, and smiled, but I could see that their eyes were still troubled.

When white-haired Gorgo hobbled in, I sat on a stool and listened. Her tale was about our ancestor Aegestus and his arrival in Sicily from Troy. Having landed near Mount Etna

to water his fleet, he ventured into a dark cave, where he was
seized by Polyphemus the Cyclops, one of the immortal smiths
who live thereabouts, and carried down to the bowels of the
burning mountain. It seems that Polyphemus and his clan
needed human blood to temper a thunderbolt which they were
forging for Zeus. Cunning Aegestus, however, intoxicated
them with Pramnian wine, and having removed their shoes
(every Cyclops has notoriously tender feet) hammered them
full of nails. Then he escaped, and when the smiths pulled on
their shoes and tried to give chase, pain forced them to desist.
So Aegestus regained his ships in safety, and continued westward until he reached Rheithrum. The howling of the Cyclops
was music in his ears.

Gorgo, small, thin, and active as a bird, told the story with
such skill—lowering her voice at moments of suspense, raising it to a shout when the crisis came, and mimicking the
characters—that the delighted weaving women called for
another like it. She looked doubtful, but when I nodded my
assent, began a tale about her ancestor Sicanus and his ex-
periences in the cave of one-eyed Conturanus—a giant tall
enough to knock a hole in the sky with his staff. With his belly
resting on the summit of Eryx and his immense legs thrust
behind him on our plain, he used to plunge his great hands
into the Aegestan Sea and scoop up tunnies by the hundred.
Sicanus had entered the cave in expectation of hospitality,
followed by twelve companions, but Conturanus brained and
ate them one by one, and their egress was barred by the door-
stopper, which only he could budge. This excessively large
boulder he rolled back twice a day: to drive his flocks to
pasture at dawn and lead them home at twilight. On the third

night Sicanus blinded Conturanus with his own staff, charred
to a point in the fire, and escaped by clinging to the wool
beneath the belly of a prize ram, when Conturanus let it out
to feed early the next morning. Conturanus raged madly
against Sicanus, and threw two enormous but ineffectual
rocks at him as he swam away towards Hiera.

These rocks are still shown, protruding from the sea about
three miles to the south-west of Drepanum; and a huge cave,
now occupied by our Sican shepherds, where we go sometimes for picnics, is called the Cave of Conturanus. When
one of the women asked how so tall a giant managed to live
in a cave no larger than our Palace, Gorgo explained that
he had the magical power of diminishing his size at will by
eating a certain mushroom.

Eurymedusa said afterwards: "Gorgo, how you enthral
us! Alas, that Homer has no daughters as well as sons! If
he had, and if they turned your stories into poems, and sang
them sweetly to the lyre, what a ravishing entertainment that
would be!"

"Alas, indeed!" I thought. The Sons of Homer are so jealous of their privileges that they allow none but their clansmen to declaim before princes. Nor does anyone dare compete
with them. Yet if men sing to men, why should women not
sing to women? Athene, who invented every intellectual art,
is a woman. So are the Muses, who inspire all song. And
the Pythoness, who prophesies in unforgettable verse, is a
woman.

"Oh, Muses," I prayed silently, "enter into the heart of
your servant Nausicaa, and teach her to compose skilful
hexameter verses!"

Believe it, or believe it not, my unusual prayer was at once answered! For I heard myself saying:

"Eurymedusa, the day must dawn when the songs of a
  woman
Sound to the well-strung lyre, and are praised by the
  Delian judges."

This was an important crisis in my life, perhaps the most important, though nobody present realized that I was speaking in verse, and prophesying, too. The common people lack discernment. If the Goddess Athene were to pass through our court of sacrifice today, helmet on head and Aegis displayed, do you think that they would rush to propitiate her? They would do nothing of the kind. I can imagine them saying: "Who in the world is this hard-faced young woman in the fringed goatskin apron? And why does she wear that round shield with the ugly face on it strapped over her shoulder? The effrontery of wearing a plumed helmet as though she were a man! She must be one of those wild, lecherous Nasamonians from Libya—what ship has brought her? Does anyone know? Let us trust that her promiscuity will not create a scandal in the market place."

Sighing for disgust, I turned on my heel and went to find Clytoneus. He was nowhere in the house, nor in the orchard; so I wandered towards the town deep in thought, and met him striding along, with Argus and Laelaps at his heels.

"I took the Eryx road," he said. "Argus started a hare and had her twisting and doubling between the cornfields. Laelaps kept only a few yards behind. Presently they reached a patch of brambles and butcher's-broom, where they lost her. Then a vixen bolted from the same thicket and led them a fine chase up the hill, but went to earth in the stone quarry. So we were out of luck. Still, the hounds enjoyed their run; they seldom get enough exercise these days."

"Tell me, Clytoneus," I said, lowering my voice because a group of peasants was approaching, "have you noticed any alteration in people's behaviour since our father sailed?"

He stopped suddenly. "Since you mention it, yes," he answered. "A certain ungraciousness, amounting almost to sullenness. It is natural enough that some people should be tempted to take things easy in the King's absence and neglect their duties. Uncle Mentor is well disposed to our house but, being of lower rank than several members of the Council, cannot sit with proper assurance in the chair of state. Besides, he is a little too softhearted, and his tours of inspection are not nearly so thorough as our father's. I happened to hear Melantheus answering him back most rudely yesterday when he suggested that the goats should be restrained by some means or other from barking the young poplar trees. Uncle Mentor went off with a civil good day, to which Melantheus returned hardly a grunt; but I came up, applied my spear shaft to the insolent fellow's shoulders and advised him to mend his ways."

"What did he say then?"

"He muttered darkly that Agelaus, being now the senior Trojan prince left in Drepanum of an age to command the Elyman forces, should have been awarded the regency, and that our father had done wrong to pass him over because of some private quarrel. So I drubbed the fool again. If only I were a few years older . . ."

I pressed Clytoneus further. "Do you feel no danger threatening our house?"

"What sort of danger?"

"That is precisely what I want to find out. I read Melantheus's rudeness as a bad sign, because he would be too cowardly to talk in that strain without powerful backing. However solidly based our dynasty is supposed to be, the whole town smells of rebellion."

"Rebellion by whom?"

"By Prince Antinous. He, not his old father Eupeithes, is the real leader of the Phocaeans, who have always resented their subordination to the Trojan house of Aegestus. But his cousin Eurymachus appears to be the brains of the movement. Behind these two, willingly or unwillingly, are ranged a large crowd of the young bloods, and even a few Trojans— Agelaus, for one. I trust none of them, except perhaps the sons of Halitherses. What do you say?"

"That the exaggerated courtesy with which your so-called suitors now treat me makes me suspect a plot."

"Dear Clytoneus, the Goddess Athene often warns me clearly what not to do, or what to do. She has just come disguised as the daughter of our shepherd Philoetius, and 'Mistress,' she said, 'a Calydonian boar is to be hunted tomorrow. I foresee mourning.' "

"Explain the reference, please."

"Are you taking part in tomorrow's boar hunt?"

"Yes, I have just been asked by Amphinomus, a very honest fellow."

"You mean Eurymachus's cousin?"

"I do."

"Eurymachus has certainly made a stalking-horse of him."

"Forgive my stupidity, Nausicaa, and be still more explicit."

"I am suggesting that in the course of the hunt, to which Eurymachus, Antinous, and all the Phocaean nobles will be invited, a javelin intended for the boar will transfix you; as happened to one Eurytion in the famous Calydonian Hunt. Peleus, who threw the javelin, protested afterwards that he had been aiming at the boar; but Peleus was always a dangerous companion. He accidentally killed his brother Phocus with a quoit—if, indeed, it was an accident."

Clytoneus scratched his head. "Then should I decline the invitation? Should I say that I have fever?"

"My advice is: go boldly to Amphinomus, and tell him in the presence of his kinsmen: 'Friend Amphinomus, I have been warned by a female soothsayer not to hunt tomorrow, unless I place myself under your protection. She declares that it is one of my unlucky days. If I am pierced by a misdirected javelin, will you swear to take vengeance on the house of the man who flung it?' As you speak, watch their faces."

Clytoneus, though inexperienced and unsure of himself on public occasions, never shrank from any difficult assignment. Screwing up his courage, he stalked into Amphinomus's courtyard as if about to hurl a spear at the sacred images, and his request sounded almost like a declaration of war. Amphinomus, who showed no sign of guilt, remarked in quiet tones that it would be folly to disregard the female soothsayer's advice, and that since tomorrow was an unlucky day, by all means let him stay at home and offer propitiatory

sacrifices to the Infernal Gods. But Antinous avoided Clytoneus's eye, while Eurymachus glared defiance.

"You have forestalled a plot against my life," Clytoneus
told me later. "I must reward Athene with thanks offerings
for the warning she gave me, and placate the Infernals as
well."

"Athene deserves your gratitude," I said. "Continue to
keep on guard. Until our father returns, you would be wise
not to go hunting alone, or accept invitations to dine out.
Beams have been known to collapse, eaten through by mag-
gots; and brawls to start, in which goblets and stools fly
recklessly about, hurled by anonymous hands, killing innocent bystanders."

Clytoneus asked: "You do not think, do you, that any such
accident could take place in the Palace? The staff are trustworthy enough, surely?"

"All but a few. What troubles me is this: since Halius went
to live among the Sicels, only two lives stand between you
and the throne, namely Laodamas and our father. Do the
conspirators know, then, that Laodamas has been put safely
out of the way—not murdered, let us hope, but sold to
Phoenician slavers—and hopefully expect our father to meet
with an accident as soon as he sets foot again on our quay?"

"He should never have sailed. Perhaps we ought to send
him a warning."

"Sandy Pylus is distant and the winds are fickle," I reminded Clytoneus. "Besides, he proposes to make enquiries at
the court of King Pheidon the Thesprotian. Have patience,
Brother, be wary, trust in the Gods."

We walked slowly back to the Palace, and parted at the

gate with looks of affection. Clytoneus went to take a warm
bath, which Eurycleia had prepared; and I drank half a cup
of wine to fortify myself against another miserable visit
to Ctimene's bedside. Ah, to hear the same confidences, complaints, and reproaches delivered for the hundredth time in
a flat, whining voice!

CHAPTER

FIVE

WASHING

DAY

I COULD NOT SLEEP. Despite a spectacular storm out at sea on the previous night, which had kept the fishing fleet in port, the air was still heavy with thunder. Another sirocco had been slowly rising since late afternoon, the third or fourth that same month, and was now blowing everything to pieces, banging doors, stripping the trees of green fruit, and fetching tiles from the roof. We could expect a shower before morning, though not one smart enough to make up for the damage done by the wind. Our siroccos are of two kinds: hot and cold. The cold seems the more bearable but scorches the flowers and vegetables just as cruelly.

I began reckoning our chances of success, should Antinous and Eurymachus raise an armed insurrection, and should

Agelaus, aggrieved at having been slighted by my father, support them. Could we hold our end of the peninsula, even though forewarned of the assault and reinforced by the islanders of Hiera and Bucinna, the herdsmen of Hypereia and the scattered loyalists of Eryx, Aegesta and Drepanum? It seemed unlikely. Once the enemy reached the Palace, our main gate would soon be battered down by a great log of wood, and fire arrows shot into the open attics, which were highly inflammable. Granted, the common people were on our side, because my father always dispensed equal justice, protected their liberties, and had shown himself a considerate employer. But the common people are notoriously slow to act, and being armed only with clubs, wooden hayforks and suchlike, are easily cowed by men with broad shields, long-plumed helmets, and deadly sharp weapons of war. Would my women be raped? These things happen in real life, not merely in old tales. Procne and I had, as a matter of fact, discussed this unpleasant topic a few months before. My contention was that it would be almost impossible for a man to violate a determined woman against her will, unless he first knocked her insensible. Of the fifty sons of Aegyptus, whom their father ordered to violate the Danaids, I said, the only one who lived to see the dawn was the wise youth who respected his bride's virginity. But now my argument did not sound quite so convincing as it had done.

About midnight I was roused from an uneasy doze by something which struck the stool by my bedside. The wind had dropped, and I could hear the roar of the sea as it broke on the point. It was good to be awake, because I had been dreaming of how an eagle swooped down on the geese which

Gorgo keeps in a shed for me and feeds on mash; he tore them to pieces before my eyes. I sprang out of bed and hurried to the window which gave on the garden. Someone must have tried to attract my attention. Could it be a drunken suitor? But nobody showed himself, and the fruit trees were bathed in moonlight.

On the floor I found a strip of sheepskin wrapped around a stone and covered with pictures drawn in cuttlefish ink. A woman burning a ship and a swallow whispering to her. In bright sun, a cart, and a row of washerwomen; also three scorpions consulting together, with a Cretan axe planted above them. Easily read: Procne—namely the swallow—was suggesting that I should take my women to wash clothes in the morning. She would meet me, Nausicaa, "Burner of Ships", at the Springs of Periboea—the cart indicated that we should meet at some distance from the town—where she would tell me of a plot hatched by three murderous people, namely the scorpions, for the usurpation of royal power. Procne had never learned to write, but managed to convey her message well enough . . . It seemed that I was not far wrong in my assessment of the situation!

A sudden cool gust of air. A dark cloud rose up from the north, blotting out the moonlight, and heavy drops of rain began to strike the dusty orchard leaves. I fell asleep soon.

An hour or so after dawn I washed my face and went downstairs to a breakfast of barley bread, oil, pickled samphire, slices of pork sausage, mulled wine, and honey cake. My mother was seated, distaff in hand, beside the hearth among her sleepy women, spinning purple wool with deft twists of her long white fingers.

"Good morning, Mother. Have you seen my uncle Mentor?"

"Yes, child. He is on his way to attend a special meeting of the Drepanan Council. You may catch him, if you run."

I had no difficulty in overtaking him. The slowness of his limp suggested that he was not looking forward to the meeting. "Uncle!" I said, "could you provide me with a mule cart today? It promises to be fine for a change, and there are piles of soiled linen waiting to be washed. Unless we attend to it now, we shall have nothing presentable to wear. You have gone around in the same tunic this last month—I recognize the wine stains on the hem—and Clytoneus complains that he is ashamed to appear publicly in such dirty clothes. We Elymans have always been famous for our love of clean linen."

"Who attends to the laundry?"

"It is really Ctimene's business, but she spends so much of the night weeping that she is never in a condition to start work until the sun has travelled a third of the way across the sky. If I do not go to the Springs, who will?"

"Surely the maids can manage the laundry by themselves? I like to have you around the house to keep an eye on the linen factory and the dairy."

"No, Uncle Mentor. I cannot trust the maids with the clothes, many of which are of the finest wool; they would do more damage in a morning than could be repaired in a year. Some of our handsome old bedcovers have escaped being washed for a couple of winters, and are filthy from brazier dust or the smoke of torches. Then there is a pile of robes which my father has set aside as wedding gifts for when I marry—if I ever do. They will make shabby enough pres-

ents until the torn embroidery has been darned; but how can
I match the colours before they are washed?"

He sighed: "Very well. Tell the grooms to give the cart a
good scraping—it last carried dung—and to harness the
mules. Do you need a driver, or can you control the beasts
yourself? We are shorthanded in the fields at present."

"Thank you, Uncle Mentor, but I know how to drive."

"Good-bye, then, and a happy working day to you!"

"Good-bye, and a peaceful council meeting to you!"

He pulled a comically wry face. I kissed him on both
cheeks and ran to ask my mother for the loan of six women,
besides my own three.

"You can have three. The rest you must borrow from
the linen factory; I do not suppose Eurymedusa will mind
very much. I am grateful to you for taking on the task, though
I doubt whether you realize how formidable it is. Tell Eurycleia to make up your hamper and fill a wineskin. Here, take
this bottle of scented oil. You will want to bathe in the
harbour, I expect, and anoint yourselves afterwards."

I thanked her and found Eurycleia. "Quick, pack us a
hamper, dearest Nurse," I said. "Bread, meat, cheese,
pickles, fruit and salad from the garden—no, I can choose
the salad myself . . . And a goatskin of that dark raisin
wine. We are off to the Springs of Periboea!"

The Springs are called after my Sican great-grandmother,
whose son was Nausithous. They rise behind Rheithrum, and
their water is unusually soft. Most of our washing is done in
huge stone troughs through which the stream has been led.
First we rub the clothes with a mixture of wood ash, fuller's
earth, and urine, to remove stains; and then we jump on

them, as when one treads grapes in a vat. Obstinate stains we beat out with flat wooden cudgels, laying the clothes on smooth stone slabs. The more delicate woollens we wash in warm, slightly salted water, to prevent their shrinking and to fix the colours. Our drying ground is a pebbled beach, which catches the whole heat of the sun. Washing days are quite enjoyable if the weather is kind. And should a thunderstorm come on, we can take refuge in a cave near by called the Naiads' Grotto; at the back are stalactites and stalagmites looking like looms, and a row of ancient stone vessels, which the Sicans occasionally fill with food and drink for the Naiads.

"Oho!" cried Eurycleia, as she hurried to the storeroom. "So now you are going to wash at the Springs of Periboea? Is the wind at that door? I have a notion that you will bring home a baby from the thicket."

Not considering this a joke in very good taste, I made no answer. Eurycleia was referring to the story of childless Queen Periboea who, having one day taken her laundry women to a stream near the Corinthian seashore, happened to find an eight-day-old infant washed up in a chest. She retired to a thicket, and afterwards told her women that she had just been delivered of the child, whom, according to the Corinthians, she named Oedipais, the "Child of the Swelling Wave"—though the Sons of Homer change the name to Oedipus, or "Swollen Foot". This Oedipais subsequently captured the city of Thebes. He is said by some to have killed his father and married his mother: an obscene and improbable story.

I collected the women, climbed into the cart—where the

hamper, oil bottle, cudgels, washing and all had been carefully stowed—touched the mules with my whip, and clattered
away. The women ran alongside, laughing and singing. Not a
cloud was to be seen in the sky, and the rain had cooled the
air.

Rheithrum is a landlocked bay a quarter of a mile wide
and over a mile long; behind it stretch clover meadows dotted
with clumps of olives suitable for picnics. At the farther end
rise the Springs of Periboea, which are Palace property and
run into the harbour. I unharnessed the mules and sent them
off to graze—when evening came, a lump of bread would
soon tempt them back—and made the women gather sticks
and light a big fire to heat up stones. Live charcoal for this
purpose had been brought in a pot. A second breakfast of
bread, cold meat, olives and onions, over which we wasted
little time; then as soon as the stones were red-hot, they were
plunged into a shallow trough to warm the water for the
woollens. We worked on these and the finer pieces a good two
hours or more.

Presently I heard my name called, and saw Procne running
towards us. "What a surprise," she cried. "I had no notion
that you were out washing today. My father is breaking in a
colt by the Naiads' Grotto. Would you care to watch him?
He is making the beast trot round in circles at the end of a
rope; but it is still very frisky and obstinate."

"I cannot come until the woollens are done; but we shall
not be long now. Lend us a hand, will you, dear Procne?"

"With all my heart," answered Procne, and we washed
silently for a while. Then I set the women to scrub the sheets
and plain tunics and the white presentation robes, while she

and I strolled off. We were no sooner out of earshot than I asked: "Darling, may I guess the names of your three scorpions?"

"I should be delighted. Afterwards I can deny on oath ever having mentioned them: I need only nod or shake my head when you ask me."

"Well, let me guess: Antinous, Eurymachus, and that lout Ctesippus with the twisted mouth."

Procne nodded vigorously.

"Is Agelaus in the plot?"

She fluttered her hand and pushed out her lower lip, meaning "Not exactly".

"Who gave you this information?"

"I heard it by accident. While I was gathering strands of wool from brambles and thorn trees near our house—I like to have an excuse for a walk—I happened to be posted behind a thicket when the second and third scorpions came by and lay down in the grass at the verge. I had not noticed their arrival until they began to talk, and then it was too late to escape. So I stood quietly, rooted like a tree. I heard Eurymachus—I should say the second scorpion—insisting that their chance had come at last to revenge themselves on your dear father."

"Oh, Procne, why do you sweeten Eurymachus's bitter words? He must have called the King by some very disagreeable names."

Procne blushed. "Yes, 'miser', 'skinflint', and 'bloodsucker', were among the less flattering of them, and he suggested that since the King had invited all eligible bachelors to court you and then sailed away to Greece in undignified haste, leaving as his Regent your uncle Mentor, to whom they owe no allegiance, rather than Agelaus, on whose knees the Elyman sceptre should properly have been laid . . . How did this eloquent sentence begin? I forget. But Eurymachus suggested that the said bachelors should show their disapproval of the way in which the clans have been treated by the King: for instance, being forced to give the Hyrian merchant public presents in acknowledgement of a private benefit —that is, if telling barefaced lies could be regarded as a benefit—and denied even the satisfaction of seeing the promised gold goblet added to the pile. He also complained that the King had refused to provide you with the traditional dowry of cattle, tripods, cauldrons, chased swords, gold-mounted scabbards, silver mixing bowls and the like, offering commercial privileges, priesthoods and other intangible gifts instead."

"How are the clansmen to show their disapproval?"

"Eurymachus and Antinous suggest that it will be a great joke if the whole company assemble at the Palace and announce themselves as your suitors. They intend to make free with the palace flocks, herds and wine, camping in the two courts and forcing Lord Mentor to offer them such hospitality as befits their rank."

"And then?"

"Then, I gather, they hope that your brother Clytoneus will be provoked to violence, because he is a touchy and head-strong young fellow, and be killed as soon as he reaches for his sword. Little Telegonus will die accidentally—a boat will overturn and spill him out into rough water. Then Antinous will marry you and demand a splendid dowry; and Eurymachus will get Ctimene, with Laodamas's inheritance added; and your father will be ambushed on his return from Sandy Pylus by a vessel lurking in the Straits of Motya. His rich lands, for want of an heir, will be divided and sold to the highest bidder. They have everything planned to their own advantage."

"I see. And who will be the next King of the Elymans?"

"They have promised Agelaus the sceptre, on condition that he does not oppose their wicked plot."

"Procne, you are a true friend! You have told nobody but me, have you?"

"Not even my mother."

"Oh, if only I could decide what to do! If only I had some reliable friend of fighting age! My uncle Mentor is a man of peace; my grandfather Phytalus is too old; Clytoneus is too young . . . And your father sails for Elba in about five days' time, you say?"

"Though he is loyal to your house, what could he do if he stayed?"

"And you, Procne?"

"Need that be asked, Nausicaa? I love you as I love no one else in the world! Trust me to the last drop of blood."

"That is what I wanted to hear, although I have heard it before. Perhaps now, if Athene will inspire me with some extraordinarily cunning plan . . ."

"My father is waving. I must go at once. Good-bye, my best friend."

I watched her running across the clover, and then walked slowly back to the washing women. It was midday, but by making an effort we should finish the linen within the hour.

My father has always maintained that the only known way
to make servants work well, short of threatening them with
torture, is to work by their side and set them an example. So
I was soon jumping on the sheets in the trough, or banging
at them with a cudgel; yet let the domestic chatter flow past
my ears, as the water flowed past my feet, while I silently
prayed to Athene for a sure sign of her favour.

The sign came. A covey of small birds had gathered to
quarrel over the breadcrumbs which we had turned out of
the basket after breakfast. And suddenly a hawk pounced,
scattered the uninvited guests, and carried off one of them in
his talons to eat at leisure. My heart leapt, and I began to sing
a hymn of praise to the Goddess, which the women took up;
and a beautiful sound our voices made!

I inspected the sheets and tunics already washed, set a few
aside for further scrubbing, and helped the women to spread
the rest on the beach; the sun would dry them by evening.
Then I clapped my hands. "Girls," I cried, "since we seem
to be alone, we can bathe naked in Rheithrum, and then run
around to get the stiffness out of our backs and raise an
appetite for dinner. You have all worked pretty well and we
need not go home until just before sunset."

This put everyone in a happy humour. We climbed down
the bank on which the washing had been and, after a long
careful look in all directions, unclasped our girdles, shed
our clothes, and went splashing about in the cool water.

"Oh, how fat you have grown, Glauce," shouted one of my
maids, pointing at the plump stomach of a weaving-woman.
"For shame, and your wedding not for another month! Did
this happen at the Ascent of Aphrodite?"

"I'll drown you for that!" answered Glauce. "Don't you know honest fat from dishonest? I keep only beans and good bread and figs inside."

"Here, let me feel! No, child, you can't deceive me! There's more here than ever went in at your mouth. Who is the fortunate father?"

They tussled, screamed, pulled each other's hair, and laughed wildly. Glauce soon forced her opponent under the water, holding her down by the shoulders. "So you think I behave like your friend Melantho!" she yelled. "Is that it?"

"Let her go, Glauce," I ordered. "The joke has gone far enough."

Up came the maid, choking and spluttering, and pretended to be thoroughly subdued; but soon she caught Glauce off her guard, and pushed her backwards into a pool. It was only high spirits, and neither bore the other any ill will. However, I took Glauce aside to ask her: "What did you say just now?"

"Nothing, mistress."

"Glauce, that is untrue. You were angry for a moment, and said more than you intended. I know, because you looked guiltily around to see whether I had overheard."

"I bear Melantho no grudge."

Then the Goddess Athene put these words into my mouth: "Yet it was about Melantho that you weavers were gossiping when I visited the factory yesterday morning."

"I did not gossip, mistress."

"Glauce: tell me the truth, or I shall take one of those cudgels and bang you across the face until your own mother will ask 'Who can this be?' "

"I swear by all the Gods that I did not gossip! I only listened."

"Very well, then, what did you hear?"

"Lies, I daresay. It must have been a lie. You know how much scandal is talked in the market place."

"Indeed, I do; but I insist on hearing what this particular scandal was! Melantho is the daughter of our cattlemaster Melantheus and also the Lady Ctimene's maid; I am bound to protect her good name."

I frightened the truth out of Glauce. One hot day, it seems, at siesta time, Melantho had been seen stealthily leaving a boathouse on the far side of the southern harbour, and though nobody knew whether she had enjoyed anyone's company there, three days later she was wearing a valuable gold bracelet. She claimed to have found this in the vegetable patch behind her cottage when she went to pull a lettuce, and to have got Melantheus's permission to keep it.

I asked Glauce: "To whom does the boathouse belong?"

"I am not sure."

"Well, to whom do they say that it belongs? All marketplace stories are circumstantial."

"Please, mistress . . ."

"The cudgel is handy; what do you say?"

"That your suitor, my lord Eurymachus, owns it."

"Very good, Glauce. Like you, I refuse to believe this story, but it is always best to know what people are saying." I forced a gay laugh, and shouted: "Now, girls, out you come! Wash off the brine in the spring water and then anoint yourselves. I have the oil, and scallop shells make useful scrapers."

So we trooped back to the Springs, where we washed,

anointed and scraped ourselves, dressed our hair, and set the
cloth for dinner. The wine was strong, and though I had tempered it well, the girls grew excited and wanted to dance,
even after eating like mares in a clover field.

"Not now," I said. "This is when you rest. But if you will
promise to keep quiet until the shadow from this stick touches
the edge of that stone, I will join you in the ball dance afterwards."

They all lay down obediently and dozed. I stayed awake,
watching the shadow creep slowly towards the stone, and
marshalling my thoughts. So Melantho was having a secret
affair with Eurymachus, was she? It must have been going
on for some months, if Eurymachus had bribed her to tell that
story of the Sidonian ship, as obviously he had. But why?
What would he gain by the lie? And why should his mother
have supported him? I already guessed the answer. The immediate problem was how to face a dangerous and intolerable
situation. Once more I prayed silently to the Goddess, rose
encouraged, and roused the women.

We ran to the beach again, scratched a labyrinth pattern
on the smooth white sand, and began our famous Trojan ball
dance, in which we perform complicated movements, singing
as we wind in and out of a maze, and throwing the ball from
one girl to the other, at each change of the tune. All was going
perfectly, when I tossed the ball to awkward Glauce, who
jumped too high, knocked it with her thumb, and sent it flying
into the water.

Rheithrum has a currrent caused partly by the stream
which feeds it, and partly by the lunar tide; the difference
between ebb and flow may be as much as a yard in depth. We

watched the ball drifting into deep water, and the girls
shouted for dismay, because none of them could swim.

I swim pretty well and was on the point of stripping off
my tunic to retrieve the ball (made of white leather stitched
over cork and painted with red rings) when the shouts suddenly rose to a general scream and the women stampeded.
Only Glauce remained, clinging to me in terror. I turned, and
saw to my amazement a naked young man staggering towards
me down the bank; one hand modestly concealing his private
parts with a branch of oleaster; the other spread out, palm
upward, in a suppliant gesture. He must have been lurking
in the thicket close to where we had dined.

A momentary silence followed, broken by Glauce's giggle
and her quavering cry: "Oh, mistress, here comes your baby!
The boy that Eurycleia foretold you would bring back from
the thicket by the seashore."

I could have strangled the fool.

The young man seemed exhausted and, in any case, we had
little to fear; ten sturdy women armed with cudgels are not
to be underrated as a fighting force. So I stood still and let him
approach, wriggling prostrate across the sand to clasp my
knees in the well-known style of suppliants. But he halted a
decent distance away and, propping his head on both elbows,
gazed steadfastly at me.

"Now, whom in the world has Athene sent me?" I
wondered.

CHAPTER
SIX
THE NAKED
CRETAN

NOTHING COULD HAVE BEEN MORE CORRECT
than the naked young man's approach.

"Madam," he said, in an unfamiliar but musical Greek
accent, "forgive me! My eyes being dimmed alike with exhaustion and salt water, I cannot trust them to inform me
whether you are a goddess or a mortal. If a goddess, you can
only be Artemis the Huntress: your body is so slim, so strong,
so regal. But if a mortal, how I envy the parents of such a
paragon! From my thicket I watched you dancing, and each
movement, each gesture, was perfection—you outshone your
companions as the moon outshines the stars. Yet infinitely
more enviable than your parents will be the man who suc-
ceeds in persuading them, with lavish gifts, to accept him as

a son-in-law! The mere thought of such good fortune deepens the misery of my present plight. Look: I am poorer than an infant of one day old; he, at least, has a cradle of his own and a warm swaddling band upon which loving kinswomen have embroidered his clan mark. I have not even a loincloth to hide my nakedness; the greedy sea has stripped me of everything but courage and these two strong hands."

He paused to observe the effect that these words had on me; I granted him a half-smile, since both his language and manners showed that he came of distinguished family. Besides, though his body was bruised, swollen, cut and salt-encrusted, he had an athlete's shoulders and thighs, and curly yellow hair, tinged with red, which recalled Apollo's in the temple frescoes.

"The sea has also left you an eloquent tongue," I remarked, "which I do not altogether despise."

Lowering his eyes, he continued: "Then let me confess, without fear of causing displeasure, that a sort of religious awe creeps over me as I grovel before you. Never have I seen anything so wildly beautiful as your slender figure and upright carriage. Artemis must look just like that when she dances with her maidens on Mount Erymanthus; though it were death to watch her. In this dizzy and famished state, I find it hard to convey my feelings; yet let me compare you to the young palm tree at Delos, which rises tall and straight beside the altar of Apollo—the altar built entirely of wild goats' horns by the God himself—for there the sea breeze plays with the palm's delicate fronds, as here it stirs your long fine hair."

"You have visited Delos then?" I asked, much amused.

"Or is this a secondhand compliment borrowed from one of the Sons of Homer, who make Apollo's holy island their headquarters?" No one had ever compared me to a young palm tree; probably because I am neither tall nor slim, and my hair, though long, is by no means my best feature. This stranger was far from being a fool. My suitors had always kept on what they considered safe ground by admiring my teeth, nose, brow, ankles and fingers; all of which, I flatter myself, pass muster.

"Certainly I have visited Delos, in more prosperous days, dedicating spoils of battle to Leto's divine twins. When first I set eyes on that sacred palm sapling, I let the gold and silver drop to the ground and stood rapt in silent wonder at its beauty. It seemed a thing so far removed from mortal life and charged with such limitless virtue that I dared not touch its bark lest I might tumble senseless for very ecstasy. The same feeling overcomes me now; which is why I venture to clasp your knees, though offering myself as your suppliant and slave."

"What has brought you to Sicily?"

He shrugged his shoulders. "The Blessed Gods alone know why they have saved only one man from the wreck of a gallant ship and cast him ashore at your feet, more dead then alive. Could they have had some heroic task in mind that I must perform on your behalf?"

My heart leapt again, but I replied as casually and distantly as I could: "Who knows? I am not even sure yet whether to offer you my protection. How long have you been hiding in that thicket?"

"Since dawn. The ship was struck by lightning two nights ago, about a mile from the coast."

"You owned her?"

"It would be easy to pretend that I did, but ill fortune is hardly an excuse for boastful lying. No, she was a large, well-found Corinthian, homeward bound from Libya; and how I came to be aboard her is a painful story. Let it suffice to tell your ladyship that the storm, a brief though violent one, broke suddenly, soon after dusk. You must have seen it yourself. Asleep in the waist at the time, the first thing I knew was that my ears were ringing with the crash of thunder, a strong smell of sulphur assailed my nostrils, and cold sea water had drenched my naked body. I dived overboard, and swam off as fast as I could to avoid being sucked down by the wreck, which sank almost at once. The water was alive with bobbing heads, like ducks on a pond, which the continuous lightning flashes revealed. Then rain fell hissing, and for a while I paddled about wildly, appalled by the choked cries of my drowning shipmates. I remember shouting to the God Poseidon: 'Save me, Earthshaker, and you shall have sacrifice upon sacrifice, the costliest obtainable, even if I must do violence to placate you!' These words were cut short by a jolt in the ribs which knocked all the breath out of my body, and I thought that the end had come: the crabs would have my flesh and the depth of the sea my bones. But I clutched desperately above me as I sank, and caught hold of something round and solid: the ship's mast, or four fathoms of it, with a couple of stays attached, blackened by the lightning stroke. How I contrived to get astride this divinely sent timber, Heaven alone knows; but it kept me afloat until dawn, when I saw an empty barrel drifting not far off, and the ship's companion ladder close beside it. The stays enabled me to lash the barrel to the mast and make a deck of the ladder, on which I could lie half in the water and half out. Having nothing to use as a sail, I tried to paddle towards the distant coast with my feet and hands. Dolphins sported around, a cormorant skimmed by, drenching its plumage as it dived for fish; but no ship came close enough to be hailed, and I drifted miserably from dawn to sunset."

I nodded. "And last night," I suggested, "the southern gale caught you?"

"It did indeed. I heard huge seas pounding against the ironbound coast, and each time my mast rose on the crest of a wave, the line of surf, deadly white under the moon, seemed to creep nearer and nearer. I renewed my plea to Poseidon. But an enormous breaker, the mother and grandmother of all breakers, came rushing down, unshipped barrel and ladder and whirled them from me. Swept onwards into the surf, I abandoned my mast to grasp a protruding jag of rock and scramble ashore; however, the backwash dragged me away when I had already secured a handhold. I felt like a cuttlefish in the month of March, which the fisherman takes pitilessly by the neck and wrenches from its breeding hole in the cliff, with pebbles still clinging to its suckers. A great strip of skin was torn from my right palm—look!—but despite the smart I managed to battle my way out to sea once more, clear of the toothed rocks; searching, as I mounted each wave's crest, for a gap in the long deadly battle front of surf. At last I saw the very thing and swam towards it. The water seemed colder, as if this were the debouchment of a brook. With desperate strokes I reached the gap, and found myself in a calm, land-locked harbour. Not another yard could I have swum, though dear life depended on it; but, sinking, I felt sand beneath my feet and stumbled forward in a daze, coughing and vomiting sea water. I reached that bank and crawled up it, inch by inch, until I came upon the thicket and there was a sheltered nook between an olive and an oleaster growing from the same stock. I scraped away the fallen leaves, lay down and heaped them over me again. Almost at once I slept, and have only just awakened."

It is impolite to ask a suppliant for his name, clan or country until he has received the entertainment that the laws of hospitality require. "You are safe among us," I assured him, "and shall be given food and drink without delay."

He clutched my knees ecstatically, pouring out incoherent words of gratitude, and at last pleaded: "If I have said anything amiss, Goddess, may the north-easter whirl the offending words to perdition."

The women gathered closer, and now that I had decided to take mercy on this stranger, ventured to utter cries of pity and encouragement.

He released my knees and, turning his head, said with a gallant attempt at a laugh: "Ladies, though valuing your kindness, and though tormented by hunger and thirst, I dare not offend your modesty. I feel sufficiently ashamed to expose my bare buttocks in so public a manner; to rise were worse. Perhaps that old sack yonder, which seems to have contained your laundry, would serve to cover my nakedness."

Someone handed him the sack, and he discreetly wrapped it around his waist before rising.

"Girls," I said briskly, "take this suppliant to the Springs for a wash, and choose him a cloak and tunic, of the better ones. They are all dry. Also find the oil bottle and a scraper; and bring him back here when he is decently dressed."

He made a point of asking them to retire while he bathed—which proved his delicacy of feeling—and when he appeared again, wearing one of my father's embroidered tunics, and a scarlet cloak which belonged to Laodamas, I thought I had never seen anyone so soldierly in my life, though his legs were a trifle short in proportion to his muscular body. But, of course, a man may be as handsome as a god and yet deceitful or muddleheaded.

We set a meal of roast beef, bread and wine before him—plenty had been left—and oh, how hungrily he tore at the beef with his strong white teeth, and how the wine gurgled down his smooth brown throat!

When he had done, I asked: "Who are you, my lord—for you must surely be of noble birth—and what is your country? To avoid any awkwardness, it would be well to let me know at once whether you have ever fallen foul of my people, the Elymans?"

"Fortunately, never," he answered. "You and your well-trained women happen to be the first Elymans whom I have had the honour to meet. But I know you as the most westerly of civilized nations, and have heard of the great reputation for energy and good faith which you have consolidated among the maritime peoples of the world. I am a Cretan, and Aethon son of Castor is my name: a true Cretan from the far west, and a fugitive homicide. I killed a man in self-defence, a treacherous son of the King of Tarrha, and was sentenced to eight years' exile by the Council; seven of which I have now completed, wandering from country to country. May I, in turn, ask your name, benefactress?"

"I am Nausicaa," I answered, "the only daughter of the Elyman King and Queen. My eldest brother, Laodamas, is feared lost at sea; and my father has recently sailed to Sandy Pylus, hoping for news of him there. Lord Mentor, my maternal uncle, is acting as Regent, and I have one grown brother at home, hardly more than a youth, named Clytoneus, and my little brother. Telegonus is still under the charge of women. Listen to me! If I protect you, this must be conditional on your obeying me implicitly throughout your stay here."

"That goes without saying," Aethon agreed. "You have saved my life, which is now yours to direct for as long as you deign to do so. What are my orders?"

I paused before answering, and he bent his head resignedly: somehow he knew that I had a difficult situation to face. "To begin with," I said, "you must not come home with us, but follow at a prudent distance, keeping the cart in sight until we reach a fortified wall which runs across the neck of yonder headland. The town of Drepanum lies on the other side, between two harbours, and near the gates rises a Temple of Poseidon, facing a paved market place, with docks and shipyards on either hand, and an oar factory, marine stores, two rope walks, and a great deal of activity and gossip. It is this gossip that I want to avoid at all costs. Do not think that I am ashamed to be seen in your company, my lord Aethon, but my position is already extremely delicate. A number of young Elymans have asked my father for my hand but, to be frank, I entertain a strong dislike for the more influential of my suitors, yet have so far formed no attachment elsewhere. If I were to bring you into the town, the sensation caused by such a sight would embarrass both you and me. Rope-maker would shout to net-mender: 'Look, look! Who is that tall handsome stranger with the Princess Nausicaa? Where has she picked him up?' And then they would go on: 'Have any of you ever seen him before? Either some god has descended from Olympus in answer to her prayer—everyone knows that she considers herself too good to marry a mere mortal—or, less improbably, she has rescued a shipwrecked sailor and lent him some of the clothes from that cartful, and is now taking him along to her mother and uncle. "This is my future husband," she will announce. "I have just given him my carefully guarded maidenhead, for I love him with all my heart." A fine trick to play in her father's absence, eh?' No, Aethon, do not blush, and neither will I. You must understand that this is how loutish minds work hereabouts. I hate them all. And please do not think that I approve of indiscreet behaviour. A young woman's reputation for chastity is of the utmost value to her, and I have always been at pains to keep mine irreproachable; moreover, if I am ever lucky enough to bear a daughter, she will have to do the same, or forfeit my love."

Aethon smiled. "So be it, Princess," he said. "Pray continue with your orders. Am I to lounge at the town gate, complaining that I have been clubbed on the head by robbers and forgotten everything about myself; so that I am obliged to wander in search of a friend who can tell me my name and city?"

"That is not a bad idea," I answered, "but might have unwelcome complications. Some scoundrelly foreign captain might claim you as a runaway slave, and who could contradict him? Not you, certainly, if you deny that you remember even your own name. No, listen: at a little distance from the town wall we shall pass through a poplar grove sacred to the Goddess Athene (whose priestess I am), growing in the middle of a park; you will find a well there, with a rope and an oaken bucket, and beyond it a patch of chick-peas and vetch. The park is crown property, and nobody would dare disturb anyone who went to pray in the grove. So wait by the well until you judge that we have reached the Palace, which stands near the point of the headland. Then go boldly to the guard at the gates and announce that you have a personal message for the Queen. Any little child will guide you to the Palace, because it is by far the largest and noblest building in the town. My grandfather used dressed stone; all the other houses, even the Temple of Poseidon, are wooden constructions with lath-and-plaster walls in Sican style. Enter the court of sacrifice as though you knew it of old, then cross the banqueting court and pass between the two red marble dogs into the throne chamber. These clothes are good enough to prevent any slaves from challenging you. My uncle, Lord Mentor, will doubtless be seated on the royal throne drinking wine. Bow your respects to him, but go straight up to my mother. Her tall ivory chair, with the footstool attached, stands against a pillar near the hearth, and she will be weaving sea-purple, or perhaps doing fine embroidery, a wheeled workbasket by her side. Clasp her knees, and speak as you have spoken to me. In her sympathy lies your best hope of success. I should be vexed if you were to fall into the clutches of the Town Council, not a very merciful body of men—unless my father is present to control them—and find yourself auctioned as a slave to the highest bidder."

"To be auctioned is a fate that has never yet overtaken me. May Zeus grant that it never will. Benefactress, I shall do as you say, and may your patroness Athene favour me!"

This much being settled, I told my women to fold the linen neatly, lay it in the grass-strewn cart, and collect all our belongings—the ball had drifted across Rheithrum, and Glauce retrieved it at the outlet with a long branch of oleaster—after which Aethon helped us to catch and harness the mules. I mounted and cracked my whip; and off the cart bounced over the meadow until we struck the coast road again.

With a backward glance at Aethon, I thought: "What a singular day this has been, full of signs and wonders . . . Dear Mistress Athene, I thank you a thousand times for having listened to my prayer! Can Aethon be the man whom you intend me to marry? I am half in love with him already— but perhaps only because he is my own personal suppliant and trusts me . . . (So Laodamas loved the hound Argus, which used to fawn and cringe at his coming as though he were a god.) And have you sent him to rescue our house from disaster?"

Another strange event: both mules suddenly baulked, for no apparent reason, and though I flicked them with the whip, backed at least twenty paces and halted shivering. I told Auge to hold their heads while I climbed down and found out what had scared them. Nothing. The road lay empty, without even a white stone or a fluttering rag to frighten them —unless it were that filthy old goatskin wallet, abandoned in the ditch, which they mistook for a lurking dog.

I stood still awhile, my arms outstretched as if praying, much to the bewilderment of the women. Then I called them together and said, kindly though severely: "Loyal servants, gentle playmates! The mules baulked at the sight of the Goddess Athene, who appeared shining by the roadside, visible only to her priestess. She addressed me in oracular verse, of which this is the substance: 'Princess Nausicaa, if one of your women blurts a single word to her family, or to friends, or to acquaintances, about the Cretan champion whom I have sent you in your need, I will blind that slut and cover her upper lip with thick black hair! And now, child, you may inform the stranger that I have cancelled your instructions: he is not to advance another step towards your well-built town of Drepanum, but must turn inland while it is yet light and follow the road which skirts the town of Eryx and winds up the mountain from the east. He will find your father's swineherd at the Raven Rock among the esculent oaks, where great herds of hogs are fattening; and I have ordained that honest servant to protect him. Let Aethon place himself under Eumaeus's care and lodge at his homestead until you send him whatever message I may put into your mouth. But first he must take off those glorious clothes, which the Queen will instantly recognize as palace property and conclude to have been either stolen or bestowed on him as a love gift. Then he must daub his handsome body with cow filth and wrap around him the old sack for which, at my prompting, he pleaded; nor must he reveal his name or country to any of the swineherds. It is as a nameless, unkempt beggar that I shall bring him to the Palace of the Elyman kings.' "

Aethon seemed puzzled by this sudden divine command, but accepted it unquestioningly. I then instructed him how to reach Raven Rock, advising him to cut himself a stout staff as a defence against Eumaeus's savage mastiffs, and to take up the discarded wallet; into which we thrust a few crusts of bread and parings of cheese, and the scrag end of our leg of mutton, so that he now looked a real beggar.

Nobody else witnessed this transformation, and soon a villainous ruffian was toiling through our willow grove, staff in hand, waving good-bye to us. I disliked having to send Aethon on that long climb in his weakened condition, but he was young and bold, with good food in his belly, and I had to play for safety. If Eurymachus and his companions found out that he was an exiled Cretan nobleman, a homicide too, who would stop at nothing to show himself deserving of my protection, his life would be worth little. "It will be far better," I thought, "to hold him in reserve as an unsuspected ally." And my women could be trusted. They believed me to have occult powers, as one who was in constant treaty with the Blessed Gods. None of them would risk blindness and a thick moustache by blabbing.

I patted and made much of the mules until they started again; and kept them going smartly, but not too fast for my women. After skirting the Grove of Athene we were admitted into the town by the gate watch. Our progress through the docks excited no great interest; and at last I pulled up outside the Palace, clapped my hands for a groom, and ran indoors to enquire what had happened during the day.

My uncle Mentor, gloomily waiting on a bench in the throne chamber, began to weep when he saw me.

"What has happened?" I exclaimed. "No ill news of death or sickness, I hope? Or have the Sicels invaded our frontiers? Uncle, why are you not sitting on the throne?"

"Niece, the news is bad! Though by the grace of Artemis, neither death nor disease has been reported, nor have any Sicels, or Phoenicians, or other strangers threatened us, it is very bad. This enemy works from within. When today I attended the Drepanan Council, I met with unkind looks and cruel words. The clan leaders ordered me to surrender my regency on the ground that in the King's absence the Elyman sceptre always passes to the most honourable of his own clansmen. I declined to obey until compelled by an all-Elyman assembly; because, after all, the King himself conferred the regency on me. And then, as I left the council chamber, Antinous gave notice that, in accordance with your father's wishes, he and others of your suitors will before long visit the Palace; where they expect to find a feast of roast meat and lavish wine spread for them in the banqueting court. And that this entertainment must continue day after day, for a month, or two months, or even more, until a husband is chosen for you from the company. He also said that I am qualified under Elyman law to make the choice, since your mother and I come of Aegadean stock, and—as the King himself admitted —uncle disposes of niece in our islands. My dear, I may be an easygoing man, but there are certain occasions when I dig in my heels and will not budge. I refused point-blank to choose you a husband without your father's consent."

"I am grateful to you, Uncle Mentor. Did Antinous discuss the case of Ctimene?"

"He did: impertinently asking me to presume the death of Laodamas and send her home to her father on Bucinna. Again I answered no: because Ctimene is determined to stay and has already planted herself on the hearth as a suppliant. To drive her out now would be to visit this house with a curse; besides, what business is it of theirs whether Ctimene goes or stays? Oddly enough, Eurymachus supported me in this, and Antinous gave way. But you do not seem in the least surprised, Nausicaa?"

"It takes a good deal to surprise me these days, Uncle. Well, what are you proposing to do?"

"First tell me: have you set your heart on any of these young men?"

"Certainly not. The least dull are the most detestable and, contrariwise, the least detestable are the dullest. If I am allowed to marry for love, my choice will necessarily fall on a stranger."

"Then I am resolved to keep hold of the sceptre until it is wrested from my hands. When your suitors enter this house I shall offer light refreshments and then courteously ask them to retire; and if they defy me, I shall lay the matter on the knees of the Immortals."

"I am assured, Uncle," I said, "that the Immortals are already concerned in our affairs and, when we take care not to offend them either in word or deed, will protect us behind a wall of unbreakable shields."

He looked shrewdly at me, but I gazed back at him with expressionless eyes.

"I hope that you are right, child, for I have begun to smell blood and the smoke of burning rafters. But we need hardly anticipate immediate trouble. Tomorrow I will get out your father's fast chariot and visit the elders of Aegesta. Perhaps they will take a different view from those of Drepanum."

CHAPTER

SEVEN

THE GREEDY

SUITORS

THE VERY NEXT DAY my impudent suitors sent
word, as if from my uncle Mentor, to our chief swineherd
Eumaeus at Raven Rock, and to Philoetius, our chief shepherd, who was grazing the flocks near the Cave of Conturanus.
They were instructed to drive down, respectively, eight fat
boars and a dozen fat wethers for slaughter without delay.
Suspecting no fraud, these honest servants sent what was demanded, and Melantheus the cattlemaster willingly added a
couple of prime bullocks. I was superintending a group of
women at work in the court of sacrifice when these beasts
reached the Palace. It happened to be the day for remaking
the mattresses. Once a year we pull out the lumpy wool from
the linen ticks, flog the yellowish-white heap with long canes

until it fluffs up; then we refill the ticks, distributing the
handfuls evenly so that the whole surface becomes smooth,
soft, and buoyant, and sew the ends together again, neatly
turning the hems. It is not an agreeable task. Wool dust gets
into noses and makes them sneeze, and if a wind rises, as it
did on this occasion, and blows the wool wantonly about the
court, tempers grow short. I ordered the gate to be barred until
we should have finished, but presently heard a violent knocking, and hoarse cries of "Open, open in Lord Mentor's name!"

I sighed and waved to the porter. He unbarred the gate, and
in surged a confused crowd of men and animals: Melantheus
with the bullocks, Eumaeus's son with the hogs, Philoetius's
cousin with the wethers, and behind them a disorderly group
of domestic servants, none of them wearing the Palace badge,
who sang and laughed in a most ill-mannered way, staring
around them and shouting ribald jokes at my women. A furious
gust of wind swept into the court, scattering the wool in all
directions and creating a small white flurry in front of the
sacrificial altar.

"Shut that accursed gate!" I screamed. The porter was still
holding it open for a hog which had taken fright and bolted
out again.

"Who is in charge of this rabble?" I went on. "Melantheus!
What are you doing with those bullocks? Have you lost your
wits? The Feast of Apollo is not due for several days yet. Bar
that gate at once, I tell you, porter! Never mind the wayward
hog. Have you no sense? Look at this waste of good wool!"

Melantheus had slipped off, as though to retrieve the hog;
but Eumaeus's son came forward, touching his forelock, and
apologized very decently for letting in the shameless wind,

over which, as he observed, even Father Zeus had no control, but only the three deaf Fates.

"Why in the world has your reverend father sent us those hogs?" I asked in gentler tones. We Elymans always call swineherds "reverend," because Sican swineherds give oracles from the behaviour of their sows, and Eumaeus, though Ionian by birth, had become more Sican almost than the Sicans.

"A messenger came from my lord Mentor," he answered, "demanding six of our fattest porkers. My reverend father being away at Aegesta, I wanted to know what good news was to be celebrated. Had an embassy arrived with rich gifts from a neighbouring city? Or could it be that the King had landed unexpectedly with Prince Laodamas? But the messenger explained that the beasts were wanted for your wedding feast. So I obeyed. Philoetius's cousin, here, was told the same."

"Someone has been making a fool of you both, friends. You had better drive the hogs back as soon as you have rested. Meanwhile, take them outside and tie them by their hind legs to the hitching posts. The waste of it all: walking so much weight off them to no purpose! And that goes for the bullocks, too. Lead them out immediately! They will foul this newly swept court."

Then I turned to the masterless servants. "You, my lads, what is your business? Has the same idiotic joke been played on you? No, I am not being married either today, tomorrow, or on any subsequent day before the return of the King. I say so myself, and surely I should know? And pay attention: some of you are behaving as though this were the shrine of Aphrodite on a morning of high festival, and my chaste and well-mannered maids were her temple prostitutes. Remember, your boorishness reflects on the lords whom you serve; and off with you all—or all except you two lads wearing my lord Agelaus's badge! Wait here, pray, both of you, and when the court is empty again and the gate barred, I shall require you to salvage the wool which your rude entry has sent flying about."

Eumaeus's son touched his forelock a second time. "Begging your pardon, mistress, I fear that my reverend father will tan my back with his heaviest cudgel if I bring these porkers home without direct orders from the Lord Mentor. You would not have me beaten, mistress, I am sure."

"My uncle is away until tomorrow. Like your reverend father, he has gone to Aegesta. This should be proof enough that the orders are not his. And if you doubt my words, would you perhaps prefer to consult the Queen?"

The boy shifted his feet and looked uncomfortable. "If it please your ladyship, I should like to consult Prince Clytoneus. My reverend father and I honour your mother beyond all women, and your self hardly less, but orders for our hogs always come from the men of your noble house—no disrespect intended."

"And no offence taken," I said. "Put someone in charge of the herd and go to the tower room. You will find Prince Clytoneus there, touching up the device on one of the palace shields—though why he cannot leave the task to a skilled painter is more than I can say."

I turned to the intruding servants again. "Why are you waiting? I told you to be off."

A tall, curly-bearded man, wearing Antinous's badge, answered boldly: "We have orders to prepare a feast here for our masters." He tapped the sharp sacrificial knife at his girdle.

"Have you, indeed? Well, then, my orders are exactly the reverse: get out, and get out quick! You are interfering with the morning's work!"

The servants glanced doubtfully from one to the other, and I clapped my hands for the porter. "Porter," I said, "call Medon the herald and desire him to clear the court. Since these dolts will not listen to me, perhaps they will listen to him."

Some of the servants had raided the woodpile and were lugging out faggots. It would only have made matters worse if I had intervened, so I paid no attention to what they did and continued to direct the wool beating until Eumaeus's son returned with Clytoneus. Clytoneus's hands were stained cinnabar red from the painting and, in the light of the first words he spoke, this accident struck me as pleasantly ominous.

"I warn you wretches who have broken into our Palace, with butcher's knives at your girdles, that when the time comes, my men and I, not you and your masters, will do the butchering!"

Medon then entered, blinking and yawning, newly awakened from sleep, his favourite pastime. He raised the white wand, which, like his plumed sandals, showed that his person was sacrosanct, and made a long, eloquent speech. He began with a preface in praise of the Elyman people: their courage, honesty, tenacity, gentleness and good manners, the deeds of their forefathers, the favour bestowed on our nation by the Gods, the wisdom of our rulers, the solidarity of our clans, the beauty of our princesses, the extreme rarity of riots, quarrels or brawls in our market place. Next, he enlarged on his own position as royal herald, the sacred duty imposed on him to keep the peace, and the surprise which had overcome him when informed that certain sacrifical beasts were spontaneously offering their necks to the knife . . .

Would he ever reach the point? I wondered. But it was soon obvious that he had no intention of doing so—he was playing for time. Presently the servants' masters would arrive, and the dispute must enter upon a new and more interesting stage.

So I asked Medon to desist, and addressed the men myself for the last time. "Lads," I said, "if you leave this court now, your masters will beat you for disobeying their orders. If you do not leave, however, then as sure as my name is Nausicaa, the Furies will pursue you with their brazen scourges and hound every man to death, though he run a thousand miles. I am a priestess of the royal hearth, and when I summon those daughters of Uranus, they come crowding at my back." Here I took Medon's wand from his hands and advanced towards them with slow menace, glancing frequently over my shoulder and smiling encouragement to the invisible Furies. Antinous's bearded valet folded his arms and stood his ground, but I struck him across the head and kicked him hard in the groin. He cried "Oh! Oh!" and stumbled away, doubled up with pain, and there was a concerted rush for the gate, through which Eumaeus's son and Philoetius's cousin had already driven their beasts. The two fat bullocks took fright and charged after them, bellowing, and this added to the fun; but it was not long before I had cleared the court and barred the gate myself.

"Dear companions, let us collect the scattered wool," I ordered cheerfully. Suppressing their mirth, they obeyed, all but Melantho, who sat and scowled on a bench, as though she had not heard me. She was a tall, well-built girl who walked like a princess—as I do not; and this beauty of gait encouraged ambitions in her which she lacked the intelligence to make good.

"You will come to an unlucky end, daughter," I prophesied. "What begins in the boathouse, as they say, ends in deep water." I added "as they say" to pass it off as a proverb, and pretended to be mystified by the sniggering of the other girls. "What's the merriment?" I asked severely. Melantho bent to chase a whirling strand of wool, but I read the hate and fear in her eyes.

I drew Clytoneus aside. "Our enemies are showing their hand at last, dear Brother, yet I can trust you to preserve my honour, and that of the house. You must act for our father now, because I have a notion that Uncle Mentor will be detained at Aegesta, so that you are the only man left about the Palace—except grandfather, of course, but he is deaf and his memory is failing."

Clytoneus embraced me tenderly, and I was back working at the wool when Medon's loud voice sounded again from close behind: "Mistress, allow me to present a number of distinguished suitors whom your beauty and the King's reiterated invitations have drawn together out of all the clans of our nation. They come here in hope of lavish hospitality, and in the confidence that, after a careful review of each suitor's merit, one of them will be chosen and garlanded as the fortunate sharer of your bridal couch." There they stood in a solid mass, grinning like naughty children who have broken into the larder and find themselves faced by a staid housekeeper.

Melantheus had led them around by the garden door, and they numbered no less than one hundred and twelve—fifty-six Phocaean clansmen, twenty-four Sicans, twenty from the mixed clans, and twelve Trojans.

I greeted them with an imperceptible nod and beckoned to Clytoneus. "Brother," I said, "as acting head of the royal household, will you be kind enough to inform these impetuous young noblemen that, though they appear without warning, in unprecedented numbers, and at a very awkward time, they are welcome to our palace commons: namely, spruce beer, bread, cheese and olives, which will duly be set before them if they have the patience to wait awhile."

"My sister's words are mine," cried Clytoneus, staring straight in front of him.

"Princess," drawled Antinous with a superior smile, "can you be so young and ignorant as not to know what is expected of you? When suitors for your hand arrive in such a flatteringly large company you should offer them roast meat and the best wine."

"No orders have been given to our swineherds, cattlemen, or shepherds; consequently there is no meat to roast, and even if I had authority to draw good wine for you, it would be wasted on a snack of bread and cheese. Spruce beer is a healthy drink, and economical, too."

"But unless my eyes deceived me, I observed more than a dozen fat beasts tied to the hitching posts outside the gate."

"Ah, those! But they are not for sacrifice."

"You are your father's own daughter," exclaimed Antinous.

"So the Queen has always maintained, and since it is a wise child that knows its own father, I shall not dishonour her by doubting my legitimacy. I must therefore ask you to retire. The King gave me his solemn promise, which the Queen witnessed, that my inclinations would be consulted in this matter of suitors as religiously as if I were an oracle. He has since sailed to the east on domestic business, and even if he were here, your visit could not justify the expense of a banquet; for I should be forced to admit that a cursory review of your faces disinclines me to accept a single one of you. They express nothing but insolence, vanity, greed, mockery and rebellion. However, because I am, as you say, my father's own daughter, and because Clytoneus is my father's son, neither of us can waive the common claims of hospitality. If you are hungry enough to make do with what you deserve, go to the banqueting court and sit down at the cloister tables; when I have completed this mattress stuffing, I shall attend to your wants. Clytoneus, please find Eurycleia and ask her whether she has sufficient cheese for about ten dozen corpulent young men. And perhaps Phemius will consent to sing to them."

I turned my back on the company and resumed work. "What a little spitfire!" cried Ctesippus, not troubling to lower his voice. "To think that more than a hundred of us are competing for the pleasure of having our cheeks scratched by her long nails!"

"The pleasure would be wholly mine," I flung over my shoulder, as they trooped past me into the banqueting court.

I realized that, physically, we were powerless to cope with

the invaders, but pride forbade me to show the least sign of accepting so absurd a position. When Melantheus went to the entrance gate, unbarred it, and called in the servants, I ran and shot home the bolt at once.

"Melantheus," I said, "if you defy my orders by bringing back that fat stock, let me warn you that when the King returns, he will not hesitate to disembowel you, afterwards cutting off your extremities and feeding them to the dogs."

"I act at the orders of Prince Agelaus," he answered pompously, "whom the Drepanan Council have elected as Regent."

"Indeed? Then fetch him to me, unless you want to be beaten as a liar."

Melantheus hurried off, and presently brought Agelaus, a small, sullen, dark-faced man who had nothing to commend him but his birth, a luxuriant head of hair, and a certain dexterity at cottabus. Cottabus is a game for banqueters: each in turn throws what wine is left in his goblet at a number of minature silver cups floating in a basin ten paces away; whoever sinks most of these is the winner. My father, however, allows nobody to play cottabus in the Palace—prince, guest, servant or slave—because of the splashed clothes and walls, and the waste of good wine.

I greeted him with: "Why, kinsman! Have you come to play cottabus in the King's absence? You have my special indulgence, so long as you stick to spruce beer and keep to the middle of the court. But first tell this scoundrel Melantheus that the beasts tied up outside must stay there until they are rested and can be driven back to the pastures from which they were brought in error."

Agelaus flushed. "I shall tell him no such thing! Those beasts are to be sacrificed; and, once the fat and thighbones have been offered to the Blessed Gods, we promise ourselves the satisfaction of eating their roast flesh. And, mark you, when I play cottabus, I play it only with the best wine."

"Who, may I ask, are 'we'?"

"Your suitors, Princess."

"Have a care, Agelaus," I said. "Resentment at some fancied slight has clouded your intelligence. As soon as my father lands at Drepanum, he will seek you out and strike off your head . . ."

"If he ever lands," Agelaus interjected.

"And if he does not, kinsman, I doubt whether your position will be in any way improved. Antinous and Eurymachus have already agreed to betray you. What if the javelin intended for Clytoneus at the boar hunt drives whistling between your shoulder blades, and the Phocaeans usurp the sceptre which Zeus himself placed in the hands of our Trojan ancestor Aegestus? Call off your rebellious clansmen, before it is too late!"

"You seem to know a great deal," he sneered.

"The Goddess Athene has been gracious enough to make me her confidante," I answered.

Agelaus paused irresolutely, then "Melantheus!" he shouted, in what were meant to be kingly accents, "command the servants to make ready our sacrifice!"

"Very well, kinsman," I said. "You have chosen as you have chosen. But theft is no less reprehensible in a Trojan prince than in the cheapest Sicel slave."

The servants re-entered boisterously with the beasts. Leodes, priest to Zeus, and one of my suitors, thereupon dedicated the bullocks to the Thunderer and to Poseidon, and the other beasts to Hera, Apollo, Aphrodite, Hermes and the rest—but pointedly omitted Athene, as if scornful of my trust in her. This caused me deep satisfaction, since Athene is the best ally imaginable and quick to take offence. Zeus, though the stronger, is apt to be indolent or preoccupied and, as they say, his mills grind slowly.

We sewed up the last mattresses, in hurry and confusion because the court was soon filled with the swirling smoke of log fires and all the bustle of cooking. I went to find Clytoneus.

"I have done my best, Sister," he said. "On our mother's advice, I have given the clerk of the Drepanan Council notice to convene it again for tomorrow morning. I am not yet old enough to qualify as a member, yet Halitherses tells me that any royal prince may call a Council in the absence of the King or his authorized Regent. I shall protest strongly against this invasion of our Palace. Meanwhile, the rogues have browbeaten Pontonous the butler into fetching them wine, although he was expressly warned to take orders only from me. I have sent Eumaeus a message by his son, and Philoetius a message by his cousin, to send down no more beasts unless they receive a written demand bearing the imprint of my seal."

"You can do little else at present. Whether the Council will reverse its judgment is another matter; but your protest must be placed on record, if only to satisfy our father."

"Hush, Phemius is tuning up. It is to be *Odysseus's Return,* the last fytte of the cycle."

Phemius's delivery was neither so dramatic nor so com-

pelling as Demodocus's. His voice, however, was younger and
more resonant, and he had lost none of his front teeth, which
made for clearer enunciation, and his self-assurance improved with every performance. It is my view that he will
one day become the most famous of all his guild, and I have
entrusted my epic poem to him partly for this reason.

After the conventional invocation of the Muse, he gave a
summary of the tale: how the anger borne by Aphrodite
towards the Greek leaders who had attacked and burned the
holy fortress of Troy and, by killing her favourite, Paris,
had dealt a blow to devoted lovers the world over, was expressed in her peculiarly savage treatment of Odysseus. Being
the Goddess of the Sea as well as of Love, she was content,
in some cases, to wreck her enemies' ships and drown them,
as she drowned Ajax; others she drove by adverse winds to
distant lands from which they took years to return, as did
Spartan Menelaus; still others she so wearied by bad weather
that they despaired of seeing their wives and children again,
but stayed to found cities beside outlandish rivers, as did
Guneus in Libya, and Elphenor in Epirus. Her usual revenge,
however, lay in allowing the victorious champion to reach
home, only to find that his wife had set her lover on the
throne; as happened to Argive Agamemnon and Cretan Idomeneus, joint leaders of the Greek expedition. On Diomedes
and Odysseus who, between them, had done more than any
of the Greeks to earn her hate, she visited a double punishment—a wearisome return after shipwreck and similar perils,
and the subsequent discovery that their wives had been false
to them. Yet Odysseus's sufferings were far harsher and
longer drawn out than those of Diomedes; and whereas Dio-

medes's wife Aegialeia had taken only a single lover, Odysseus found that Penelope, supposedly so faithful to his bed,
was living in riotous and promiscuous love with no less than
fifty of his own subjects; and that his son, Telemachus, had
been sold into slavery, none knew where.

Phemius stopped to rinse his throat, and Clytoneus applauded. "Well sung, Phemius," he cried, "best of bards
next to the venerable Demodocus! I hope that you will enlarge on the subject of those rascally fellows who camped in
Odysseus's palace and made the swineherds and shepherds
slaughter his fat stock for them. Have their infamous names
survived, to bring a blush to their descendants' cheeks? And
was it they who, to detach the Ithacans' affection from their
rightful prince, plotted to sell him in the Sidonian slave
market?"

Antinous sprang up with an oath, but Eurymachus restrained him. "Clytoneus's question is a very pertinent one,"
he grinned. "Let us hear how Phemius answers it."

Phemius gulped, and seemed ill at ease; however, his good
sense and ready wit did not desert him. "My ancestor Homer
has given us little information on this point," he said apolo-
getically. "But you should remember, I think, that Penelope's
fifty lovers, the leading citizens of the islands over which
Odysseus ruled, were all bewitched by Aphrodite, who had
lent Penelope her girdle of irresistibility: though she was by
now fat, ungainly and well past the age of childbearing, they
could not refrain. Each awaited his summons to her couch,
sitting expectantly in a ring, as dogs do when a bitch is in heat.
They found Telemachus's presence awkward. Stung by his
taunts, which they felt keenly, yet unwilling to turn murderers,

they begged him to sail away. Then, since he would neither go nor keep silence, they sold him to a slave trader who undertook to find him a considerate master. It would have been better had Telemachus disregarded the situation at the Palace, unpleasant as it must have been to so spirited a prince, and spent his time in the chase. Now, if you will allow me, I shall proceed."

"Very well, Phemius!" muttered Clytoneus. "If you have gone over to the enemies of our house, your wand and feathered sandals will not protect you for ever."

Phemius told the familiar story of Odysseus's journey: how he sailed to Thrace, a region which had provided King Priam with bold allies, and sacked the city of Ismarus. His foolish crew would not hurry their spoils of gold, silver and captive women into the ships; but delayed on the shore, slaughtering sheep and fat cattle and drinking heady wine. Other Thracians from the hills flocked in chariots and on foot to the support of their suffering neighbours and broke the Greek ranks; so that Odysseus was lucky to get his men aboard again, full-bellied if empty-handed. A storm soon blew all his canvas to ribbons, and drove him towards Cape Malea at the foot of the Peloponnese, which lay on his course; yet would not let up until, after nine days, he sighted the coast of Libya, where the lotus-eating Nasamanians live. There some of his men tried to desert when he sent them inland to fetch water; he clapped them in irons, and put to sea once more. Then Aphrodite sent a storm which wrecked his entire fleet. Odysseus alone managed to swim ashore to the desolate isle of Pantellaria, or Cossyra—on fine days we can see it from the summit of Mount Eryx far to the south—and he

spent the next seven years there, living off shellfish, asphodel
roots, and the eggs of sea birds. Every day he used to sit on
the strand, chin against knees, gazing at the blank horizon;
yet no ship, of the few that passed, ever heeded his frantic
signals. At last a Taphian thirty-oarer put in, not for trade,
because the island was uninhabited; not for water, because
it was waterless, except for occasional rain puddles; but to
maroon one of the crew whom they judged hateful to the
Gods. They consented to engage Odysseus instead of this
sailor, pretending to sympathize with his misfortunes, took
him by way of Italy to the head of the Adriatic, where they
were buying Hyperborean amber—and treacherously sold
him to the priestess of the Goddess Circe, who had charge of
Aeolus's oracle on Aeaea. She forced him to act as her man
of all work and to share her bed, which he soon found almost
as distasteful as his solitary confinement on Pantellaria, the
priestess being both ill favoured and insatiate.

At last he secretly sent a message to the priest of Zeus at
Dodona, who ordered his release, and a Thesprotian ship
fetched him off, half dead with exhaustion. At Dodona he was
advised to placate Aphrodite by extending her empire, and
therefore shouldered an oar and trudged inland, until he
came to a village whose inhabitants, never having heard of salt
water, mistook the oar for a flail. Having told the local shepherds of Aphrodite's birth from sea foam, he offered public
sacrifices to her, implored pardon, and was granted a favourable augury of mating sparrows. Thence he hastened home to
Ithaca, where he took vengeance on Penelope's lovers with a
bow which had once been Apollo's, killing all fifty of them
at a marriage contest. She was sent back in disgrace to his

father-in-law, King Icarius. One day the seer Teiresias prophesied that death would come to Odysseus from the sea, and
so it did. Telemachus returned without warning, having
escaped from slavery and travelled far and wide in search
of his father. Landing by moonlight, he mistook Odysseus for
one of Penelope's lovers. There, on the stony beach, he transfixed him with a sting-ray spear.

Phemius's account of the slaughter was brief and uncir-
cumstantial. I should have preferred to hear how Odysseus
managed to shoot down fifty swordsmen one after the other.
To draw a bow and let loose an aimed arrow takes time.
Though he might perhaps have killed four or five of his
enemies, in the meantime what were their comrades doing?
If brave men, they would have surrounded and overwhelmed
him by sheer numbers, even though unarmed; if cowards, at
least thirty or forty would have made good their escape. It
is not enough to say that Odysseus was the wiliest of men and
the best of archers; such praise needs detailed proof.

That evening I discussed the question of Odysseus's bow
with Clytoneus, and our conclusions gave me an idea which I
was feverishly anxious to see translated into action. We also
had a famous bow in the Palace. I have purposely not mentioned it hitherto; but the fact is that while the Phocaeans
were building Aegesta, as described at the beginning of this
story, a group of their kinsmen arrived from Italian Crimissa.
They possessed the very bow which Hercules had bequeathed
their ancestor Philoctetes when he died on Mount Oeta; and
with which Paris was mortally wounded, just before the Fall
of Troy. For Philoctetes, having been driven from his own city
of Meliboea in Thessaly, I suppose by his wife's lover—all

these tales follow the same pattern, but why did he not shoot him at sight?—sailed to Southern Italy and founded Petelia and Crimissa. The Crimissans brought the bow to Aegesta and presented it to my ancestor, the King of Hypereia, as a token of allegiance. It had hung in our storeroom ever since.

CHAPTER
EIGHT
THE COUNCIL
MEETING

THE BANQUET ENDED AT NIGHTFALL, and my suitors went staggering away, gorged, befuddled, and splashed with erratic cottabus throws. In the court of sacrifice I plucked at Antinous's sleeve. He mistook this for an endearment, but I soon undeceived him, saying: "My lord Antinous, I address you as ringleader of these drunken young noblemen, and originator of an insolent plot against our royal house. If, as they tell me, it is your intention to come here every day to gluttonize in our courts, I must try to make two things clear, though in your present condition you may find it hard to follow the simplest Greek sentence. The first is that we are carefully counting the fat beasts you eat, and the gallons of wine you drink, and that Elyman law requires a thief to restore his theft fourfold—I repeat: not once, but fourfold. The second is that the palace servants have been ordered to refuse you the least assistance, and that your own servants are therefore expected to clean up your sordid messes. Pray instruct them accordingly, before they help you home to bed."

He belched in my face. I spat in his; but my eyes shone with such fury that he dared not lay violent hands on me. Trying to belch again, he vomited half a pint of wine and some gobbets of undigested meat. "And what of this?" I asked, pointing in disgust at the befouled threshold.

"You may keep that," he hiccuped. "Write it off the account."

Back I went to the throne chamber, where my mother sat at the loom with her usual imperturbability. "Nausicaa, my dear," she said, "I wish you would go up to comfort Ctimene. She was at her window listening to Phemius's song, and when he described how Odysseus sat, chin on knees, in his desolate island, staring at the unbroken horizon, she broke down and began to tear her hair and scratch her cheeks. Now she is convinced that a similar fate has overtaken Laodamas, and talks of commissioning a ship to visit all the known desert islands, from Troy to Tartessus, in the hope of finding him."

"Tell me, Mother, do you think that something serious can have happened to Uncle Mentor?"

"Why, no! Obviously he has been held up on the Aegesta road to prevent him from provoking a quarrel between the two town councils. He is now perhaps a prisoner in Eurymachus's house—not fettered, nor exposed to indignities, merely detained—for fear that he may lose his temper and rouse the loyalists to armed resistance. Your uncle Mentor is

a patient man, but everyone knows that when he sees himself
unable to consult the elders of Aegesta, his anger will break
out as fiercely and twice as murderously as that of an im-
patient man like your dear father. Yes, Daughter, I realize
the awkwardness of the situation, yet our enemies seem in
no hurry to bring matters to a head. They propose to bleed
and humiliate us first. By the way, though I see no reason
why you, as the excuse for their presence here, should treat
them otherwise than as thieves and interlopers, I have advised
Clytoneus not to draw his sword against any of them nor insult
them directly. It is difficult, I know, for a boy of spirit to
keep his hand from the pommel, but once he draws, he is lost:
they will claim to have killed him in self-defence. Be patient:
the Gods are protecting us. Now, please, go to Ctimene."

I did what I could for my wretched sister-in-law, saying
that when Laodamas returned, he would be disappointed to
find her so thin and pale, with torn cheeks and black-rimmed
eyes. "It will look like a confession that you were in the
wrong that night," I suggested cunningly. "Whereas, if he
finds you plump, merry, and dry-eyed, he will respect you
for it and avoid provoking you again. For I cannot think
that his adventures away from home have been altogether
pleasant."

Delighted by this new point of view, she embraced me
convulsively. "So you have changed your opinion and agree
that he put himself in the wrong?" she asked.

"I decline to take sides in a dispute between husband and
wife, the more so when they are members of my immediate
family," I answered. "But it is quite clear that he did not
understand you, even after so many months of marriage."

This contented her, and I refrained from adding that I understood Ctimene all too well myself. I knew her to be lazy, small-minded, and hysterical; and had just been telling Clytoneus that her only use in this world would have been to breed children—and then make them over to my mother for bringing up properly—had she been capable of conception, which it seemed she was not. I heartily wished her back on Bucinna, even for a brief visit; we had trouble enough on our hands without her perpetual whining.

Clytoneus told me that the Drepanan Council had consented to meet—a good sign in a way, though he could scarcely hope them to give him any satisfaction—the venue being, as usual, the Temple of Poseidon, a large, whitewashed wooden building with carved columns. The benches of the Council Hall are polished stone, and frescoes on the walls depict the principal scenes of our national history: from the birth of Aegestus to the foundation of Drepanum. In a smoky inner shrine stands Poseidon's figwood statue: his face painted cinnabar red, his body first lacquered and then sprinkled with the blue dust of powdered lapis lazuli, his hands gilded. He holds a double axe and wears a long grey wig. Outside are the Courts of Justice, where my father spends a great deal of his day settling litigious cases, and generally comes late home for dinner, cross and tired.

Some forty councillors of all ages had gathered, when Clytoneus, in the ragged clothes of a suppliant and displaying an olive branch, entered and sat down on the bench nearest the door. The president of the Council was Aegyptius the Phocaean, a man more than eighty years old. As a child he had witnessed the building of this temple, and we thought him a good friend of our house, though one of his three grandsons was among my suitors. He welcomed Clytoneus with a vague smile. "Why, my boy," he said, "this must be the only time in our annals that so young a prince has convened the Council; but the action is perfectly in order, and I salute your civic spirit. Perhaps you bring us good news of your venturesome brother Laodamas? Or has our glorious King cut short his voyage and turned his helm about, as an eagle returns to his eyrie after a daring flight into the eye of the sun? No? There is little joy in your face, I fear, and you are dressed as a suppliant. Well, then, you must intend to raise some other matter of public concern. Whatever it may be, my dear Prince, I pray that the Gods will grant your heart's desire."

Clytoneus left his seat and strode into the middle of the Council. Peisenor, the town herald, who claimed descent from the God Hermes, handed him a white rod as a token that he might plead without interruption; whereupon Clytoneus bowed his respects to the Elders and began speaking in a loud, shrill voice.

"Venerable lord Aegyptius, tried ally of our royal house," he said, "I shall not waste your time with what poor eloquence I may possess. My business is a public one only if you consent to make it so, which is my plea, and explains these ragged clothes and this olive branch. A double affliction has fallen upon us, and of the first, at least, you have shown yourself sympathetically aware. My father, the King, has sailed to Sandy Pylus in the hope of establishing the whereabouts of my brother Laodamas, who vanished mysteriously a year ago. As though this were not anxiety enough, a gang of idle young men have taken advantage of the King's absence to pester my

sister Nausicaa with unwelcome attentions, and to insult the
Regent, Lord Mentor. They arrived yesterday in a great
jostling mob, and refusing to take no for an answer, or to
accept the simple fare hospitably set before them as unexpected visitors, slaughtered our bullocks, hogs and wethers,
helped themselves to our wine, spent a riotous afternoon in
our banqueting court, and blundered away at nightfall without even clearing up their spilt wine and vomit. Now my uncle
Mentor has also disappeared while driving to Aegesta; where
he proposed to consult the city fathers on a legal point arising
from the decision reached by this honourable Council two
days ago. It is my view that he has been detained against his
will by a member, or members, of this very Council."

"My dear boy, can you prove any of these wild allega-
tions?" asked Aegyptius. "Are you seriously suggesting that
your uncle Mentor has been abducted and kept in confinement
by one of us? What I have heard of last night's banquet is
altogether different. My valued colleagues Antinous and
Eurymachus—for both of whom you should entertain the
highest respect, since the King himself accepted them as your
sister's suitors, and conferred unusual privileges upon them
—have explained the whole circumstances to me. They de-
clare that your royal father wept tears of sorrow when he said
good-bye, kissing them repeatedly and begging them to make
free of his table while he was away. 'According to ancient
Aegadean custom,' he said, 'I am leaving my dear brother-
in-law Mentor to arrange for Princess Nausicaa's marriage.
Nor will I hamper his liberty of choice by favouring any one
suitor above the rest, even you two distinguished noblemen.
So let the eligible bachelors of Drepanum, Eryx, Aegesta,

Halicyae, and of all lesser settlements in my domain, come courting at the Palace; there to eat and drink of the best until one of them is chosen, I hope speedily. Whatever Mentor decides, I approve in advance.' "

"My lord Aegyptius," Clytoneus protested, "if my father indeed addressed those words to the persons you mention, he certainly spoke in a very different sense to my revered mother, my chaste sister, my noble uncle Mentor, and my unworthy self. He advised us to be frugal in his absence, to entertain no more than decency required, and to postpone all important decisions."

"Ah, but where a man leaves conflicting orders, it is the last of these that counts in law! And here we have two witnesses ready to swear that he changed his mind before the ship weighed anchor."

Clytoneus felt like a young boar trapped in a net, while the hounds bay about him and the huntsmen close in with their shining boar spears. Yet he lost neither his courtesy nor his courage. "May I suggest, my lord Aegyptius," he said, "that these men have failed to honour your venerable grey hairs and deceived you shamelessly? My uncle Mentor, for whose disappearance you offer no explanation, my revered mother, my sister and my sister-in-law were all present when the King sailed. None of us saw him take my lords Antinous and Eurymachus aside to kiss them and whisper in their ears. Nor can anyone else have done so, since both noblemen absented themselves conspicuously from the weeping throng on the quay. Oh, that my father were with us once more! This is an intolerable outrage to the dignity of the Crown, which you, my lords, should resent not only as reflecting upon yourselves, his trusted councillors, but as being nothing short of a universal scandal. Have you no fear of divine vengeance when this case comes to the notice of the Olympians? I hereby adjure you in the name of Almighty Zeus and his aunt, the Goddess Themis, who assembles and dissolves councils throughout the civilized world, to intervene in this affair and take cognizance of the truth! If this Council as a body were responsible for the depredations, as it has been for denying my uncle Mentor the regency, I should feel far more at ease. The case would demand a public settlement; nor would you fail in the end to pay compensation, because we should appeal to the Elyman Assembly, and itemize every loss and damage. As it is, we are subject to private marauders, who appear in irresistible force and, though the ringleaders happen to be members of this honourable Council, belong to no organization which we can sue. Forgive my natural bitterness!"

He burst into tears, and the white rod rattled to the floor.

Most of the Council were plainly touched, and a murmur of condolence arose, but no one ventured to speak until Antinous strode forward and picked up the rod.

"Clytoneus, my congratulations!" said he. "You are a born rhetorician, and it is a pity that your cause is bad and based on mere spite; your pretended grief has deceived some of my tenderhearted colleagues. Is ours the blame if your sister obstinately refuses to disclose her preference for one or other of us suitors? She cannot even dare complain that too small a choice has been offered her. Lord Mentor himself, sick of the whole business, and unable to imbue her with a sense of duty, has sailed to his own island of Hiera, swearing to stay there until she makes the decision expected of her. Tell me the truth, Clytoneus: did the Princess Nausicaa not promise your revered mother to choose a husband as soon as she had completed that purple wedding robe? And is it not a fact that for every three pictures which she embroidered, at the slowest possible rate, she unpicked two; and presently ceased work altogether?"

Clytoneus sprang up, shouting: "From whom have you culled this domestic information, my lord Antinous? Was it from Eurymachus? And did Eurymachus get it from dark-eyed Melantho in the boathouse?"

Cries of "Oh! Oh!" were raised, and all eyes were fixed on Eurymachus, who felt obliged to take the floor. "I have no idea who this dark-eyed Melantho may be," he said blandly, "unless, as her name suggests, she is a daughter of your cattlemaster Melantheus. He, certainly, was the source of the information which, as you guessed, I passed on to my colleagues here. But nothing was said about a boathouse. Does his daughter perhaps patch sails?"

Aegyptius then called Clytoneus to order, warning him that while Antinous held the rod he was entitled to speak without interruption.

Clytoneus apologized, and Antinous went on: "My lord, pray show indulgence to this young man, who is still ignorant of procedure and whose self-control is no stronger than his memory for facts. Let me repeat that we suitors visited the Palace at the King's direct invitation, and that we propose to come every day until the Princess Nausicaa gives her long-awaited answer—though it must necessarily disappoint one hundred and eleven of the one hundred and twelve. She had better not, in effect, try our patience further, nor presume on the remarkable gifts which the Goddess Athene has showered on her: such as beauty, intelligence, skill in handicraft, and an extraordinary knack of getting her own way, despite the opposition of her kinsfolk. No priestess in legend outshines her in these respects: not Tyro, Poseidon's bride, nor Zeus's bride Alcmene. Nevertheless, this remarkably clever girl has overreached herself: so long as she fobs us off with 'one day soon,' we shall continue to enjoy the hospitality promised by her father when he kissed Eurymachus and me good-bye; which will mean great and needless expense."

Clytoneus beckoned for the rod and, having by now regained full control of his feelings, spoke slowly and quietly: "It is not my sister alone who refuses a forced marriage; it is also my mother, the Queen, whom I am bound to obey in such matters as this, and who can claim to be better informed of the King's intentions than anyone else in Drepanum; and my uncle Mentor, the Regent, whose attitude Antinous has misrepresented; lastly myself. We all find the conspiracy outrageous and will not be imposed upon. I beg you, my lords, to register our view in your memories, so that my father can be acquainted with it on his return: namely, that the action of my sister's pretended suitors—some of them wicked, some greedy, some foolish, some merely thoughtless like my lord Aegyptius's grandson—is robbery in the first degree, for which Elyman law demands a fourfold restitution. Antinous and his fellow criminal Eurymachus—who broached the plot three days ago under a yew tree, where one of Athene's owls perched listening—are in their own estimation cleverer even than my sister Nausicaa. But they, not she, have overreached themselves! Their antics (laughable though they may seem today) will eventually cost them more than anyone in this Council suspects.

"My lord Antinous, my lord Eurymachus, and you, my lord Ctesippus, if you have the least shame in your hearts, or reverence for the Blessed Gods, avoid the Palace and feast elsewhere, play cottabus with your own sweet dark wine, and vomit the surfeit of your crammed stomachs on some other floor! But if you have neither shame, nor reverence for the Gods, then eat and drink your fill, as you propose; and I will entreat Zeus, whom I honour, to bring closer the day of reckoning: the day when all enemies of our ancient house shall be utterly destroyed. My lords, how do you read this augury? Yesterday, while the Princess Nausicaa supervised the laundry women beside the Springs of Periboea, an eagle swooped down and made havoc among a covey of impudent sparrows which were feasting on the palace bread. All present saw the sight and wondered."

Old Halitherses rose and accepted the rod. "Men of Drepanum, if this augury was indeed seen (and it will be simple to check the report), it can admit of only one reading. The sparrows are suitors who make merry at the King's expense. They should be restrained—for these signs are warnings rather than prophecies, and doom can be averted in good time by men of experience—before the eagle swoops and makes havoc among them. Signs must always be respected. One evening last year, I saw a strange sight: a young he-goat had slipped into the sea from a cliff and was struggling desperately to scramble ashore in a heavy swell. It is a common opinion that goats are too sure-footed ever to fall, but perhaps part of the cliff had become loosened by continuous rain and given way—and it grieved my heart that I could not save this poor creature because of my great age and the surliness of the sea. So I pondered and asked myself: 'What young man goes in peril of his life?' By dawn Prince Laodamas had disappeared!"

Eurymachus replied: "My lord Halitherses, like all augurs you observe half a hundred sights daily, and those which can be twisted into a prophecy, months or years later, you advance as proof of your prescience; the rest are conveniently forgotten. Birds can always be seen idly fooling about in the sky, or in trees, and a great many of them are birds of prey. If every time a lark flaps her wings or an eagle breakfasts on a sparrow I must spend the next month wondering what trouble it portends, life would become impossible. And then the behaviour of weasels or hares or foxes or goats— there is no end to the divinatory study of animals. Why, look yonder at those two dogs misbehaving behind that pillar! Run home, old man, the sign is meant for you! make sure that your grandchildren are not getting into serious mischief! But first let me warn you against provoking this headstrong young buck, Prince Clytoneus, to violence, in the hope of a handsome present from the royal family. If he attempts to use his budding horns on us, the King's guests, force will be used, and you will find yourself ordered to pay a heartbreaking fine for incitement to murder . . . Meanwhile, the more you preach at us the less we shall respect you; it is like shouting into the north-east wind. Antinous and I propose to enjoy the royal hospitality, and nothing can stop us: neither this Prince's boyish threats nor your tedious auguries."

Clytoneus took the white rod for the last time. "My lords,"

he said. "Having recorded my suppliant protest before the Gods, and before the people of Drepanum, I await your considered verdict, for which, since I am not yet one of your number, you will not need my vote. If you decline to act in the matter, I shall appeal to the Elyman Assembly. But first let me restate the case point by point . . ."

He had only just embarked on his exposition when he became aware of a stir and a murmur from the benches. My uncle Mentor entered, bowed to the Council, and took his accustomed seat. His presence strengthened and encouraged Clytoneus, who held forth with increased eloquence. When he had done, Mentor beckoned for the white rod and spoke as follows: "My lords, some of you are perhaps surprised to see me here. Yesterday I was driving in the royal chariot to Aegesta when a messenger detained me, saying that I was urgently wanted in my own island of Hiera, where a convulsive disease had attacked our red cattle—and that a six-oared boat was waiting on the shore not far off to take me there at once. Suspecting no fraud, I interrupted my journey and clambered aboard. But when, set ashore on Hiera, I ran to my brother-in-law's house and asked him anxiously how many cows had died, he replied smiling that all the beasts were in good health. He had, however, been sent a message —I could not discover by whom—to expect my arrival: I was supposedly in flight from Drepanum, having been warned that it would be death for me to remain in the town! Retracing my steps to the beach, between relief and annoyance, I found that the six-oarer, the crew of which wore my lord Eurymachus's house badge, had disappeared. Nor would any of the local fishermen ferry me back to Drepanum, even for

a high price, because of certain threats made against my life
if I left Hiera. I spent the night with my brother-in-law, but
when dawn came, decided to return here, where my business
lies. I keep a skiff of my own on Hiera, which I launched on
rollers, then stepped the mast, hoisted sail, and ran across in
less than two hours.

"My lords, I beg your close attention. Though no longer
the Regent in your eyes, I am still the Regent in the eyes of
all honest Elymans who respect and obey the King; and if I
choose to visit Aegesta, it will go hard with the man who tries
to stop me by force, since trickery has failed. I shall ask the
Aegestans to find out on my behalf why you did not challenge
the King's choice of Regent, publicly announced on the morning of his departure; and why you have since approved of a
plot to maroon me on Hiera. As for the matter of the suitors,
raised by my nephew Clytoneus, I support him wholeheart-
edly. Not that I wish to do battle with these so-called suitors
of my niece. I shall do no more than ask them once again to
begone and warn them that to slight me may mean death
when the King returns; for the joke has gone too far. They
are gay young bachelors and few of them realize the serious-
ness of their deeds. But the same is not true of you elder men,
fathers of families, who connive at the brutal invasion of your
King's Palace, the stealing of his goods, and the insults offered to his family. During Clytoneus's speech, has a single
expression of sympathy escaped your lips? Has any one of
you dared condemn the suitors' action for what it is—daylight robbery, treason and rebellion?"

"Come, come, my lord Mentor," said Aegyptius. "These
are strong words. Doubtless you feel aggrieved because the

honour which you enjoyed for a few days proved to be
illegally bestowed; but do not confuse the issue. This Council
can hardly take cognizance of a practical joke played on you
by some person unknown: the underlying suggestion being, I
suppose that, since you are a Hierian, Hiera is the best field at
the moment for your activities. Moreover, the suitors, among
them—I admit—one of my grandsons (and I hope that he
may prove the successful candidate) appear to be well within
their rights. It has been established by two of the councillors,
for whom you evince a sudden implacable hatred, that on the
morning of his departure the King invited . . ."

Because the suitors were many and drawn from almost
every family in Drepanum, the meeting took its expected
course. The elder councillors did not care to antagonize their
kinsfolk, and decided that if as many as one hundred and
twelve young men had joined in the banquet, they must have
had good grounds for doing so.

Leiocritus, another of my suitors, made the closing speech.
"Have done with this nonsense! What a tempest has been
raised on account of one supper! The King could offer a
similar banquet every day for a year and notice very little
depletion of his immense flocks and herds; though, being the
meanest man alive, he asks his daughter to offer them bread,
cheese, and spruce beer; and demands an immense dowry
from the fortunate suitor as well. Break up this meeting, my
lord Aegyptius, and let us all go about our business! If
Clytoneus insists that his father's presence is necessary for the
marriage agreement, he has only to take ship and fetch him
back from Sandy Pylus. My lords Mentor and Halitherses can
arrange the matter between them, though I very much doubt

whether Clytoneus, despite his bragging, will have the spirit
to leave Drepanum. Come, Antinous, come Eurymachus and
Ctesippus, it is time we were off for the day's banquet at the
Palace. The royal herdsmen have been warned to send more
beasts."

Clytoneus stalked glumly down to the seashore, where he
washed his hands in the surf and prayed to Athene for guid-
ance. Athene, as before, was quick to help. She sent Mentor in
search of him, and when Clytoneus turned around, there he
came.

"My dear nephew," cried Mentor, "I am here to tell you
how proud I am to find that, as I always hoped, you are
neither a coward nor a fool, and that you inherit both your
father's strong-mindedness and your mother's passionate love
of justice and decency. So forget the suitors, their greed and
dishonesty; they are fools, led by knaves, and the Gods will
destroy them. Your course is to pretend acceptance of Leiocritus's advice: go to the Palace, collect provisions as if for a
voyage to Greece—wine, barley, cheese, and so forth—and I
will do what I can to raise a crew among the common people
who remain loyal to your father and myself. Any longer stay
in Drepanum, even at the Palace, would be dangerous, after
your insults to the enemy."

Clytoneus asked: "Why 'as if for a voyage to Greece?'
You mean that I should not, in fact, sail to Sandy Pylus?"

"I mean exactly that."

"Where then? You are not suggesting that I should desert
my family?"

"No: I want you to seek immediate armed assistance. And
only one quarter remains where you can hope to find it, be-

cause the suitors have now, I hear, sent representatives to
Aegesta and Eryx and poisoned the citizens' minds against us;
Eryx has already ruled that my regency is unconstitutional.
You must approach your brother Halius, who has been elected
war leader of the Sicels in Minoa, and appeal to him. Even
resentment of your father's stern action long ago will surely
not prevent Halius from running to the defence of his beloved
mother and your sister Nausicaa. He used to carry Nausicaa
on his back when she was a little girl, and wept bitter tears
when he had to leave her."

"And you, Uncle? You disregard their threats and have
not insulted them less openly than I did."

Mentor shrugged his shoulders. "I think that I know what
duty I owe my King," he said in firm tones.

CHAPTER
NINE
CLYTONEUS
SAILS

CLYTONEUS RETURNED heavyhearted to the Palace, where he found the suitors rejoiced by the turn events had taken, many of them having been afraid that the Council would intervene decisively. They were lounging about in the cloisters of the outer court, tossing small quoits or playing backgammon, while their servants skinned goats and singed fat hogs around the great altar. Antinous sauntered up with a cheerful smile and clasped Clytoneus's hand. "My dear Prince," he cried, beaming, "how glad I am that you have come to join us! You were seething and walloping like a stewpot back there in the Temple of Poseidon; but now, since the Council have rejected your protest as frivolous, you must be sensible and realize that we are not here without good cause. Well, well: public speaking exhausts a man who has not made it a lifelong practice, and I daresay you are feeling peckish. Dinner will soon be served, and I shall see that you are offered the choicest cuts. By the bye, I am surprised to hear that you are sailing in search of the King. But though he cannot fail to admit that we are within our rights, the novelty of the voyage will keep you from brooding, and if you have trouble in finding a suitable vessel, please come to me—I shall perhaps be able to supply one."

Clytoneus gave Antinous's hand no answering grip, but snatched his own away. "If you think," he said doggedly, "that I have the least intention of eating and drinking in your company, which would be to connive at shameless thefts from my father, you are much mistaken. The Council have by no means spoken the final word, and well you know it. Moreover, when I reach Sandy Pylus, you may be sure that what I tell the King will not redound to your credit; and should I find difficulty in securing a ship, you are the very last man to whom I would apply for either help or advice."

"If you want a quarrel," said Antinous, "I shall be pleased to oblige you. By rejecting my hand you have not improved your chances of a long life."

The other suitors began taunting Clytoneus. Ctesippus shouted: "He talks boldly enough of sailing to Sandy Pylus, but somehow I think that he has a different voyage in mind. Perhaps his destination is Corinth, where Queen Medea left her famous drug cabinet; he plans to bring back a little bladder full of deadly poison and squeeze its contents into the mixing bowl when we are too sodden to notice."

Leiocritus chimed in. "You are right, by Hermes! But what

a pity it would be if, like Laodamas, Clytoneus never returned! Then we should have to send off the youngest brat in
quest of him, leaving only women to run this Palace. And
if he fell overboard, that would oblige us to carve up the
property and throw dice for the various lots. I have my eye
on the orchard as serving a double purpose: fruit store and
sporting house. By Hercules, Prince, those fillies of yours
are fine leapers! Did you break them in yourself?"

Leiocritus's jokes confirmed my fears that an attempt
would be made to kill our father on his return, and to wipe
out our whole male line.

Clytoneus entered the house without answering and took
Eurycleia aside. "Nurse," he said, "I need twelve jars of
wine, not the best, but the next best; and twelve stout leather
bags of bruised barley meal—twenty measures in each. At
Lord Mentor's suggestion I am off to recall my father from
Sandy Pylus. And understand: you must breathe no word
about this to anyone, even my mother, until I am clear of the
harbour."

Eurycleia burst into tears. "My dearest child, you also?"
she blubbered. "Are you leaving us utterly defenceless? What
is to prevent these shameless young lords from murdering
us in our beds and sacking the Palace?"

"My uncle Mentor will be here to protect you. He is a
councillor and the Queen's brother, and while he rules the
household, who would dare to harm you? The estate may
suffer, perhaps, but my grandfather can keep an eye on it,
and the labourers are loyal. So are all the chief herdsmen,
except Melantheus."

"Ah, that wretch Melantheus!" she cried. "This morning I

had to take him by the scruff of his neck and kick him from the storeroom. He came wandering in as if he owned it! And his daughter Melantho—there's a harlot for you! The worst of it is that her example has already corrupted several of the other girls. Yesterday they were drinking in the cloisters: holding the men's hands, kissing and pressing feet underneath the table. I watched them through the window. After a while they slipped out by the side door into the garden and began rabitting with the suitors in the rank grass. Upon my word, a nice way for young noblemen to behave when they are supposed to be courting your sister: to debauch her maids! And who will rear the bastards they breed? The world seems to be tumbling about our ears! I told the Queen of the rabitting, and her only comment was: 'Poor girls, they have chosen a brief pleasure. Aphrodite is a powerful Goddess, and who can withstand her? Those girls are no longer children: they know that they are doing wrong. Now it is too late. A broken maidenhead cannot be patched.' Oh, my child, you are very unwise not to tell you mother where you are going."

"I promised my uncle to tell nobody, even her."

At this point I walked in, having been listening behind the door. "Clytoneus," I said, "play fair, and so shall I. Since neither of us can cope with these troubles alone, each must take the other into his confidence. Sweet Eurycleia, leave us alone together—I should not like you to hear secrets which you will burst your heart in trying to conceal."

Eurycleia went out, sniffling, and I pressed Clytoneus: "Brother, are you really off to Sandy Pylus, as the rumour goes? If so, that would be very stupid. But if you are sailing somewhere else, I must be told: when hand washes hand, both come clean."

"Have you any private information to offer me in exchange?"

I frowned. "We are not merchants bargaining," I said. "We are brother and sister, confronted by formidable odds. Unless we trust each other completely, we are lost. What would have happened at Mycenae—answer me that—had Orestes and his sister Electra made separate, unrelated plans for the destruction of the usurping Aegisthus? If you think me a coward, or a fool, or incapable of keeping a secret, say so at once and I shall know where I stand."

Clytoneus apologized. "Of course I trust your discretion," he cried, "and of course I intended to share my secrets with you. Just now it was important not to let Eurycleia think that I was confiding in you rather than in our mother, whom I dare not tell that I am appealing to Halius at Minoa. Halius might help us; and neither Uncle Mentor nor I can think of anyone else who could."

"I had myself considered approaching Halius," I answered, "but only as a last recourse. To invite foreign soldiers here, especially Sicels, seems a dangerous precedent. Even if successful, it would create the impression that our dynasty governs the Elymans by force of arms, not by force of affection; which would strengthen the Phocaeans in their rebellious plot. Besides, though I long to embrace Halius again, and though he owes loving obedience to our mother, he cannot have forgotten the curse that was laid upon him at his departure. What makes matters worse, in a way, is that he was innocent of the fisherman's barbarous murder. Ctesippus killed the poor fellow, as I accidentally discovered a month or two ago."

"Can that be true? Then why did you not denounce him?"

"I tried, but as soon as I mentioned Halius's name our father flared up in such a rage that it was impossible to say another word. I asked myself: 'Why rub salt into half-healed wounds? Halius, no longer a homeless wanderer, has married the Minoan King's daughter and become heir presumptive to the throne. He is happy enough, no doubt, and by this time must be thinking and acting as a Sicel, not an Elyman.' Also, I lacked irrefragable proof that Ctesippus murdered the fisherman. I had only the confession of a dying woman who, it seems, was bribed by Ctesippus to witness against Halius. I told our mother all I knew, and she agrees that nothing can be done to reverse the injustice."

"Do you think, then, that I ought not to go?"

"How soon could you reach Minoa?"

"Unless the wind changes, in two days, with oars and sails. We have to make some eighty or ninety miles. The return journey will take a good deal longer, if we have to fight a head wind."

"Since it is unlikely that Halius will be able to supply a naval squadron at short notice, you had better come back by land. Your reappearance must be a surprise. Halius, whatever else he may do, cannot fail to escort you to the frontier, and if you come back by sea, the crew may accuse you to the Council of treating with the enemy. I shall expect you home in seven days, trusting Athene to continue favourable. Take the inland road, and meet me at Eumaeus's hog farm. If I am nowhere about, weep: you may be sure that I am either dead or ravished."

"What do you want me to bring you from Minoa?"

"Threats of a Sicel raid unless the suitors leave the Palace without delay and compensate us in full."

"But if Halius refuses to offer any such threat?"

"He will not refuse."

"And the ship, if I manage to borrow one, which is by no means certain? What orders shall I give the crew when we reach Minoa?"

"I leave that to you, but they must keep away from Drepanum until you have been back here at least two or three days."

Clytoneus, though tough, is malleable. Having no ideas of his own, but only indignant anger, and finding that my plan agreed with our uncle Mentor's, he was willing to do as I suggested. The immediate problems—where to borrow a ship and pick up a crew; who could be trusted to exercise Argus and Laelaps in his absence; what gifts to offer Halius, and so forth—engrossed him so thoroughly that he forgot to ask me the secret cause of my confidence, or how I should spend the interval between his return and that of the ship. But I proposed to play fair: Clytoneus would meet Aethon the Cretan soon enough. And until then it seemed pointless to burden his head with schemes which were not yet clearly formulated even in my own.

Clytoneus had unexpected luck. One young nobleman, a member of our clan, Noemon by name, happened to have a ship available. This long-legged, pale-faced boy had fallen in love with me, and it occurred to him that by lending Clytoneus this vessel, which lay beached in a deserted part of the southern harbour, and hiding the matter from Antinous and Eurymachus, he could show his loyalty to our house, and me, and stand well with us when these troubles were over. Unfortunately, however, he disregarded my warning to avoid the Palace; though telling my uncle Mentor in private that he was prepared to pay for all he ate and drank, and that he came there in the sole hope of catching an occasional glimpse of me at the window. I felt a certain pity, and gratitude, too, for Noemon, who had large, prominent eyes, like a hare's; but he could never have become my husband. I had sworn a solemn oath by the Infernal Goddess Hecate, whom Zeus himself holds in awe, not to marry any man, whatever the circumstances, who entered our house uninvited and abused our hospitality.

Very well, then: here we had the needed ship. Eurycleia provisioned her; my uncle Mentor signed on a crew; and the secret was so carefully kept that, a few hours later, while the suitors were rioting in the cloisters, Clytoneus slipped out of the Palace by the garden door, hurried to the harbour, went aboard unmolested, and was soon making good progress with oar and sail to the south-east. Not until too late did our enemies notice his absence; and it caused them some concern. Antinous and Eurymachus had flattered themselves that nobody would dare lend him so much as a four-oarer; or that they could, at any rate, keep her in port by threatening the crew. The last thing they wanted was that the King should learn how things stood at home. What if he enlisted armed help at Sandy Pylus, and sailed back with a large punitive force? They had planned to cut him down as soon as he set foot unsuspectingly on the quay. Now they must modify their plans. Yet they could not openly reproach Noemon without giving themselves away, and for most of the suitors this reckless distraint on our cattle and wine was still a mere joke at the expense of an overthrifty king who had issued a general welcome and forgotten to cancel it at his departure. Thus Noemon remained unaware that he had struck a severe blow against our enemies. They decided to post watchmen all the way down the coast, with instructions to make smoke signals when the King was sighted—he could be recognized by his sea-horse prow and purple-striped sail. Then they would hurry out ships to ambush him off Motya.

My mother greeted me ironically next morning and, having dismissed the maids, asked: "Who put Clytoneus up to this adventure? Was it you or Mentor? Or was it perhaps both?"

Never having yet successfully deceived my mother, I said: "My uncle Mentor arranged it and made Clytoneus promise to tell nobody. Not even you or me."

"Not even Eurycleia, I suppose?"

"Eurycleia had to provide the barley and the wine."

She sighed. "But he is obviously not going to Sandy Pylus?"

"Why do you say 'obviously'?"

"Would he dare face his father without bringing a message from me? Besides, my enquiries show that the helmsman whom Mentor engaged has only coastal experience; Clytoneus would not risk the Ionian gulf unless with a helmsman who had made the run a dozen times before. And his fear of taking me into his confidence must mean that he does not want to cause trouble by asking my approval of certain actions which your father would forbid. In fact, he has gone to Minoa: am I right?"

I nodded.

"Well," she sighed, "loyalty to your father alone prevents me from praising his courage."

She said nothing to my uncle Mentor. He now went about with a bodyguard of two Sicel slaves, who had a strong attachment to him and carried carving knives in their girdles. The suitors were careful not to insult him in the Sicels' hearing, but a day or two later, egged on by Eurymachus, Agelaus ventured to enter the throne chamber, reach for the royal sceptre and seat himself on the throne. My mother sprang up from her loom and cried sharply: "Boy, out of the King's throne at once! That is no ordinary chair. If I catch you sitting there again . . . !"

She ran at him, boxed his ears and pulled him down by the legs. Having never before seen my calm, queenly, beautiful mother angry, Agelaus was so surprised that when he found himself sprawling on the marble pavement with a bruised spine, he scrambled to his feet and blundered away. Shame kept him from telling his friends of this misadventure; but the throne thereafter seemed no less terrible to him than the fiery chair, wreathed about by serpents, in which Theseus (another arrogant usurper) endures the eternal torment imposed on him by Persephone, the Queen of Hell.

That was the day of the suitors' boar hunt. A big tusker had been reported in a mountain thicket some two miles from Drepanum, and the suitors rose early to go after him. I need record no details of the chase except that, Antinous having borrowed Argus and Laelaps for the occasion, poor Laelaps was disembowelled after gallantly seizing the boar by the snout—if only it had been Antinous himself! And because the bunglers had netted the thicket in too great haste, the boar escaped and did considerable damage to crops and vineyards —fortunately not palace land—until our shepherd Philoetius, meeting it by chance in a narrow lane, earned glory with a shrewd javelin cast.

The suitors' servants, meanwhile, had been preparing the usual enormous meal in the court of sacrifice. I gathered, from scraps of conversation overheard, that since Eumaeus had lately resisted all demands on him for hogs, the servants had been ordered to take them by force; that this morning it had come to a fight with Philoetius, who refused point-blank to supply further sheep or goats; and that his cousin had been severely wounded about the head. I heard no news of a beggar staying at Eumaeus's farm, but was certain that Aethon had obeyed my instructions and prudently kept out of the way. For he was a natural fighter, a champion, who could have routed the rabble of servants with a mere faggot, if so inclined. His clear eye and muscular arms . . . Cautiously examining myself, I decided that I must have well and truly fallen in love, else why should I place such confidence in Aethon's strength and courage? Having been denied this experience hitherto, I began to feel a little strange: not unsure of myself, but perplexed. Since Aethon's life and honour had suddenly come to mean as much to me as my own, I possessed (to speak fancifully) both an interior and an exterior soul . . . So it was good to remember that I had treated him firmly, which I must continue to do; and then, if Athene granted us victory over our enemies, and if I agreed to become his wife, he would never despise me, however undisguisedly I loved him. Soon we should meet again, all being well, and I could then find out whether I had not been mistaken in my first favourable estimate of his powers . . .

My reflections were interrupted by shouts from the court of sacrifice: the hunters streaming in. I took refuge in the Tower to avoid them. Eurymachus had stepped into a muddy pool, which the boar used as a wallow, and now rudely entered our women's quarters, his legs black with filth, demanding a foot bath. My mother was in the orchard giving directions to Dolius the gardener; my uncle Mentor was down the street looking over a team of mules which had been offered for sale; so that none of the family happened to be at home except Ctimene. I should have sent Eurymachus about his business; but being grateful to him, I suppose, for his intervention on her behalf, she told Eurycleia to fetch hot water and attend to him. Eurycleia knew her place and did not question the order, though obeying it with obvious distaste; she poured a bucketful of cold water into a large copper basin and sent a maid to the kitchen for the same amount of hot. When all was ready, Eurymachus seated himself on a stool and put both feet in the basin.

"You are very silent, old lady," he sneered.

"I have little to say, young nobleman."

"And sulky, too."

"Do you blame me?" Eurycleia picked up a brush, seized his foot and began to scrub off the filth.

"Hey!" he cried. "Give over! Do you wish to flay me alive? What brush is that?"

"The hard brush for cleaning hogskins. Did you expect me to use a lady's sponge?"

Suddenly she screamed, let go his foot, grabbed the hem of his undershirt and pointed an accusing finger at a neat darn.

Eurymachus's heel struck the side of the basin, which upset, flooding the room with dirty water.

He caught her by the throat. "If you dare!" he muttered murderously.

Ctimene, standing by a window, misunderstood the situation.

"Upon my word, Eurycleia!" she exclaimed. "Have you gone mad? Is this the way to greet a nobleman? First you scrub his feet until you almost skin him and then you drop one of them and overturn the basin! Be careful or I shall have you whipped, for all your grey hairs."

"And unless you keep your toothless mouth shut," shouted Eurymachus, "you may get worse than a whipping: you may find yourself strung from a rafter!"

"My lord, I will be very discreet in future," Eurycleia whimpered, pretending to be scared out of her wits. "I shall be as mute as a stone or a nugget of iron."

"You can count on her perfect servility, my lord Eurymachus," echoed Ctimene. "Fetch more warm water, at once, Eurycleia, and a soft cloth!"

The fact was that Eurycleia recognized the darn as her own handiwork, and the undershirt as one of the three taken by Laodamas when he disappeared. But how had it come into Eurymachus's possession? Was it murder?

A forced promise being no promise, Eurycleia gave me her news without delay, and asked whether my mother and Ctimene ought to hear it too.

"Ctimene is not to be trusted with a secret," I said. "And perhaps it would be best to wait until Clytoneus comes home before telling my mother anything. We must soften the blow."

"You think then that Laodamas . . . ?"

I nodded miserably.

"Only let Eurymachus ask for another bath!" she cried. "I'll take net and axe and butcher him, as Clytaemnestra butchered Agamemnon. My heart growls in my breast like a bitch with puppies when a stranger approaches."

"No, dear Eurycleia, the blood vengeance falls to Clytoneus and me. If we delay, my brother's ghost will plague us mercilessly; indeed, it must be he who has brought all this recent unhappiness into the Palace. We shall call on you when we need your services."

CHAPTER
TEN
THE OLD
WHITE SOW

I N SUMMER, as I reminded my uncle Mentor, the best times for slipping unobserved out of the Palace are an hour after midnight, when everyone but the porter is asleep; and an hour after dinner, when everyone is taking a siesta, the porter included. We chose siesta time. I had told my mother where I was going and why. She kissed me fondly but made no comment, except: "Ctimene will have to be persuaded that you are down with a dangerous fever."

"If only Halius will help us!" my uncle muttered as we skirted the stables, keeping under cover of the olives. Both of us wore stout shoes and the clothes we kept for rough work: darkish frieze unrelieved by any trimming that shone or sparkled. He took his sword with him and a bag of provisions; I had a dagger concealed beneath my dress.

We contrived to reach our private jetty unobserved. The
dinghy was ready, and in it we rowed across the southern
harbour to the farther beach, thus avoiding the town gates.
Then we struck inland, and by the grace of Athene did not
meet a soul in our walk over the marshes. Presently we had
left the city of Eryx on the left hand and were on the slowly
rising track leading to Hypereia and the Temple of Aphrodite
beyond. The sun shone blisteringly hot, but this was a journey
from which we could not turn back, though the sweat broke
from my brow and rolled in rivulets down my dusty cheeks.

"Uncle," I said at last, "when Clytoneus and I were little
children and went on picnics, you used to help us along by
telling us stories. My favourite was the one about the King
who would not die. Tell it me again."

"In this heat, and up this hill? Panting like hounds after a
chase?"

"I will carry the bag if you do as I ask. I want to be reminded of the days before I had a care in the world."

"Very well, I consent. No, my dear, I can manage the bag
as well. Soon we shall be among the sweet-smelling pines,
and then I shall not mind so much . . . Yes, the King was
called Ulysses. Ulysses is said to have been the grandson
of Autolycus and an ancestor of the Phocaeans."

"Like Odysseus."

"Like Odysseus," my uncle agreed, "and some people
therefore confuse Odysseus with Ulysses. This is the story as
I heard it from the mystagogues of Aegesta, in explanation
of the ballet formerly danced there in the height of summer:

"Autolycus the Phocian was a past master in theft, Hermes
having given him the power of transmogrifying whatever

beasts he stole from horned to unhorned, or from black to white, and contrariwise. Thus, although Sisyphus, King of Corinth, his neighbour, noticed that his own herds grew steadily smaller, while those of Autolycus increased, he was for months unable to convict him of felony; and therefore, one day, engraved the inside of all his cattle's hooves with the monogram C Ɔ or, some say, with letters spelling 'Stolen by Autolycus'. That same night Autolycus helped himself as usual, and at dawn hoofprints along the road gave Sisyphus sufficient evidence to summon witnesses of the theft. He visited Autolycus's stables, identified his stolen beasts by their marked hooves and, leaving his supporters to remonstrate with the thief, hurried around the house, entered the portal, and while a hot argument raged outside, seduced Autolycus's daughter Anticleia, wife to Laertes the Argive. She bore him Ulysses; the manner of whose conception accounts for the cunning that he habitually showed, and for his nickname, 'Hypsipylon', which means 'Of the High Portal'.

"Now, one day Zeus fell in love with Aegina, the daughter of the River God Asopus, and disguised as an Achaean prince, secretly carried her off. Asopus set out in grief to search for Aegina, and first visiting Corinth, asked King Sisyphus if he knew her whereabouts. 'I do,' answered Sisyphus, 'but you must buy the information by furnishing my citadel with a perpetual spring.' To this Asopus agreed, and made the Spring of Peirene bubble up from behind Aphrodite's temple. 'You will find Zeus embracing your daughter in a wood five miles to the westward,' said Sisyphus, 'and, by the bye, he has forgotten to bring along his almighty weapons.'

"Asopus started in pursuit, surprised Zeus in the very act

of seduction, and forced him to flee ignominiously. But Zeus, when out of sight, transformed himself into a boulder and stood motionless until Asopus had rushed by. Then he stole back to Olympus and from the safety of its ramparts pelted Asopus with thunderbolts. The poor fellow still limps because of the wounds he received, and pieces of coal are often fetched from his river bed. Zeus then ordered his brother Hades to drag Sisyphus down to Hell and there punish him eternally for the betrayal of divine secrets. Yet the undaunted Sisyphus put Hades himself in handcuffs by persuading him to explain their use and then quickly locking them. Hades was thus kept a prisoner in Sisyphus's home for some days—a ridiculous situation, because nobody could die even if he had been beheaded or torn to pieces. At last Ares, God of War, whose interests were threatened, came hurrying up, set Hades free, and delivered Sisyphus into his clutches.

"Sisyphus, however, had another trick in reserve. Before descending to Hell, he forbade his wife Merope to bury him, and on arrival at Hades's palace, went straight to Persephone, complaining that as an unburied person he had no right in her dominions: he should have been left on the farther side of the River Styx. 'Let me return to the upper world,' he pleaded, 'arrange for my burial and avenge the neglect shown me. My presence here is irregular. In three days' time I shall be at your service.' Persephone was deceived and granted his plea, but no sooner did Sisyphus find himself once again under the light of the sun than he repudiated his promise. Finally Hermes was called upon to drag him back.

"Ulysses proved to be a true son of Sisyphus: for he would not die despite the continuous hostility of all the gods and

men whom his father had gulled. The God Apollo, in the like-
ness of a boar, rushed at him while he was hunting on Mount
Parnassus and ripped his thigh, as he had ripped the thigh
of Adonis. But Ulysses, though he carried the scar to his
grave and, indeed, won his name from it—for Ulysses means
'Wounded Thigh'—cured himself with the herb moly, the
gift of his great-grandfather Hermes, who alone protected
him. On Hermes's advice he enlisted a band of exiles and
adventurers with whom he took ship and escaped from Greece,
hoping to found a colony in some region over which the
Olympians had no power. They sailed to many islands: first
to the island of Ogygia, whose queen Calypso enticed Ulysses
into a huge cave and offered him the apple of immortality if
he would lie with her, which he did. Yet he was not deceived
and though eating the apple, also ate of the moly and thus
counteracted Calypso's spell of death. Thence they sailed to
the Island of the Cimmerians in the extreme north, where
night and day meet in twilight and massive icebergs, as they
are called, float about in a foggy sea, crushing ships between
them. Next, they cast anchor in the harbour of Far Gates,
where Charybdis, the daughter of a cannibal king, welcomed
him to her bed: and that evening would have sucked his
blood and eaten him raw, but the taste of moly was on his
breath and she desisted.

"Thence they sailed to the Island of Wailing, whose queen
Circe entertained him well, then struck him with a wand, in-
tending to turn him into a hog; but against the moly her spells
had no effect. And thence to the Island of the Sirens, where the
bird women sing sweetly among the bones of the dead; but
he stopped his ears and those of his comrades with wax. And

to the Aeolian island, where the souls of men are winds; there
the queen who entertained him tried to steal his soul and
confine it in a leathern bag; but again the moly preserved
him. And to the Island of Dogs, where the lovely Scylla, having taken him as a lover, suddenly transformed herself into
a pack of six white, whimpering, red-eared hounds, and pursued him with foam-flecked jaws; but the moly threw them
off the scent. Finally the same herb preserved him from the
White Goddess Ino, who sat on the gunwale of his ship disguised as a fascinating mermaid, then wound her scarf about
him and dragged him to her deep-sea cavern; having moly
between his lips, Ulysses did not drown. Seven times during
his voyage he had avoided death, and on every occasion had
sacrificed a propitiatory goat to Father Zeus. Now he reached
Ogygia in the far west, where the sacred cattle of the Sun
are herded by the Nymph Lampetië. These he stole, as Hercules had previously also done, and came safe away, though
Lampetië had tied his hair to the bedpost while he slept, and
summoned her brother Eurytion to behead him. But the hair
untied its own knots, the moly being all-powerful. Then the
Gods, in admiration of Ulysses who had sacrificed the stolen
cattle to all of them together, invited him to live on Olympus;
for it was fated that he should never die."

Listening to this story again, I was surprised to find how
my childish imagination had transformed it, confusing the
incidents and attaching them to familiar scenes. The Far
Gates, for example, were the harbour and fortress of Cepha-
loedium, up the coast from Aegesta, where my father had
taken me during one of his royal progresses, long ago; and
Circe's palace was our own, but somehow set in the middle of

Eumaeus's hog farm; and the sacred cattle of the Sun were
a speckled herd, much prized by my father, which a pirate
crew had once tried to lift near Rheithrum. The Aeolian
island was Osteodes, lying all alone to the north-west, and
visible in fine weather from the top of Eryx; being waterless,
it is good only for seal hunting and lobster catching. And
Calypso's island was Pantellaria, which one can see on exceptionally clear days, far to the southward, halfway to
Libya.

"What is moly?" I asked.

"A sort of garlic with a yellow flower."

"And I always imagined it snow-white and perfumed like
the April cyclamen! Why has it become so famous in magic?"

"Doubtless because of its golden colour and because, unlike
other plants, it grows faster when the moon wanes, resisting
the magic' of the various death-in-life Goddesses whom
Ulysses encountered. The pilchard, also unenticed by the
moon, has a similar virtue, and its liver is therefore sovereign
against the evil eye and witches."

"Are you sure that you used to tell me this story in exactly
the same way?"

"Quite sure. And if I were to repeat it ten years hence,
there would still hardly be a word changed. This is a myth,
rather than an old wives' tale like the one about Conturanus."

"I do not understand."

"Well, the mythographers explain that a certain Corinthian
king refused to die when his reign ended. In times past, a
new one had been appointed every year and at its close was
castrated with a boar's tusk and sacrificed to the Moon Goddess Hera. But this Corinthian Ulysses defied tradition and

went on reigning for eight years. And he instituted an annual
Demise of the Crown, as when your father lies in state for a
day and a goat is sacrificed to Zeus, also hogs to the Infernal
Gods. Those visits to the seven islands are an allegory of his
seven annual escapes from death. At the close of the eighth
year, Ulysses should have gone down to the Underworld, as
did his father Sisyphus; but by a divine dispensation he was
allowed to live out the term of his natural life. The Gods
were thus said to have granted him immortality. However,
every ninth year, to commemorate ancient custom, he offered
a speckled bull to Zeus instead of a goat; as your father also
does."

Ungratefully I wished that he had not spoilt the story by
his explanations. "I detest allegories and symbols. By the
way, Uncle, what if the King fails to appear in time for the
Demise of the Crown?"

"The Regent takes his place, though that is considered unlucky. We can therefore expect your father back within thirty
days, unless . . ."

"Unless what?"

"Oh, Nausicaa, sometimes I think none of us will survive
this trial!"

We toiled gloomily upwards, making frequent halts because the ascent was hardly short of three thousand feet. I
seldom climb, and my uncle Mentor had a game leg, the result
of a chariot accident. But we met nobody and the view was
glorious, with the islands stretched out before us like the ones
that Ulysses visited: Hiera at last wholly detached from
Aegusa, after riding on its back for a while, and marked
clearly against the western horizon. We drank at a roadside

spring and ate a little food, and presently sighted Hypereia
at the eastern end of the summit, which, though walled and
ranking as a city, now houses only a few families. A couple
of hundred feet below it lay Raven Rock, and the Fountain of
Arethusa, and Eumaeus's hog farm, reached by an exceed-
ingly rough path. Oh, what a fearful barking greeted us from
his four savage hounds! My uncle halloed to Eumaeus to call
them off; then, as they bounded ferociously towards us,
dropped his staff and forced me to sit down on a rock beside
him.

"Keep as still as an image," he said, "or you will be torn
to pieces!"

Fortunately Eumaeus recognized my uncle's voice. He had
been cutting two oblong pieces of dressed pigskin and boring
holes at each corner to make himself a pair of sandals; but
dropped the leather and dashed through the gateway after
the hounds, yelling imprecations and hurling stones after
them. Though they slunk back to heel obediently, how scared
I was! Eumaeus, you see, had been visited almost every day
lately by the suitors' messengers, whom he would not dissuade
his hounds from treating as if they were Sican bandits; each
of the four creatures was as big as a calf and fanged like a
wolf. Eumaeus apologized gruffly, and when he had made the
dogs smell us, to learn that we were friends, they accepted
food from our bag and wagged their tails.

The farmyard was spacious. One of its rough stone walls
ran along a sheer precipice; the others were topped by a
stockade of wild-pear branches, and protected by an outer
fence of oak rails lashed closely together. Eumaeus had built
a dozen large sties inside the yard, where the sows and pig-

lings slept at night, while the boars were driven into the space between the stone wall and the oaken fence. When he invited us into his cottage, my heart suddenly began to beat violently in the hope of seeing Aethon again, and the fear that he was no longer about.

The cottage was a dark, smelly, windowless place, unfurnished except for a trestle table, a stool, and two large wooden boxes on the floor, strewn with straw, which served as beds. Eumaeus's wife had died in giving birth to his only son—the boy who used to drive the hogs down to us—and no touch of a woman's hand was to be seen anywhere. It occurred to me that the Greek camp before Troy must have been in a pretty filthy condition by the tenth year, unless the women captives taken in raids set themselves to improve it—by clearing away refuse that would attract flies, planting flowers and sweet-smelling shrubs around the huts, polishing the metal, sweeping the floors, making window frames and stretching them over with ʼoiled vellum to keep out the wind and let in the light. These swineherds wore only leather, using sheepskin coats and sheepskin bed coverlets in cold weather, ate like hogs, slept like hogs and grunted rather than talked; but nevertheless had a simple, penetrating wisdom and displayed a more humane spirit by far than reigned among the noblemen of Drepanum.

Eumaeus was making his reverence to me as my father's daughter, when someone passed behind me in the gloom and let fall a load of faggots with a crash. I leaped nearly a foot into the air, but turned and recognized Eumaeus's son, who now gathered an armful of straw from one of the beds, spread it across the fallen faggots, covered it with an old bald goatskin and begged me to be seated. I was only too glad to do so, though the fleas were already eating me alive and, being a princess, I could not scratch.

"Well, well, my lord," said Eumaeus, rubbing his horny hands together. "What about taking bacon, bread, and wine with us?"

"Dinner is not a bad thing at dinnertime," my uncle laughed.

"But, by Cerdo, you had a narrow escape from my hounds! They would have made short work of you and our little Princess, if you had not kept your heads; and then I should have been held responsible. As though I hadn't a sufficiency of troubles: the King gone off in search of Prince Laodamas, and Prince Clytoneus gone off in search of the King, and those cursed noblemen scheming to ambush and kill them both on their return . . ."

"How do you know that?" asked my uncle sharply.

"The old white sow told me several days ago," Eumaeus answered. "And then these wretches demanding my best hogs in your name, and threatening to cut my throat if I refuse! It is enough to turn my hair white. They have plotted your death too, my lord."

"How do you know that?" asked my uncle again.

"I had it from the old white sow. Now let me tell you something really remarkable. A beggarman came here the other day whom the hounds did not bark at—knowing him, I suppose, to be a friend, though hounds are stupid creatures; and the old white sow, when she saw him, rose from her wallow and offered her neck to be scratched. 'Old lady,' I said, talking Sican to her, as she expects, 'who is this beggar that you love so dearly?' And she answered in her own way: 'A homicide, a wild man, my chosen champion!' "

"Is the beggar still here?"

"Under the oaks with the boars," said Eumaeus, "and what is more, he has contrived a lyre from a tortoise shell and the guts of a dead stoat and is playing beautiful music to them and singing in an outlandish language. He declines to tell me his name or country, and because I have a suspicion that he is a god of some sort—Hermes, or Apollo perhaps—I dare not press him to reveal it."

"What does the old white sow say about him now?" asked my uncle, as Eumaeus hurried to fetch the goatskin of wine, the ivywood mixing bowl and the beechwood drinking cups.

"The same as she said at first, my lord."

"Will you invite him to join us in this splendid repast?"

"I have already sent my son on that errand, my lord, by your leave."

Seldom before have I felt so elated. Oracles from birds, oracles from the entrails of bulls, taken by priests of noble family and long experience—these are all very well; but I have Sican blood and the Sicans say: "The old white sow can tell which way the wind will blow, and is never mistaken."

We heard the distant throbbing of a lyre and a loud, sweet melancholy song with many unexpected grace notes. Though knowing as little Cretan as any Greek woman of Sicily, I recognized it as a love song and bit my lip to choke back my emotion. "Nausicaa," I said to myself, "be careful! Do not give yourself away. The room is dark and by leaning back you can keep your face in shadow; but at least control your voice."

Aethon entered and had the sense to do no more than courteously incline his head in my direction before greeting my uncle. He now wore a filthy, tattered, smoke-begrimed tunic lent him by Eumaeus, and a cloak of undressed deerskin.

"Eumaeus's son tells me, my lord," said Aethon, "that I have the honour of addressing the Regent of Drepanum, the famous Mentor of Hiera. These rough clothes which I wear need not mislead you as to my quality: I am a person of rank in my own country; and though at the moment the Gods are chastening me for having lived too fortunate a life, I trust that before long they will lift their curse and return me to the ivory chair from which I was unseated."

My uncle offered Aethon his right hand and introduced him to me. He bowed deeply, I bowed slightly, and at this point Eumaeus excused himself, and went out to resume his sandal-making. He did not wish to vex my uncle by listening to a conversation between his betters.

Aethon thought fit to tell the truth about himself. "My name is Aethon son of Castor," he said. "I am a Cretan of Tarrha. My mother was a concubine bought at a high price from pirates: a native of Hiera, and of noble family. She was named Erinna, and my father loved her more than his lawful wife . . ."

My uncle Mentor rose and solemnly embraced Aethon. "Is it possible?" he cried. "Does she still live? My little cousin Erinna, whom the Sidonian pirates stole as she played with her ball on the beach?"

Yes, she was alive and in good health when Aethon had last heard of her, a few months before this.

Everything at once became delightful, except that I could

no longer regard Aethon as my personal property who owed
his life and his hopes of safety to me. He was now an acknowledged kinsman, and my uncle might, I feared, take my place
as his protector.

"Tell us more, Cousin Aethon," I said, greatly reassured.

"My father," he continued, "treated me as honourably
as his legitimate sons, but when he died they divided the
estate and cast lots for the shares, allowing me and my mother
only a couple of fields and a dilapidated cottage. However,
I won a wealthy wife by skill in boxing, wrestling and
archery, and soon could look down on these half brothers as
poorer and less distinguished than I. When she died in pre-
mature childbirth, bewitched by a sister-in-law, I sorrowfully
took to sea and began raiding the Phoenician coast to avenge
my mother's wrongs. In three voyages I came off safe with
a huge hoard of treasure and, though loathing the slave trade,
did not hesitate to capture wealthy women (whom I treated
courteously) and hold them up for ransom. One day the son
of the King of Tarrha invited me to join him in a large-scale
descent on Ascalon; unfortunately we were beaten back from
the city by superior forces, and brought home a dozen
wounded comrades, having left as many more behind as
prisoners. When the King of Tarrha tried to make me responsible for the disaster, I spoke out fearlessly and charged his
son with having affronted the Ascalonians by the rape of their
wives and daughters; and the God Hercules, too, by the sack
of his treasury. I also blamed him for having failed to leave
soldiers behind to guard his fleet, or to make wine-drinking
while on active service a capital offence—precautions which
I had taken myself. 'The ships under my command,' I said,

'did not lose a single member of their crews, and we have
brought home quantities of copper ingots, sard and mal-
achite.'

"Every captain spoke in my support, and the King's son
earned the royal displeasure. That night he waylaid me in
a dark alley. I wrested the sword from him and drove it
through his belly. Since nobody witnessed the incident, I was
accused of having been the aggressor; but the Council, though
kindly disposed towards me, did not wish to offend the King.
I was therefore banished for eight years.

"One year I passed in the Achaean settlement at the mouth
of the River of Egypt, a stream which separates the Jewish
Kingdom from Egypt, and pretended to be a Cypriot. I was
then captured in a border war with Egypt, and became a
mercenary officer in Pharaoh's army. Six years later, I agreed
to captain a Phoenician merchant ship on a voyage to Libya.
As soon as she sailed, however, the owner, having heard that
I was the same Aethon who had once raided Ascalon and
stolen his copper ingots, stripped off my fine clothes, replaced them with rags, and thrust an oar into my hands. I
learned that he planned to sell me as a slave. We sailed along
the southern coast of Crete, put Tarrha well astern—how my
heart ached at the beloved outlines of the hills!—but in the
narrows between Sicily and Africa met with high seas and
rough weather. The mainsail split and carried away, and
while we were struggling to turn the ship's head into the
wind, a heavy sea jarred her timbers, and we began making
water faster than we could bail it out. I had given up all hope
of survival when a fast Corinthian unexpectedly appeared
and stood by, fifty yards to windward, not daring to close with

us for fear of a collision. 'We sink, we sink!' screamed the Phoenicians in their own tongue. 'Is any Greek sailor there?' bawled the Corinthian captain. 'If so, let him leap into the sea and clutch this line.' He made fast a long stay to the foot of the mast and threw it out into the wind; whereupon I leaped over the gunwale, swam stoutly, grasped the life line, and was hauled aboard. Then the Corinthian veered off, leaving the Phoenician to founder."

I waited for Aethon to tell the rest of the story as I had heard it—how the ship was struck by lightning and he drifted ashore at Rheithrum. But he knew that I should not like my uncle to ask embarrassing questions, and therefore invented a tale of how the Corinthian captain had also decided to sell him as a slave; and how, halfway down the coast towards Motya, they had landed to fetch water, leaving him tightly lashed under the benches. "I managed to bite myself free with my strong teeth," Aethon said, "swam ashore and took to the hills. The Gods guided my feet up a rough track until I reached the house of this noble swineherd. My lord Mentor, I was rich once, and though I am now impoverished, perhaps you can guess at the harvest by a survey of the stubble. Well, I have escaped black death from drowning, and slavery, which is worse than death, and here I am, good Cousin, at your service. If a bold heart, a strong sword arm and a marksman's eye can be of use to you and my kinswoman, the Princess Nausicaa, in your present misfortunes, you know on whom to call. Eumaeus has told me about the cruel wretches who are plotting your ruin and the ruin of the royal house."

My uncle came to a sudden decision. "Aethon," he said, "your features are the features of our clan; your courage is our courage; your pride, our pride. With your permission and that of my niece I propose to inform her suitors that you have been sent here from Sandy Pylus by my brother-in-law the King to be Nausicaa's husband; that she consents; that I consent; and that they no longer have any excuse for camping in our courts. This announcement, you understand, will be one of expediency alone. Although I should be happy indeed to find that the King would accept you as his son-in-law, I am unable to guarantee anything of the sort. Besides, he has promised my niece not to force any husband on her whom she dislikes; and who knows whether she shares my high opinion of you? I shall therefore add that you have sent to Crete for the bride price and that meanwhile the marriage cannot be consummated. This will enable us, if all goes well, to stave off our troubles for a while. Now I must be off, leaving Nausicaa under your charge until my nephew Clytoneus keeps his tryst here, which may be tonight. He has sailed to Minoa in the hope of armed assistance from his elder brother Halius."

"I accept the charge willingly. What are my instructions?"

"If the suitors do as I ask, then I shall send up embroidered robes and handsome red shoes so that you can make a good impression on your entrance. If not, stay here in hiding until I send arms and armour instead. And when you accompany him, Nausicaa, wear moly, rather than roses, in your hair; and rub moly on his palms, that Hermes may protect him. But whatever news I send, let me know as soon as possible what message Clytoneus brings from Halius. Cut it with a knife on a strip of bark and give it to Eumaeus's son to hide in his wallet among the bread and cheese. And let us all trust in the Blessed Gods!"

"Wait, rest. You are forgetting your dinner."

"I cannot wait. There is still food in the bag to eat as I go, and my feet feel no longer tired; they will skim down the mountain as if shod with the winged sandals of Hermes."

He kissed me tenderly, grasped Aethon by the hand, and went to tell Eumaeus that I would be staying in the cottage for safety's sake, and that nobody except the family must know of my presence there.

I watched him out of view, and sighed gently. When I returned to the cottage, Eumaeus was weeping, but he would not say why.

CHAPTER
ELEVEN
ARROWS
FROM HALIUS

T HAT EVENING, after the sows and piglings had been driven, dismally grunting and squeaking, into their several sties, and the boars into their pen, Eumaeus, his son, Aethon and I sat drinking wine together in the cottage for an hour or so until suppertime, while the noise of the beasts gradually subsided and they settled down for the night. Supper was a splendid meal because Eumaeus had chosen to slaughter his best boar in my honour, a fat five-year-old with a heart-rending squeal. His men dragged it to the hearth, where a great heap of dry firewood already blazed. Eumaeus shore off and threw on the fire a tuft of the boar's bristles, at the same time praying to the Immortals for the speedy reunion of our family and a fortunate close, as he said discreetly, "to the dispute about the Princess's marriage." Then he brandished a faggot, which he crashed down on the base of the boar's skull, knocking it senseless; whereupon his son, having slit its throat, singed, flayed and jointed the carcase expertly. A slice cut from each of the joints was then laid on a cushion of fat, sprinkled with barley meal and thrown into the flames as an offering to the Goddess Cerdo. When the meat had been reduced to small square pieces on the hacking block—an up-ended pine log—we all squatted around the fire with wooden spits in our hands, toasting the succulent pork. Eumaeus then told Aethon the story of his life, which I had never heard before except in fragments.

"Being certainly no worse born than yourself, my lord," he began, "I incurred the Gods' jealousy at a far earlier age. Ctesius, my father, ruled two small Ionian cities, Syraco and Ortygia, the latter built on an island which lies across the great harbour to the east of Sicily, the former on the mainland near by. It is a very salubrious region, and rich in flocks, herds, barley and grapes. I was not yet six years old when Phoenician traders brought to Ortygia their cargo of pretty things from Egypt, and my nurse, a Phoenician captive, fell in love with the mate. Having seduced this fine strapping creature, the mate undertook to bring her home to Sidon and marry her if she could supply an adequate dowry. One evening, therefore, while he and my mother bargained over an amber and gold necklace which had caught her fancy, and all the maids crowded around to watch the fun, my cruel nurse clutched me by the hand and slipped out of the palace. In the banqueting court she passed a number of tables heaped with broken meats where a feast had been in progress. My father and his fellow feasters were away at the Council Hall, so she snatched up three valuable goblets, hid them in her bosom, and hurried me to the harbour, promising to show me the Phoenician ship if I kept quiet. I trotted happily along at her side, but no sooner were we aboard and my attention had been distracted by a beautiful little toy—a jewelled horse with movable head and tail—than the ship weighed anchor and I found myself a prisoner. They even gagged my mouth to keep me from crying out, and the nurse, who had always hitherto treated me with exaggerated affection, slapped my face and said: 'And now, spoiled and peevish brat, you will learn the bitterness of servitude as I have learned it.' Though a mere child, I knew enough to answer: 'Nurse: I never wronged you, and may the Gods avenge me!' For this she beat me so cruelly that the captain intervened and took me under his own charge. When we were only seven days out, the wicked woman lost her balance as a gust of wind made the ship heel, and falling from the steering deck into the hold, broke her skull.

"I was now all alone, and the Sidonian captain sold me to a Rhodian merchant who, in the following year, brought me back to Ortygia confident of a great reward because I was my father's only child. My father, however, having meanwhile died, the throne had passed to a cousin of mine, and this godless rascal swore that I was not the lost prince but a pretender, and refused point-blank to let my mother go aboard the ship. The Rhodian then sold me, at a modest price, to the King of Drepanum, Princess Nausicaa's grandfather, who treated me kindly and brought me up in the Palace with his own children. Being a slave, I could not aspire beyond my station—though I dearly loved the eldest princess, and she me—and when old enough to earn a living, instead of idling about in a fine mantle and tunic, with a couple of hounds at my heels, and sleek perfumed hair, I had to put on working clothes, forget my delicate upbringing, and learn the trade of hog farmer as apprentice to the King's Sican swineherd. A good life in its way, admittedly, and I could always count on the friendship of the old King and Queen; and having married the chief swineherd's daughter—now long dead—I inherited his position. But occasionally I remember that I was born a prince and dream of doing great deeds with sword and shield. Before coming up here I used to perform military exercises in the company of Nausicaa's splendid father, and I may still perhaps have the knack and strength to shine in battle. Last year, however, what little hope remained of winning back my paternal inheritance finally faded. The Corinthians, taking advantage of dynastic disputes, seized Syraco and Ortygia and founded their proud new city of Syracuse, which they hold with thirty war galleys."

"Old man," said Aethon, "the blow which you struck that hog would have sent a helmeted man down to Hades just as quickly."

When the roasted meat had been pulled off the spits, Eumaeus produced seven beechwood trenchers and heaped each of them high. The first for me, the second for Aethon, the third for himself, the fourth for his son, and the fifth for Mesaulius, a Sicel slave whom he had bought cheap from a charcoal burner because he seemed to be dying, but soon cured with mountain herbs and good feeding. The sixth and seventh platters were reserved for the mountain Nymphs and

Pastoral Hermes, who hold orgies together in the groves of
Hypereia at every spring equinox. Mesaulius doled out quantities of barley bread, and had it not been for the fleas I
could hardly have desired a better meal. But they were eating
me alive, and the prospect of spending the entire night in the
cottage appalled me. Aethon, I could see, was suffering almost as much as I, which gave me some comfort. At last
Mesaulius cleared away the food and Eumaeus announced
that the time had come to turn in. Though it was cold, gusty
weather and rain came pelting down the smoke hole, hissing
on the embers, he had decided that it would be improper for
any man to remain in my company, even if a curtain were
rigged up. He offered me his bed, and his best duffle cloak as
a blanket, showed me how to bolt the door against intruders,
solemnly bade me sleep well, and led his companions out,
leaving me alone with the fire and the fleas. They went off to
the shelter of an overhanging rock near the gate, where they
had piled a heap of straw on a wide bed of brushwood. Each
took a watch in turn, because Sican bandits might be about;
though Eumaeus's hounds would have given the alarm in any
case. I envied Aethon! A fireside attracts fleas, and unless he
brought away any from the cottage he must have slept com-
fortably enough. Eumaeus and his men no longer noticed
fleabites, their blood being habituated to the poison, or their
skin too tough for the insects' jaws to puncture.

I could not sleep a wink but sat on a stool by the fire,
scratching and picking the black torments off my white body.
Strangely enough, my head was flooded with beautiful,
smooth-flowing hexameter verses: the story of how Ulysses
visited Aeaea and encountered Athene, who presented him

with moly; which I made like cyclamen, of course, not garlic. "To be a poet is easy," I thought. "I could compose a whole fytte in a single night, I believe." However, I stopped after sixty lines, and memorized them; had I attempted more, I should probably have forgotten all. This was the beginning of my grand epic, though it had not yet taken shape in my mind. Eumaeus, when I told him later about my experience, gave the credit to the Goddess Cerdo, who inspires poetry and oracular utterances as well as protecting swineherds; but I had the fleas to thank for keeping me awake. As soon as the first signs of dawn showed through the smoke hole I shot back the bolt, went out into the cold farmyard and climbed a little way up the wall to watch for Clytoneus, who should soon be coming along the tortuous western road from Halicyae. I had been waiting only a short while when he startled me by calling my name, and there he stood close behind me. The hounds, knowing him well, had not announced his arrival with their usual bloodcurdling hullabaloo. Eumaeus was now shouting for Mesaulius to bring wine and bread and a trencher of cold meat. We entered the cottage, fanned up the fire and breakfasted; but since Clytoneus made no mention of his journey, except that he had sheltered from the storm in a wayside shrine, and since I refrained from questions, though obviously burning to hear his news, Eumeaus went out and attended to the hogs.

"Good news?" I asked, as I closed the door.

"Good news," Clytoneus answered without much enthusiasm. "I saw Halius and he promises help. Let me tell you what happened. The wind was dead astern as soon as we passed Cape Lilybaeum, and we made Minoa on the after-

noon of the following day. Naturally, the Sicel harbour
guards were suspicious—ours must have been the first Elyman
ship to touch there for five years—but on hearing that I had
an urgent message for Halius, they changed their attitude.
Halius has built the King a palace in Greek style, rather
like our own though smaller, and when I arrived some pretty
slave girls bathed me, rubbed me with oil and fetched clean
linen. Then a chair was set at a polished olivewood table,
and the same girls brought a variety of fish and game and a
long chine of beef, and sauces, and sweetmeats; and wine in
a golden goblet. By the way, the horns of the heifer that provided the beef had been gilded in honour of the Sicel Moon
Goddess Cardo, who is much the same as Eumaeus's Cerdo.
At last Halius appeared and sat down opposite, pretending
not to recognize me and too polite to say a word until I had
finished eating; but studied me intently. He looked well and
prosperous and the Minoans seemed to hold him in greater
awe than any Greek ever earned at home. The meal ended;
a girl brought a silver bowl of warm water, washed my greasy
hands and wiped them with a linen cloth.

"Then Halius asked guardedly: 'Who are you, my lord?
That cloak is evidence of your royal blood, and so is your
equipment. I gather that you have a message for me, but I have
not yet learned the sender's name.'

" 'Dear Halius, do you not recognize me?' I cried. 'I am
your brother Clytoneus, come here from your own mother,
and from your sister Nausicaa.' His expression grew tender,
and he drew his purple robe over his eyes to hide the tears.
Then he enquired after your health. I must tell you, by the
way, that Halius has become so Sicelized that nobody would

take him to be an Elyman, if it were not for his great size.
He had extraordinary luck when he first arrived. The King,
you see, was ordered by his Council to choose a son-in-law
and heir presumptive at the annual games celebrated for the
founder of Minoa. Yet of the only two candidates who came
forward, one had an eye gouged out in the wrestling match
and the other an ear sliced off in the sword fight. At this
Cardo's oracle pronounced that none but whole men must
reign at Minoa, and that the heir chosen by the Goddess was
hastening from the west, with anger in his heart, which must
be assuaged at all costs. The priestess meant Halius and, according to him, relied on divine knowledge rather than on a
well-organized intelligence system."

"If your news were as good as you pretend," I grumbled,
"you would have left the less important parts of the story to
the last. What did Halius say or promise?"

"When I told him about your loyal attempts to plead his
case and our father's refusal to listen, he answered with a
deep sigh: 'My father believed me capable not only of a
barbarous crime, but of perjury: for I swore by Zeus and
Themis that I was innocent. And having cursed me, he drove
me away from home. Therefore, until he comes in person to
absolve me of the curse and make amends, what filial duty
do I owe him? However, for you I feel profound affection;
and for my mother and little sister I would willingly lay
down my life.' So saying he summoned his lieutenant and
ordered him to fetch one hundred and twelve new bronze-
headed arrows in their military quivers, eight to a quiver.
These he handed to me solemnly and said: 'Warn the suitors
by the token of these Sicel arrows, one for each heart, that if

they do not abandon your Palace at once and restore their thefts fourfold, not one of them shall live. I will sail against them myself.' He also sent you a gift: this ivory comb from Caria—look at the red sphinxes on it! And this carved mirror for our mother. My own presents were embroidered blankets and a silver mixing bowl and a boar spear, which I left aboard the ship. Halius drove me in his chariot as far as the boundaries of Halicyae."

"How strong a fleet does he propose to bring to our help?"

"When I asked him that question, he frankly confessed that his threats were empty ones: no Sicel vessels would face our Drepanum fifty-oarers except with odds of at least two to one in their favour. Nor could he raise a fleet of any size except by appealing to his coastal allies and promising them a share in the spoils of Drepanum when he had sacked it— which was hardly what I wanted."

"In other words, we are back where we were?"

"It seems so: unless his threat frightens your suitors, as is possible."

"Clytoneus: something important has happened in your absence. It may even prove important enough for you not to tell the suitors about these arrows. Tomorrow at dinnertime our uncle will announce that I am already given in marriage to a maternal cousin, who has unexpectedly arrived here from Sandy Pylus."

He looked blankly at me; but incredulity changed to attentive interest, and interest to excitement as he heard about Aethon and myself—though I omitted the story of our first meeting at Rheithrum, if only because Aethon had given my uncle a somewhat different account of his adventures and I did not wish to cast any doubts on his truthfulness.

"I will, perhaps, form the same high opinion of this Cretan as our uncle has done," Clytoneus said at last. "But what if he makes common cause with Antinous and Eurymachus? What if he buys his way home by renouncing his claims to your hand?"

"He is under the oaks," I said. "Go and judge for yourself whether he is a double-dealer. The old white sow, I may say, thinks the world of him."

Clytoneus came back after a while to tell me how sincerely he hoped that the marriage agreement between Aethon and myself would prove to be no mere pretence; never had he met a man to whom he took a greater liking at first sight.

This embarrassed me. I hastened to say: "Yes, he is very engaging, but could you expect him to be otherwise in the circumstances? A friendless, ragged beggar, a refugee from the slave ship, who has landed in a foreign country and finds himself greeted as cousin by two rich noblemen! Is it probable that he would display his defects, whatever they might be: ill temper, laziness, cruelty or jealousy? In these circumstances, how can I judge of him as a possible husband? Come, Clytoneus, be practical! He is not avaricious or treacherous, I grant you; and if I thought so, I should certainly have refused to let Uncle Mentor use him in this way. I agree, too, that he is good-looking by popular standards, and well set up. But apart from certain members of our own house, beginning with our father, do you know any handsome man who is neither stupid nor vain? Hold hard, Brother! The plan has been devised solely to gain time, not to find me a husband worthy of your esteem. Aethon himself understands this. Granted, the old white sow had some very flattering things to say about him."

"In return Aethon said some very flattering things about you."

"He is getting into practice for his part. And I suppose that I must pretend to feel a certain reciprocal tenderness."

"Then you dislike him?"

"In the name of the Gods, let him suspect nothing of the kind! Though perhaps, even if you blurted it out, he would disbelieve you. A man like Aethon expects every woman to fall in love with him, even when he stinks of hog and has straws sticking in his tousled hair."

"I should like to see him properly dressed and armed. He must look magnificent."

"Let us hope that he is soon given the opportunity to display himself in all the finery at our disposal."

"Eumaeus and his son are to be trusted, do you think?"

"To the death. When we hear from our uncle what reply the suitors have made, I shall take Eumaeus more or less into my confidence. Naturally he is mystified by our meeting here, and by all this coming and going."

"What chances are there of the suitors accepting Aethon as your husband-to-be?"

"Some will go home, I have no doubt; but most will stay—Eurymachus, Antinous and Ctesippus and their party have committed themselves too deeply for drawing back. And, dearest Clytoneus, the immediate problem that you must face is no easy one: how to kill Eurymachus without involving yourself in a fight against overwhelming odds."

"Why particularly Eurymachus? Why not that scoundrel Ctesippus, whose lies banished our brother Halius?"

"Because Eurymachus murdered Laodamas!"

When I told him about the patched undershirt, Clytoneus could hardly be restrained from running down at once to take vengeance. So I took him for a peaceful stroll to the oaks and the Fountain of Arethusa, urging him to disguise his anger lest Aethon might suppose that I had said something unkind. Clytoneus was good enough to humour me, and we presently danced to the sound of the lyre, because Aethon had learned our national tunes from his captive mother, though not the dance steps. Afterwards Clytoneus and he threw javelins at a mark, and then we caught three green-backed beetles and made them race. Sulphur butterflies and red admirals flitted about; lizards sunned themselves on the warm rocks, and the day was so fine and clear that we could see Calypso's island distinctly far, far to the southward. We spent a very happy morning, and the hounds, posted around the oak wood with their ears cocked for intruders, gave us a sense of security.

A distant holloa floated up to us: "My Lord Mentor's orders. Six fat hogs are required immediately."

Eumaeus shouted back: "Come and fetch them!"

"We dare not, because of your accursed hounds."

I ran to intervene. "Eumaeus," I said, "you had better not let those men come any nearer. Permit yourself to believe, for once, that my uncle did indeed order the hogs. Your son can drive them down and take this message to him. Here; he must conceal it in his wallet."

I handed him a piece of bark, on which I had scratched: "Help promised". To write more than this would have been to discourage my uncle.

So Eumaeus, having shouted "Wait, and you shall have the hogs," went to choose the six worst in the herd.

I began cutting my nocturnal verses on the soft rind of willow billets chopped for me by Aethon, four lines to every billet, improving them as I went—and I may say that this caused a sensation among the watching swineherds, who took me for a witch. I had just finished and was about to snatch a little sleep under a tree, when Eumaeus's son, returning unexpectedly, greeted me with trembling lips and handed me back the message I had given him.

I looked to see whether the strip of bark bore a reply, but found none. "What answer did the lord Mentor give you?" I asked.

He shook his head and blubbered, brushing away the tears with the knuckles of his grimy hand.

Eumaeus questioned him in rapid Sican. Then he told me sadly: "Princess Nausicaa, I wept last night when my oracle warned me that I should never see your noble uncle alive again. His enemies lay in ambush at the foot of the mountain, where the pines smell sweetly. A javelin, flung from behind a rock, pierced those broad shoulders; and Hermes bore his ghost away, skimming the mountainside with feathered sandals. Antinous was the murderer, though his retainers swear that he was still breakfasting at home when Melantheus discovered the corpse."

As Clytoneus, Aethon and I stared dumbly at one another, each formed the same private resolution of bloody vengeance.

CHAPTER
TWELVE
THE FUNERAL
FEAST

WHOM COULD WE TRUST? And on whom could we count for armed assistance since pacific means had failed? Aethon, Clytoneus, Eumaeus, Eumaeus's son—but the last-named had no skill except with the cudgel—and Philoetius who, having been trained to arms as a young man, should still be a useful fighter. Five, against one hundred and twelve suitors, and a score of their servants. It did not seem many.

"We should stand a poor chance, I agree," said Aethon coolly, "if we fought a pitched battle. But a massacre is a different kettle of fish. We could account for several hundred in a massacre, though the repeated physical exertion of striking off a head, or freeing a spear which has transfixed a man's body, does tell on one after a while. That afternoon, for instance, not long before my capture, when I killed about forty Egyptians: we were pursuing a column of fugitives down the Pelusian highway and I had only to use the sword edge on their napes. Yet my arm ached before I had done. And it may be difficult to win so considerable a victory unless we catch the enemy off their guard in an enclosed place from which there is no escape. Dear kinsfolk, since no other one of us five has had experience of this sort, I beg you to make me your commander and let me plan the campaign in careful detail. I shall require all your services—especially yours, Princess Nausicaa—but you must give me leave to issue orders which must be obeyed without question; else I cannot promise complete success."

I hesitated for a moment when I heard Aethon—my grateful slave, dumb pawn, willing tool—confidently proposing himself as my master, my saviour, and my stern dictator. The change seemed too rapid to be wholesome, but of course he was now established as Mentor's kinsman and pledged to exact blood for blood as relentlessly as Clytoneus. And though I can organize most things, from seaside picnics to high festivals of the Goddess Athene, whose priestess I am, war does not happen to be my trade—as Andromache had to be reminded by Hector on the eve of his death. I saw no other alternative than to agree; and Clytoneus agreed with enthusiasm. Then we called Eumaeus and took him into our confidence. I did the talking. "Eumaeus," I said, "the time is at hand when you shall have a chance to strike those hard blows of which you boast. But you must be as discreet as a lapwing and as obedient as one of your own hounds. Prince Clytoneus and I have a battle in view, a vengeance of all our

wrongs beginning with the murder of our brother Laodamas
—we know now that the blood is on the head of Eurymachus—
and ending with the murder of our beloved uncle. The royal
forces are to be led by Lord Aethon here, my maternal kinsman, whom I sent to you in disguise for this very purpose——"

Clytoneus stared at me, still unaware that I had been
Aethon's protectress from the moment of his arrival.

I continued: "—to keep him out of harm's way until we
should have need of his strong right arm. Clytoneus and I
trust Lord Aethon to do what needs doing better than any
man in Sicily and we commend him to you as your leader.
Yet keep still and say nothing while he works out a plan of
action which we can all carry into effect. Now I require you
to swear in Cerdo's name that you will be bold, loyal, and
tireless."

Never have I seen such solemn joy shining on a man's
face. Eumaeus took the oath in firm tones, and sacrificed a
young boar to the Goddess, burning every scrap of the meat
to win her favour. We watched in grim approval.

Clytoneus afterwards told Aethon about his visit to Minoa,
and showed him the quivers. Aethon drew out an arrow,
balanced it on his finger tips, examined the set of the feathers
and the quality of the barbed head. "The Sicel who fledged
and armed these arrows knew his trade," he pronounced.
Then he asked Clytoneus: "Do you still propose to threaten
your enemies in Halius's name?"

"That was my promise."

"You shall keep it, to our great advantage. For if you display these arrows merely as tokens, the suitors will despise

them, knowing of Halius's weakness at sea, and never pause to consider that, given a bow and a bowstring, they can deal immediate death."

I laughed happily. "Aethon," I said, "your plan matches mine, as one half of a sliced pear matches its fellow. Listening the other day to *Odysseus's Return,* I wondered how he had disposed of so many suitors with a single bow. But Clytoneus and I talked the matter over—did we not, Brother? —and the Goddess Athene granted me a vision of slaughter."

When I spoke of Philoctetes's bow and explained the use for which I intended it, he answered simply: "The Gods seem to be as active in this affair as ourselves. We must accept with gratitude whatever help they lend us, especially Athene. She always gains the upper hand of the War God Ares, since Ares trusts to brute strength and scorns stratagems . . . Why not go down to Drepanum ahead of us, Princess, and tell your mother that Clytoneus is returned again? Eumaeus's son can escort you. Then send for Philoetius, and having revealed to him, if you think fit, all that you have revealed to Eumaeus, put him under my command. The funeral will be this morning, no doubt, because the ghost of a slain man demands to have the corpse burned without delay, as Patroclus's ghost did in the *Iliad.* Therefore, when I see a distant pillar of smoke rising from the pyre—deeply chagrined not to be present at the farewell rites—I shall know that tomorrow I can descend this mountain, spy out the position, lay my plans, and communicate secretly with you. On the third day, when you and I have made every possible preparation, let Clytoneus, accompanied by Eumaeus, carry these beautiful arrows to the appointed place; whereupon the massacre may begin."

"Not so fast, kinsman," I said. "Clytoneus has first to display the arrows and deliver his message of warning. He should order such suitors as still have some shame left, and fear of the Immortal Gods, to lead Eurymachus and Ctesippus in fetters before the Council, each charged with murder. If they obey, he should promise, in the King's name, to pardon them their follies. If they refuse, and thus plainly condone the crime, that will be another matter. Then the arrows of death may be loosed among them. By treating the young fools honourably and patiently, we shall please the Gods——"

"And forfeit the advantage of surprise," interrupted Clytoneus. "They are all guilty, without exception."

Aethon shared my views. "No, no, kinsman," he cried. "There are degrees of guilt, and if we can persuade the less criminally minded of our enemies to take our part against the murderers and rebels, so much the better. As for the advantage of surprise, neither princess Nausicaa nor I propose to forfeit that. Show them the arrows, and they will think only of a threatened Sicel invasion, not of an immediate attack by ourselves, whose powers they are bound to underrate. Meanwhile, I should like you to make me a plan of the Palace, laying it out in pebbles on the turf until I know each door and window as if it were my own. Describe your enemies to me, man by man, so that I can recognize every one of them even in the dark. List all the resources of the Palace. This is how battles are won before they are fought. I shall go as a lame beggar, for the suitors to despise as a creature no less idle and lazy than themselves."

We soon persuaded Clytoneus that he had been wrong, and

an hour later Eumaeus's son escorted me down to Drepanum,
by the same way as I had come. We found the boat still on
the beach. Eumaeus's son rowed me to the private jetty, and
by the grace of Athene no one noticed our arrival.

A steady sound of wailing, which rose now and then to a
shriek, came from the direction of the Palace. I entered by
the garden door, and when I met Ctimene in the corridor,
pretended to have just got out of bed. "I feel fairly well
now," I said. "I took a soporific and the fever has passed."

Ctimene began to weep and asked me: "Did you not hear
the wailing?"

"Yes, it work me up," I answered. "Who is dead? No friend
or relative of ours, I trust?"

"Your uncle Mentor," she exclaimed in hollow tones,
"killed by an accidental javelin cast halfway to Eryx! His
corpse lies propped on its bed outside the main gate. We have
already washed and anointed it."

"Forgive me," I said, dutifully pulling out a handful of
hair and scratching both my cheeks, "I must find the Queen
and condole with her."

Though paler than usual, my mother seemed as calm as
ever. She beckoned me close and gave me one of her rare
kisses; which made me weep. My tears are rarer even than
those kisses.

"How is your fever, darling?" she asked. "I hope I did
right to leave you quite alone from one moon to the next?"

"It was what I needed, Mother," I answered. "And, as you
see, though a little shaky on my legs, I am well again."

Because the maids were listening, I could not mention
Clytoneus's return, but when I assured her that vengeance

would soon overtake the unknown murderer of my uncle, she knew that the news must be good.

"I stupidly fainted while I was mourning for my brother," she said, "and came here to recover. I shall go outside again after a while. You had better do your turn of wailing, if you feel well enough, or people will talk. Ctimene has been revelling in it."

I did as she suggested. The corpse wore an embroidered robe and a crown of blue periwinkle. His face was benignant. Around the bed stood decorated jars containing wine and oil which would be placed in his tomb, and I noticed a honey sop to appease three-headed Cerberus. A large pyre of driftwood was already piled on the headland, and after I had wailed for rather less than an hour, the procession moved off past the linen factory. The chief male mourners walked ahead; we women followed, singing the dirge in time with the flutes. Eight sturdy slaves carried my uncle's bed, which they set down at last on the flat summit of the pyre. Beside it were laid the sacrificial victims—a cock, a black lamb, and his favourite hound—also arms, armour and an inlaid draughtboard, because he had been the draughts champion of Drepanum. My deaf old grandfather Phytalus pronounced the farewell in a weak, bleating voice. He spoke of his son's generosity, his courage, and the fearful suddenness of death; but made no demands for vengeance on the anonymous murderers, not yet having grasped what had happened. Then Halitherses applied a torch to the pyre, which had been soaked in oil, and after throwing another hank of my hair into the fire, I wept unashamedly. So strong a sea wind fanned the flames that we had to stand back thirty paces to avoid the heat. As soon as the corpse was consumed, we threw basins of water on the glowing embers, raked out the calcined bones, washed them with wine and oil and stowed them in a large bronze urn. This we handed to my grandfather, who accepted the gift dazedly; it was to be taken across to Hiera and buried under a barrow. Then we returned sadly to the Palace, still singing, to purify ourselves. None of the suitors had the effrontery to take part in the funeral banquet uninvited, and we issued invitations only to the elder members of the Council. When they arrived, we propitiated the Infernal Gods with hearth sacrifies, and grief was expressed on all sides for the cruel fate which had cut short so noble a life. "Most regrettably," said Aegyptius, "it has so far proved impossible to trace the owner of the javelin. We ought perhaps to institute a public enquiry."

"Until the wretch is laid by the heels," growled Halitherses, "a certain ghost will plague Drepanum from harbour to harbour. My lords, I advise you to act speedily."

"It was surely the work of a Sican bandit, or a revengeful slave," Aegyptius went on. "No Elyman could have committed so foul a murder intentionally or, if it had been an accident, withheld his confession."

"My lord Aegyptius," said Halitherses, "I envy you your innocency of heart. But in my mind's eye I see rivers of blood flowing to appease that ghost. May none of your own kin be present when the arrows fly!"

"You croak like a bullfrog in spring," Aegyptius answered crossly. "Pray signal to the wine pourer and have him fill our cups again. He is half asleep."

They began discussing the funeral games that would be

celebrated the next day. Agelaus, now the undisputed Regent, proposed to organize them in the field near Athene's grove: a foot race, a high jump, weight-putting, boxing and wrestling. My grandfather was expected to offer valuable prizes.

Alone with my mother in her bedroom, I told her of Clytoneus's visit to Halius, and of Halius's threat. But she cut me short. "Daughter, these things do not concern me. Your father took a decision many years ago in the case of a beloved son of mine. I swore never again to mention his name, and I am a woman of my word. If, as you say, the commander-in-chief of the Minoans has chosen to send the Elyman Queen a complimentary gift, she thanks him; but there the matter must end."

After a pause she added: "Daughter, if the threat is disregarded, can he make it good? You would surely be wiser to let your suitors eat our pork and beef for a little while longer than let those uncivilized Sicels burn and sack our Palace? Since this possibility can hardly have escaped you, it follows that you are committed to some alternative plan. In whom do you trust? He must needs be a nobleman of valour and experience: a man of men. You are only a woman, Nausicaa, and Clytoneus is only a boy. And my poor old father has one foot already in the grave—in fact, I am secretly weaving his shroud, not expecting him to last through next winter. Were there anyone else to defend us, he would have come forward long before this. And yet here you sit, in suppressed excitement, almost as though my dear Laodamas had suddenly reappeared; but that, alas, can never be. Eurycleia vainly tried to conceal her story from me; I know now that he has been murdered. I also know that you are burning with eagerness to avenge him and dear Mentor as well. And I know one more thing, because although I sit here spinning and weaving all day, I still retain the full use of my five senses: that for the first time in your life you have fallen in love, despite your oath not to accept any of the suitors who have invaded our house. So, since you are a girl of principles, who does not allow herself to be tempted into folly or to ride two horses at once, my conclusion is that the man you love, the man who has undertaken to carry out your alternative plan, is none of my acquaintance. Perhaps you will soon be good enough to introduce this courageous stranger to me?"

It is no use trying to hide secrets from my mother; her oracular little finger tells her everything. "Very well, Mother," I, said, "expect him to call on you tomorrow. As you know, I could never marry a man of whom you disapproved."

She looked searchingly at me. "But can he provide a bride price that would satisfy your father?"

I met her gaze. "Yes, Mother, though he is a beggar, he will provide the bride price—the salvation of our house."

A brief moment of doubt: was I in love with a Sican bandit chief, or someone equally unsuitable? But she soon recovered her confidence in me, and answered simply: "That will be sufficient, maybe, so long as he is nobly born."

"As a close relative of your own, Mother, he should pass muster. Please excuse me now, and when my beggar arrives remember that your brother Mentor would have already named him to you, and to the suitors, as my affianced husband, had black death not intervened."

My mother shrugged her shoulders. "Since you have worked these things out carefully," she said, "I will leave them in your hands without further questioning. If you need my help you will come to me and, short of risking your father's displeasure, I promise to do all I can for you. Come, another kiss. You are a good child, and I thank the Gods that besides sons, the cause of much grief and sorrow, I have also borne a daughter from whose conduct I seldom derive anything but pleasure."

When had my mother ever said a word in my praise before? She was being prudent as well as generous: giving me increased hope and freeing me from the one anxiety which still beset me—the fear that she would be offended when she found me making adventurous plans without consulting her. To prove her confidence, she did not even enquire the name of the mysterious stranger whom I was trusting to defend our house, nor the degree of kinship in which he stood to her. But she must have puzzled over the problem for hours.

Before going downstairs, I said: "Mother, Eumaeus and his son have sworn to fight with us to the last drop of their blood. Will you make Philoetius take the same oath? He must already guess what is at stake; but the demand would come better from you than from either Clytoneus or myself, now that my dear uncle is no longer here."

"I can foretell his answer: 'Only give me leave to kill Melantheus, for the honour of the palace servants, and I will take the oath with joy.'"

And this was exactly what Philoetius did say.

The next day the funeral games were held. Ctimene and I attended, out of respect for the dead. Ctimene was in a strange mood. She said to me quite cheerfully: "Nausicaa, my dear, I have reached the conclusion that if the King brings no news of my husband, it would be best to assume his death. What do you think? We will give him splendid farewell rites and a cenotaph, and when that it done, I can decently dry my tears. Twelve months of mourning are enough, and a bird-headed Siren perched on my bedrail last night and told me: 'Ctimene, Laodamas is no more. You are still young. Pay him his dues and marry again.' Let the King restore my bride price in full, and I will agree to go back to my father in Bucinna."

I asked: "And why this sudden change, Ctimene? Has our new sorrow anything to do with it?"

Flushing, she burst out: "To be frank, it has! I see your household slowly reduced by the ill will of the Gods. Halius is banished. My beloved husband Laodamas disappears without a trace. The King sails off to Sandy Pylus, and rumours fill the town that he is fated never to return. He is followed by Clytoneus, a headstrong youngster who does not hesitate to insult the leading Elymans in public council. Your maternal uncle is deposed from his regency and descends to Hades, struck by the hand of some god. A curse hangs over the Palace, and you have hardly improved our fortunes by refusing to choose a husband."

Ctimene's manner was so outrageous that surprise was the uppermost emotion in my heart. I decided that something new must have happened. But because Ctimene was so stupid that, if I let her talk, she would soon give her secret away, I answered carefully: "Yes, Ctimene, perhaps you are right. I too no longer feel confident that dearest Laodamas will come back to us. And it is a miserable state of affairs when a young and beautiful woman like yourself, who has once experienced the pleasures of marriage, finds herself bound by loyalty to a double bed now chilled by the cold touch of death. For myself it is different: never having been a wife I shall stay perfectly content with my own narrow bed, until I meet a nobleman whom I can love and respect as much as you loved and respected Laodamas. But look, the umpires are preparing the course for the foot race."

One foot race closely resembles another. Nine umpires station themselves is a wide circle and the runners, clad in loincloths, must keep outside them or be disqualified. Usually, after a few false starts, they pelt towards the goal as if an Indian tiger were at their heels; someone wins, a great many protests and arguments follow, finally the prize is awarded. But this race was different. The few competitors were all suitors of mine, and the lazy life they led made them incapable of running fast; moreover, their behaviour was an insult to the dead and a disgrace to the town. About a dozen of them, without even taking the trouble to remove their cloaks, ambled around the course, playing infantile tricks— punching, tripping, shouting, joining hands and cutting capers. When they reached the eighth umpire they squatted down in a ring and, with smirks or chuckles, cast lots in a helmet. The winner then strolled up to the goal, where he claimed the prize, a fine copper cauldron.

Next came the long jump. My ardent suitor Noemon specialized in this event and could outjump his nearest opponent by a good three paces; but Antinous was acting as umpire and whenever Noemon took off, called out: "A foul! You laid your foot in front of the starting mark!" So the prize went to Ctesippus.

Then the weight-putting, taken more seriously than the other sports because skill in it was aided rather than discouraged by heavy eating. Among the spectators I saw Aethon, looking wonderfully disreputable. He lifted one of the weights and set it down again with a shake of his head: which did not mean, however "Oh, how strong the competitors must be to cast a stone of this size!" but "In Crete our weights are three times as large." His face was a study as he watched the wrestling match, another scandal. Eurymachus had challenged a youth called Demoptolemus, with whom he pretended to be in love, and scorning a decent combat of half nelsons, flying mares and the rest, gave a shamelessly obscene performance: trying to kiss Demoptolemus, bite his ear amorously and straddle him. I turned my back in disgust and walked away; but Ctimene laughed until the tears ran down her face.

The boxing match was the only event worth watching, because Ctesippus lost his temper and began to maul his opponent Polybus, a tranquil young man of Sican stock. "Hold hard!" shouted Polybus. "This is a sport, not a battle." When Ctesippus continued with the rough play, Polybus brought up his knee sharply and caught him in the groin; which ended the contest, but started a free fight between the Phocaeans and Sicans who had been betting on the result.

So the umpires cleared a level place and called for a funeral dance in honour of Mentor. Old Demodocus tottered along with his lyre, and a group of boys who had just taken arms gave us the maze dance, which expresses the hope of human resurrection. The wonderful exactness of their steps and the grace of their carriage salved my wounded civic pride. We Elymans are not athletes, I own, though supreme in seamanship; and if only Halius and Laodamas had been present to perform our famous ball dance, of which they were past masters, their leaps and catches would have amazed Aethon.

As for Ctimene, it was clear that someone had offered to marry her; and it was equally clear who that man must be—Eurymachus. Once Clytoneus and my father had been eliminated, and Antinous had married me and taken a third share in the estates, Eurymachus would be in a very good position, as the husband of Laodamas's widow, to claim another third share. The last share would go to Agelaus as Regent for the heir presumptive, my youngest brother Telegonus—until it was decided to drown him. No wonder Ctimene had laughed so loud at Eurymachus's wrestling display!

I put my theory to the test. "Didn't you think Eurymachus most amusing?" I asked. "By the way, you seem to have changed your mind. Last year you accused him of taking a commission from a Libyan merchant who cheated you out of a great deal of money."

Ctimene answered: "Oh, but Eurymachus has proved to me that he had nothing to do with the Libyan's default, and promised to help me recover my entire bride price from the estate. I think quite differently of him now."

"How good-looking he is," I said, "and how clever!"

"You are not considering him as a husband, after all?" she enquired in sudden alarm.

Oh, Ctimene, Ctimene! Women like Ctimene are the undoing of the world.

CHAPTER
THIRTEEN
AETHON
GOES BEGGING

THAT MORNING, as Eumaeus and Aethon drove down half a dozen hogs for sacrifice, they had paused at a famous crossways, near the foot of the mountain, where a waterfall splashes into a stone basin. The basin, with its three altars and the ancient alders surrounding them, was dedicated to the Nymphs by our ancestor Aegestus himself. Travellers never fail to leave a small gift here, if only flowers or wild fruit, and Eumaeus now propitiated the Nymphs by burning a pair of pig's chaps on a brushwood fire. The unseemly insults of Melantheus, who came up with an equal number of fat goats, interrupted his prayers. "Foo," cried Melantheus, "what a stench! Why, whenever I drive my goats along this road, should I always have the misfortune of meeting you

and your miry, grunting, flea-ridden comrades exactly at
this crossways?"

"One remedy," replied Eumaeus without turning round,
"would be to wake earlier. Your farmyard lies not far from
here, and by starting at the same time as myself you would
miss me by two hours or more."

"Who is that foul limping biped with you?" asked Melantheus truculently.

"A beggar whom I met on the mountain. I am showing him
the way to town."

"Lout leads lout, and filth follows filth. That is a divine
law. You are surely not introducing this idle belly to the
Palace, are you?"

"Why not? So many even idler bellies gather there already
that one more will make little odds. And they all have larders
of their own well stocked with cheese and tunny, which leaves
them no excuse for dining every day on roasted meat at our
master's expense; whereas my poor fellow is hungry, lame
and homeless."

"Do you dare compare this creature with the flower of our
Elyman nobility? If he wants work, send him to me. I am
always shorthanded and he could earn a bowl of whey now
and then by cutting green stuff for the kids, and sweeping out
the stalls, and making himself generally useful. But a lout
like this fears work almost worse than death: he wanders
up the coast, rubbing his filthy shoulders against every doorpost and demanding scraps of food as the price for his absence. I know the type: if he knocks and finds nobody at home
he helps himself to clothes or shoes or something even better.
Take my warning: if you bring him into the Palace, foot-

stools will fly and he will be lucky enough to escape with a couple of broken ribs."

So saying, Melantheus took a running kick at Aethon and caught him on the hipbone. Aethon had the presence of mind not to retaliate; but groaned and nursed the bruise and grumbled under his breath as a real beggar would have done, while Eumaeus, addressing the Nymphs, cried out: "Daughters of Zeus, if my lord the King ever burned rich thighbones encased in fat on your altars, grant him a speedy return, and free me from the tyranny of strangers and the insults of fellow servants!"

Melantheus answered: "Before he returns, many improvements will be seen in Drepanum. His lands will be divided among men worthier to cultivate them than he, his throne occupied, his family extinguished. As for you, surly swineherd, I shall claim you as my slave, in reward of faithful service to my new lords, and after scrubbing you and combing your matted hair and dressing you in a clean white loincloth, sell you to the Sidonian slavers for whatever you fetch. There are always fools to buy fools, and prize fools to buy prize fools. Meanwhile, take good care of your hide, for my sake!"

Eumaeus did not deign to answer. The old white sow had already comforted him with the news that Melantheus would die soon and horribly. Melantheus then hurried his goats to the Palace, while Eumaeus and Aethon went forward at a slower pace. They watched the games, as already described, and afterwards joined the returning crowd, which enabled Aethon to drive the hogs through the town gates without drawing attention to himself. As they approached the Palace,

Eumaeus asked him: "Will you go ahead, or shall I prepare them for your coming?"

"I cannot risk being flung out," Aethon answered, "and since Melantheus saw me in your company, you had better be my sponsor—though I fear it may get you into trouble."

"First let us be rid of the hogs," said Eumaeus, "and then do whatever the Goddess suggests."

As they passed the midden heap, Aethon said: "What a fine nose that hound has! He must be a wonderful hunter. But why is he allowed to lie and scratch on a dunghill?"

"Poor Argus! Nobody has exercised him since Prince Clytoneus went away. There is nothing so lonely as a masterless hound, unless it be a fatherless child."

At that very moment Argus cocked an ear, barked joyfully and scudded off. They turned and saw Clytoneus hurrying towards them, spear in hand, though hindered by Argus's exuberant leaps and caresses. In passing he muttered to Eumaeus: "I have news of the King. Wait here until I send for you."

Clytoneus's entry into the banqueting court with Argus at his heels caused a sensation, but he elbowed his way through the crowd of suitors and paused only to greet Halitherses, who had consented to take general charge of palace affairs during his absence.

"Why, boy," cried Halitherses, "back so soon? Did you meet your royal father?"

"We never reached Sandy Pylus," Clytoneus answered. "Tomorrow I will tell you everything, but today I am weary, and grieved by my dear uncle's death. Forgive me, noble Halitherses!"

He went into the house and kissed our mother, who led him up to her bedroom. "Well?" she said.

"The King is nearly home. He has been refitting at Syracuse, and should arrive within four days. The news reached me from Minoa just after Nausicaa had set off down the mountain. But Antinous has posted lookouts all along the coast as far as the Sicel frontier, and a fifty-oarer is waiting to ambush him in the Straits of Motya; so we have no time to lose. I shall send Aethon to you this evening when the court is clear again. And, oh, Mother, my heart is bursting with grief for your murdered brother, and I have sworn in Cerdo's name to avenge him."

She asked gently: "You approve of—is his name Aethon? You do not think him too wild a man to marry Nausicaa?"

"This is hardly a situation that calls for tameness."

"I fear you are right. Run away now and ask Eurycleia to prepare a hot bath and find you a change of linen."

He took the bath, sent a maid to summon Eumaeus, and resumed his seat beside Halitherses. Up came Noemon to ask where the ship lay. "Beached on Motya," answered Clytoneus, "and having a leak patched. She will be here tomorrow or the next day. I am deeply grateful to you for the loan."

Halitherses thereupon prophesied aloud, though only Clytoneus heard it above the clamour: "I have a strange vision of a hind dropping her fawns in the den of an absent lion; I see him on his way home after a fruitless journey, unaware what will meet his hungry eye when he returns . . ."

"It would be well for your lion if the hunters had spread no net at the approaches to his den," said Clytoneus sadly.

"This lion will break any net."

"May Athene be speaking through your mouth, my lord Halitherses!"

Then Eumaeus came in and Clytoneus waved him to a near-by seat; at once a serving man brought meat on a trencher, and bread in a basket. Close behind Eumaeus hobbled Aethon but, not venturing farther than the ashwood threshold which connects the two courts, sat down with his back to a pillar. Clytoneus took a whole loaf and a slab of beef and handed it to Eumaeus. "Give this to your miserable companion," he said, "and invite him to make a tour of the company, begging for more."

"Being a beggar only by misfortune, not by trade, he will be ashamed, I fear."

"Tell him that no beggar can afford to be ashamed."

Aethon accepted the gift and began eating as though ravenous, while Phemius sang about King Menelaus of Sparta: how he went to consult Proteus, the oracular old man of the sea who rules over the sandy island of Pharos, and how he bedded down among the seals, wrapped in a sealskin. I was listening at the Tower window when Ctesippus, already drunk, interrupted the song by shouting raucously up at me: "Hey, mistress, tell us: would you also like to bed down among seals?" It should be explained that the Phocaeans call themselves "Seals." Phemius laid aside his lyre and all eyes were turned on me as I answered slowly and distinctly: "I have no such itch, my lord Ctesippus. A styful of Sican hogs smells sweetly and acts piously by comparison; and though a cloth soaked in strong perfume might drown the seals' stench, it would not protect me either from their obscenities or from their violence."

It was our agreed policy that day to foment discord in the ranks of our enemies, and this sally of mine proved success- ful. The Sicans laughed their heads off at the Phocaeans' ex- pense. When Phemius had at last been able to finish his fytte —for the Sons of Homer make it a point of pride never to sing against a babble of noise—Aethon went around begging morsels of •food from the suitors. Some of them speculated idly on his origin, and Melantheus put in his oar. "My lords, the swineherd who led this kill-joy here, uninvited, can per- haps tell you all about him."

Antinous asked Eumaeus: "Why did you do it, my man? Did you want to spoil our dinners? Or are you officiously trying to help us eat the royal larder empty? We need no assistance, thanks. Who is he, anyhow?"

"You may be well born, my lord," Eumaeus answered boldly, "but must have been badly brought up, or you would know that it is no virtue to assist the rich and fortunate, who find a welcome wherever they go. Their hosts expect some gift or service in return; but all doors are barred to a beggar save those of the royalhearted. I guided this shipwrecked merchant here in the confidence that Prince Clytoneus would take pity on him. And who are you to criticize his mag- nanimity, or to demand the names of his guests?"

Clytoneus intervened. "Steady there, reverend swineherd, pay no attention to his sour jokes! And Antinous, if you cut this beggar some bread and meat, I will ask my father to discount it from your bill."

"I shall do nothing of the sort."

"That is the answer I was awaiting," said Clytoneus. "Every Phocaean is the same: even if he were so crammed with food

and drink that his life was despaired of, and a beggar pleaded
for the leavings on the plate, he would rather die by wedging
another gobbet of meat down his throat than keep the poor
fellow from starvation."

"Beware, Clytoneus," growled Antinous. "If I gave him as
much as I should like, starting with this"—here he fished a
footstool from under the table and poised it menacingly—
"he would be out of action for three months at least."

The Sican and Trojan suitors, however, soon filled Aethon's
wallet, and he might have returned safely to his place had not
Athene prompted him to try Antinous again.

"Come," he pleaded, "you cannot be the only mean man in
this large assembly. Your dress and carriage proclaim you
one of the richest, and I expected twice as much from you as
from your neighbours. My lord, I am a Cypriot of high
birth. Seven years ago I owned scores of slaves, and enjoyed
all the luxuries that a man could desire. In those days beg-
gars came flocking to my gates and none was ever turned
away. Yet it pleased Zeus to send me on a raiding expedition
in southern waters and, before the month was out, I found
myself a captive in Egyptian Canopus, whence, years later,
after many cruel sufferings I sailed for home; but the
Thunderer, to humiliate me still further, ordained that I
should be blown off course, shipwrecked on your coast, lamed,
and obliged to beg from door to door."

Antinous shouted angrily: "Has Zeus indeed sent this
plague to stink us out? Back to the threshold, dog, or I'll give
you Egypt and Cyprus!"

Aethon retreated slowly. "Pardon me, my lord, if I drew
false conclusions about your generosity from the splendour

of your dress. A professional beggar, used to reading faces, could hardly have committed the mistake. He would have known that you never gave so much as an extra pinch of salt to one of your own slaves. I am a beginner in this vile trade."

Antinous, stung to the quick, grabbed the footstool and hurled it at Aethon. It caught him on the shoulder, but he merely wriggled a little, as if to shake off a fly, and resumed his seat on the threshold. There he made a speech: "Pray listen to me, illustrious Elymans! One expects to take a few knocks when defending one's property, or raiding an enemy town. That is all in the day's work. But never have I been so humiliated as today! A nobleman who has once enjoyed prosperity finds it hateful enough to beg for bread, without the added indignity of abuse and assault. If any god of Olympus deigns to avenge a beggar, I call upon him now!"

"Sit and eat quietly, you rogue," bawled Antinous, "unless you want to be dragged out of the Palace by the legs and flayed alive."

A roar of protest greeted this unhandsome threat and one young Trojan, Amphinomus by name, the one who had invited Clytoneus to the boar hunt, crossed the court and told Antinous to his face: "My lord, you did wrong to hurl that stool at a guest. Suppose that he should prove a god in disguise? Gods are said to wander about on earth to watch whether people are behaving with decency: Zeus himself once visited Arcadia to confirm certain reports of cannibalism that had reached him, found them not exaggerated, and let loose a deluge in punishment."

"Another deluge will flood this court, my lords," interjected Halitherses, "a deluge of blood, if you do not mend

your ways!" And when my mother heard that the reputation
of our house had been sullied by this unprovoked attack on a
beggar, she exclaimed in disgust: "May Archer Apollo strike
the striker dead!" Old Eurycleia echoed: "Ah, if my prayers
were granted, there would be few of them left by this time
tomorrow!"

My mother then sent a clever message to Eumaeus, which
a slave delivered to him in public: "Reverend swineherd, the
much travelled beggar whom you have befriended has been
barbarously treated by one of our guests. It may be that he
has heard something of my son Laodamas. Let him come into
the throne chamber and be questioned." This was both an
excuse for speaking privately to Aethon—she guessed that he
must be the beggar I had mentioned—and a seeming reassur-
ance to Eurymachus that Eurycleia had kept her mouth shut
about the murder.

Eumaeus passed on the message to Aethon. He added:
"The Queen has doubtless decided to give you a warm tunic
and cloak, even if you have no certain news for her. She
always welcomes men of good birth, however unfortunate, to
this Palace."

"As it happens," said Aethon, playing up well, "I did hear
a rumour that Laodamas had been seen, somewhere in central
Crete. The Queen will be able to judge whether it is true or
not, because I never met the young Prince myself. Pray ask
her to restrain her impatience. I shall be proud to visit her
after the banquet, but meanwhile feel safer on this threshold.
If I venture across the hall, who knows but that these noblemen may attack me with swords, not stools? Here I am neither
in the hall, nor out of it."

"As you please," said Eumaeus. "My mistress will surely forgive the delay." Then he turned to Clytoneus. "Prince, I must return to the hogs. Take good care of yourself. Is anything further required of me?"

Clytoneus raised his voice as he answered: "Yes, reverend swineherd. Early in the morning you must drive down the fattest hogs still left in your herd; because tomorrow my sister, the Princess Nausicaa, is to garland the man she intends to marry. That will be a day of days. Oh, and pass by Philoetius's house; tell him to bring in eight fat wethers. The Gods go with you!"

This announcement, upon which Clytoneus and I had agreed, caused immense excitement among the company; but he sat impassive and to the buzz of questions addressed to him replied merely: "Who knows whom my sister may choose? She will spend the night in consultation of the Goddess whom she serves."

Though less than an hour of daylight remained, and the suitors were accustomed to leave as soon as darkness fell, the banquet was far from over.

A professional beggar named Arnaeus, a Corinthian by origin, happened to have fixed his abode in Drepanum. He described himself as an odd-job man and used to wander about the market place, on the lookout for easy ways to stuff his belly. He would keep pigs from straying into the Temple, mind hounds or horses, deliver love letters, pretend to lend a hand with the catch when fishing boats put in, lead the applause whenever anyone excelled himself in public—if it was only to spit straight or break wind (forgive me) with a lusty crack. They nicknamed him Irus, the masculine form of Iris the Rainbow, Messenger of the Gods; and he had become the town butt. Antinous now sent his servant, for a joke, to tell this Irus that another beggar had collected a fine bagful of food at the Palace, and that the suitors were making much of him. He came lumbering up—he was a big man, though fat and flabby—intent on chasing Aethon away. "Get off that threshold, you idle wretch," he yelled. "Everyone here is annoyed by your presence. Can't you guess why my lord Antinous has refused you food? It's because he patronizes me, whom he knows and trusts, not you."

Aethon answered: "I have never offended you, stranger, nor do I grudge whatever alms anyone cares to throw you, if you are an unfortunate like myself. There is room for both of us on this threshold. So be quiet, or you may get hurt."

Irus screamed in falsetto: "Get hurt, eh? I wonder who will do that. Look at this fist of mine and, as you hope to keep those white teeth in your head, avoid it! What, you accept my challenge? Then tuck up your rags, come outside and fight."

"I am prepared to destroy you, if you love life so little," said Aethon wearily.

Antinous was overjoyed by the scene he had staged. "Come, friends, a match, a match! This beats all! The Gods have arranged a special interlude for our amusement. The Cypriot and Irus are challenging each other to box. I warrant the match will be better worth watching than this morning's bout. Form a ring, quick!"

His Phocaean supporters leaped up and surrounded the pair. Antinous said: "Now for the prize. I propose one of those goat-haggises roasting at the fire, and the sole right to beg in this hall."

Everyone approved this suggestion, but Aethon shouted: "My lords, though a man of peace, I would do much to win a haggis. Very well, then. I accept. Only, my lord Antinous must swear to keep it a fair fight. I want none of his supporters to trip or kick me while I am disposing of this bag of lard."

"I give you my oath by Zeus," smiled Antinous, "that if any of my companions interfere with Irus's sport, I'll half kill them."

Clytoneus broke in: "The same holds good for me, stranger. I am host here, and what I say goes."

Hitching his rags, Aethon squared up to Irus, who grew so terrified that the servants had to drag him into the ring. Aethon was in two minds whether to destroy him with a single blow or merely knock him senseless. Having decided on the more merciful course (because of the trouble and expense that homicide always brings in its train, however worthless the victim), Aethon led with his left, brought over a right swing, caught Orus on the angle of the jaw and sent him down like a slaughtered ox. He spat out teeth and blood and drummed his heels on the floor in agony. Aethon hauled him across the threshold by the feet and propped him against the nearest wall of the outer court. "Now sit there and keep the hogs and dogs away," he said. "And no more beggar-king make-believe, if you please, or I shall smash the other side of your face too."

When amid ironic cheers he limped forward to accept the haggis from Antinous's hands, Amphinomus congratulated him sincerely, and drank his health from a golden cup. "Here's to your good fortune, stranger," he cried, "and a change of trade." He offered the cup to Aethon, who looked at him with a certain pity and said in a low voice: "And for you, my lord, I wish a change of company. You are frank-faced and warmhearted. Yet your life will be short unless my wish is granted."

"Are you a prophet?"

"I am a man of experience, which comes to much the same thing, and I heard a rumour at the games that the king is on his homeward voyage."

"But tomorrow the Princess Nausicaa will announce her choice."

"Tomorrow may be too late. What if the King arrives to-night?"

Aethon drank from the golden cup, and poured a libation for my uncle Mentor's ghost. Amphinomus strolled away, shaking his head gloomily, and Aethon hoped that he would be prudent enough to take his hint.

A sudden murmur, and the whole company rose to their feet. My mother had appeared at the main door and was standing with her hand raised for silence. Everyone either loves or fears my mother; most people fear her. She speaks little and acts seldom, but when she speaks and acts, it is wise to pay attention.

"My lords," she said, "I am notoriously patient and indulgent. Hitherto I have thought of you as a crowd of irresponsible boys, tolerating your wild behaviour in the assurance that you will eventually make good the damage you cause. Certain misdeeds, however, I cannot permit. For instance, I cannot permit you to strike a beggar who comes to the Palace in search of food. Clytoneus, why did you fail to eject the nobleman who threw that stool?"

"I lacked the strength and power, Mother," Clytoneus pleaded. "No one here would have supported me."

"The Gods would have done so, child," she answered. "Surely, you know that? Another thing, my lords. Tomorrow my daughter has decided to name the man whom she proposes to marry, and if you think that these arrangements are wholly one-sided, you are much mistaken. As Nausicaa's mother, I must see that she is generously treated. The usual custom is for suitors to bring their own hogs and sheep and cattle to the house of their prospective father-in-law, not to expect free meals day after day. And they offer valuable gifts as well; so send off your servants for your gifts without delay, and let anyone who has come servantless go and fetch one himself. Afterwards I will show my daughter the gifts and a list of the donors. Your overexcited condition, and the insults to which you subjected her when she appeared at the Tower window a short while ago, discourage the Princess from showing herself to you again for the present."

Grumbling in low tones, they all obeyed, and half an hour later my mother had gathered the finest collection of bride gifts imaginable. Antinous's was a long embroidered robe of scarlet linen with twelve gold safety brooches, each representing a different beast or bird; Eurymachus's was the amber and gold necklace which Ctimene had coveted; and there were also pearl earrings, ivory combs, gold tiaras, silver bracelets set in agate, and a remarkable belt with scales like a serpent's given by Amphinomus. My mother thanked them gravely and went back into the house, whereupon the suitors began to sing, dance and play cottabus.

Nightfall found them still at it. So Clytoneus called for

tripod braziers, which two or three maids brought into the middle of the court and fed with slivers of dry pine; joking and laughing together.

"This is no place for young women," said Aethon, limping towards them. "Leave this task to me and return to your mistress upstairs."

Melantho was one of the maids. "You dare lecture me, disgusting old beggarman?" she cried. "The wine must have gone to your head. Clear off now, and make room for your betters."

"Shall I report you to the Queen when I visit her?" Aethon asked. Melantho grew frightened and scampered away with the other girls; which vexed Eurymachus, because he had planned to take her out into the garden.

"Hey, my man," he said. "Suppose I hired you to work at ditching and planting young timber? What do you say? You seem strong enough for field work. Or is begging a less laborious way of earning your livelihood?"

"My lord Eurymachus," Aethon replied, "I should be glad to challenge you one day to a reaping or a ploughing match; I know well who would tire first. Or for the matter of that, to fight side by side with you against a regiment of Phoenician militia, and count the corpses afterwards; I know well who would have killed the most. You are a boaster and bully, my lord Eurymachus, and consider yourself a big man merely because your courage has never been put to the test."

Eurymachus boiled over. "And you seem to think that just because you knocked down that windbag Irus you can talk to me as if I were a slave. Here, take this!"

He threw a footstool at Aethon's head. Aethon dodged, and

the missile struck Pontonous the butler as he was filling Amphinomus's cup. He fell, groaning, and the flagon dropped from his hand, while the Sicans and Trojans loudly reviled Eurymachus for quarrelling with a beggar and spoiling the night's entertainment. Aethon had done pretty well by making the two leaders of the plot look ridiculous and destroying the unanimity of the rest.

Clytoneus now rapped on the floor with his spear butt and shouted: "My lords, enough! This assembly is getting out of control. I suggest that you all go home to sleep off the heady fumes of wine. Tomorrow is the day of days, and we must be fresh to meet it."

"A very sensible suggestion," agreed Amphinomus. "I propose a parting cup each. Let us drink to our amity and long life, and pour a libation to the ghost of Prince Clytoneus's admirable but luckless uncle."

This was done, and the suitors went reeling away down the dark street.

CHAPTER

FOURTEEN

WITHOUT FLOWERS

OR FLUTES

CLYTONEUS AND AETHON WERE LEFT TO-
gether in the darkening court. "Come, Cousin Clytoneus,"
said Aethon, "those arms pegged on the walls must be removed. We cannot prevent the suitors from bringing swords,
but swords are for use at close quarters only, and I hope to
avoid a hand-to-hand struggle. If they get hold of javelins
and spears and shields, we lose our advantage after the first
surprise."

"What about the helmets?"

"They must go with the rest. To leave nothing but helmets
would arouse suspicions."

"Suspicions will be aroused in any case unless, perhaps, I
announce that the arms have been taken down at my mother's

orders, 'as a precaution against bloodshed, should Nausicaa's choice cause pardonable jealousy.' "

"That story might do well enough. But it would be even better, I think, if some of the women were to start whitewashing the walls early tomorrow morning, as if in preparation for the wedding. Weapons are always removed when whitewashing begins."

"I shall give Eurycleia her instructions at once."

When Eurycleia came into the court, he said: "Nurse, I propose to have these cloisters whitewashed before the wedding; so we must take down the weapons. They need a thorough cleaning and anyhow are best out of the way: my sister's suitors might quarrel again as they did this evening, and use them on one another."

"Let them, for all I care, the nasty creatures! But don't you start moving things about at this time of night. I'll send the maids along to help."

"The maids? No; they can't be trusted with valuable weapons. Yesterday when I gave Melantho my helmet to scour she dropped and dinted it. Nevertheless, I hate to have servants around when I'm doing work which should really be left to them; so I want the door of the women's quarters barred while I lug the arms across to the storeroom."

"It is dark in the passage."

"This beggarman will light my way with a torch. He owes me service for the food that I gave him. The storeroom key, please."

"Mind you return it, my child."

While she barred the maids out, Aethon and Clytoneus unhooked the whole collection of javelins, spears, shields and helmets and carried them down the passage; which was a laborious task, because we keep enough arms handy to supply the entire household in case of a sudden pirate raid. Eurycleia waited until they had finished and Clytoneus went to kennel Argus for the night. Then, unbarring the door, she called the maids into the court, setting them to clear away the remains of the banquet, sweep the floor and wipe the tables. My mother never allowed any mess to be left over till the next morning, however late the guests might retire. She came herself to supervise, and had her chair placed in its usual position beside the hearth where the haggises had been roasted.

At her orders, Eurycleia checked the cups and discovered that two of the best gold goblets were missing—those set before Leiocritus and Ctesippus. My mother smiled faintly. "Leiocritus and Ctesippus," she said, "seem to have decided that neither of them is likely to be chosen as my son-in-law. They will keep those goblets as hostages for the return of their bride gifts. What careful noblemen they are, to be sure!"

Melantho noticed Aethon engaged in shovelling ashes from the braziers and laying new fuel on the embers. Snatching up a burning torch, she shouted threats at him: "Still here to plague and insult us? Be off, rascal, or you'll find yourself thrown into the street with a singed rump."

My mother turned round and said furiously: "Drop that torch this instant, you slut, or it will be your rump that is singed." Then she asked Aethon: "Are you not the man who brings news of my lost son?"

"Mere rumours, Queen," Aethon answered humbly, "and for your ear alone. These maids might carry them in an embellished form to your daughter-in-law; and I should never forgive myself if her hopes were raised unnecessarily. Let none mistake me for the sort of man who invents lies in hope of gain. Not even were I starving——"

"Come, Eurycleia," interrupted my mother, "fetch a settle and cover it with a sheepskin for my prudent guest. Then summon the Princess Nausicaa, also Prince Clytoneus. I should like them to hear the rumours, and decide whether there can be any truth in them. But nobody else." Presently she said: "The maids seem to have finished now. Good night, girls, away with you to bed! Good night, Euryclcia!"

Soon the four of us were together beside the hearth. Seldom have I felt so ill at ease. We all waited for my mother to speak, and after a while she asked Aethon: "So you have no news of my son Laodamas?"

"None, Queen, except what I have gleaned from your son and daughter. Pray pardon my ruse for addressing you in private, and allow me to console with you as your kinsman."

"Who are you?"

"My father was a Cretan nobleman of Tarrha; my mother was your cousin Erinna, whom pirates stole."

She looked him up and down, and at length held out her hand. "You have the family underlip," she said. "My daughter Nausicaa has it too. Perhaps that is why she loves you: seeing her own face in yours, she admires it, as is natural. And since this feature denotes a quiet fixity of purpose, let us hope that you are not adverse to marrying her."

Aethon flushed as red as a split pomegranate. My face went white, I believe. The suddenness of the suggestion was terrible. Had it been anyone in the world other than my mother I should have gone for her, tooth and nail. After gulping once or twice, Aethon answered: "Queen, kinswoman, prophetess—if you are not jesting with me, how can I thank you? Indeed, my heart matches her heart as her lip matches mine; only our fortunes are unequal. Since I first set eyes on lovely Nausicaa, I have thought of little else but how to remedy this difference between her riches and my rags."

"Aethon," said my mother softly, "you can count on my perpetual favour and support. My price is that Laodamas's and Mentor's ghosts be avenged."

"They are my own kinsmen," he answered, "and I fight blood feuds to the bitter end, because of my Cretan upbringing."

He told us of Crete: the most glorious island in the whole sea, and densely populated. It has no less than ninety cities, and five separate races, each speaking a distinct dialect: the Achaeans; the Pelasgians; the Cydonians of Phoenicia; the Dorians with their three clans who worship respectively Demeter, Apollo and Hercules; the true Cretans of Tarrha. Drepanum, Aethon said, reminded him irresistibly of Tarrha, because of its westerly position, its maritime glories, its high walls and fertile shore. It was to Tarrha, he boasted, that Apollo and Artemis came to be purified as children after killing the serpent Python, who had tried to destroy their mother Leto; and in honour of these deities the Tarrhans had for centuries cultivated archery, of which they were the acknowledged masters."

"And you?" asked my mother.

"I became a servitor of Apollo when I took arms," he said.

"The mystagogues purged me with buckthorn and performed certain rites, and then a horn bow was put into my hands. I was instructed first to shoot between the recurved blades of twelve double axes set in a row, and next to pierce the throat of a gliding serpent. Both seem impossible shots, yet the initiate accomplishes them without fail in Apollo's name."

Noticing Clytoneus's surprise, Aethon explained: "An uninitiated archer relies on his reason. He allows for the strength of the bow, for the weight of the arrow, for the wind, for the tricks of light which deceive the eye when he judges distance, for the speed and direction of the object at which he aims. But by reason he will hit only a simple target; whereas the adept will strike the smallest or swiftest mark. He does not use reason, being inspired by deathless Apollo."

"I still do not understand."

"Have you ever, in fear, thrown a stone at a savage Molossian hound that came rushing towards you, and struck him full on the snout? If so, a god possessed you. Once, near Gaza, twenty Philistines ran across our company's front to outflank us. My haste made me miss their leader but, invoking Apollo, I shot the remaining nineteen dead, one after the other; and a running mail-clad man is no easy target."

When we gazed incredulously at Aethon, he seemed unperturbed. "Though they say that all Cretans are liars," he said, "who has ever dared dispute our claim to be master archers?"

A long silence followed, which my mother broke at last by saying: "Children, it is time for bed. What you three have plotted together I do not wish to hear; only let it be for the honour of this house and the satisfaction of our beloved ghosts.

Aethon, I shall send you a folding bed with blankets and sheets and a goose-down pillow."

"Thank you, Queen. I am used to sleeping rough, and any such attention would cause comment."

"At least accept a foot bath."

"If Eurycleia would consent to give me one . . ."

"Eurycleia will do as she is ordered. Good night. Come, Nausicaa!"

We went indoors, and Eurycleia, having lighted Clytoneus to bed with a taper and folded his tunic neatly for him, returned to wash Aethon's feet. They talked about me for nearly an hour; and Aethon won her heart. She burst into my bedroom in high excitement. "My darling, Aethon is no beggar after all. He is a Cretan nobleman in disguise and a very brave, talented one. From the intimate questions he asked me, the dear man seems to love you madly. Ah, if only he were one of your approved suitors! I fear that the King will never give his consent to the union—even if your feelings——" She broke off and grinned at me in affectionate enquiry.

It was bad enough when Clytoneus and my uncle Mentor decided to unite me with Aethon; and worse when my mother realized that I loved him, and said so in public; but when Eurycleia began talking in the same strain I choked for rage and snapped at her: "I trust that you gave this Cretan adventurer evasive answers, Nurse, whatever the questions were? You seem to be forgetting your station in life. Slaves are allowed to speculate among themselves on the business of their owners—who can stop them?—but to betray intimate confidence to strangers, that is sheer wickedness!"

"Darling, is this the way you should talk to the old woman who dandled you on her knees; and dried your tears when you tumbled on your nose; and taught you to make daisy chains? I told this noble Cretan nothing that you would not have liked him to know. Besides, when I washed his feet I recognized him instantly for one of your mother's family. They all have that high instep and that long second toe. Only think, he turns out to be poor Erinna's boy! I have often told you how she was stolen. It took me years to recover from the sorrow and shock. Aethon is your cousin, child. Just look at his underlip!"

"To the crows with his underlip," I cried. Then, seeing that I had wounded her feelings, I flung my arms around Eurycleia and began to sob. "Oh, Nurse, I am so miserable. Can I ever marry him? To appease the suitors and save our house from destruction, I have promised to name my husband. They insist that the wedding must be celebrated tomorrow night. Unless by some divine intervention my father returns before then, how can I attain my heart's desire?"

Eurycleia patted my shoulders and stroked my hair. "Why not announce that you have consented to marry him?"

"Don't be absurd. They would never agree."

"Well, then, darling, what Medea did at Drepane, you must do at Drepanum."

I wrinkled my forehead.

"Demodocus sang the *Golden Fleece* two summers ago," Eurycleia prompted. "Surely you remember?"

"Oh, dearest Nurse, the Goddess speaks with your withered lips. Why, that is the very thing!"

The story went like this:

Medea, fleeing from Colchis in Jason's company, took refuge at Drepane, where Alcinous was King. When the Colchian admiral, sent in pursuit, demanded her surrender and that of the Golden Fleece which she and Jason had stolen, Alcinous reserved his answer until the next day. At this, Queen Arete, taking pity on Medea, begged him to consider the cruel death which awaited her if she were carried back to Colchis. Alcinous answered that he could make no promise, but would judge the case on its merits. However, Arete persuaded him to explain the legal consequences of Medea's flight, which could be reduced to this: "If Medea is still a virgin, she must return to Colchis; if not, she has the right to stay with Jason." Arete hurriedly arranged a marriage for the lovers in the Cave of Macris, and when next morning Alcinous delivered his judgement they were already man and wife. The Colchians therefore sailed away in disgust; but Jason and Medea proceeded to Corinth, where they became King and Queen.

A whispering and the soft tread of naked feet along the passage. Eurycleia rose angrily.

"What is that?" I asked.

"Melantho and her fellow harlots have a rendezvous with their lovers, I suppose. After you had gone to bed I heard the bars of the front door being stealthily drawn. They will escape into the garden by the banqueting court, instead of by the side door, which I not only barred but locked."

"What are you going to do?"

"Catch them! And ask the Queen's leave to flog them raw tomorrow."

"No, leave this to me, Eurycleia. They might set on you."

I stole from the bedroom and, following at a discreet distance down the staircase, reached the banqueting court just as
the last of the women had disappeared into the garden. Then
I closed and barred the door behind them. A light blazed up
suddenly. Aethon had flung some dry shavings and heart-of-
pine kindling sticks on the fire. "Stop where you are," he
muttered, "unless you want your brains dashed out." He
sprang towards me, swinging a heavy faggot. I laughed.
Aethon laughed too and took both my hands in his.

"How beautiful you look in the firelight," he said.

"Yes, firelight is more merciful than the sun," I agreed.
"But why remind me of my pallid complexion and irregular
features?"

"The strong shadows thrown by the fire," he explained,
quite unruffled, "accentuate the exquisite moulding of your
nose and cheekbones."

"Which so strongly resemble your own," I said, disen-
tangling my hands.

"To change the subject, who went out by that door?" he
asked.

"A pack of she-fools headed by Melantho, the girl who
was rude to you. Their lovers are waiting under the trees.
I cannot see what good they hope to do themselves by behaving in this way. Perhaps the lovers have promised to acknowledge them as concubines and make settlements on them
when our estate is sold. Or to get them accepted as sacred
prostitutes in the Temple of Aphrodite if they prove ready
pupils in the art of love. It is a reputable profession and ex-
citing for the beginner, no doubt; but as the seasons pass they
will probably long for loom, distaff and scrubbing brush."

"I have been unable to sleep: turning round and round on my ox-skin couch like one of those haggises roasting at the fire."

"Are you anxious about tomorrow? I thought you were an experienced soldier."

"You mean tomorrow's battle? Why, no! Since the plan of campaign was settled I have not given the matter another thought, though the Gods alone know what we shall do when we have gained the victory—because it looks as if we must either flee the country or challenge the whole Elyman army. But who cares? Princess, it is you who prevent me from sleeping. You may have believed that I was speaking rhetorically at Rheithrum when I praised your beauty; and there was indeed something artificial in my speech, because the quality of rhetoric is public, not intimate. Yet it was love at first sight; only the presence of your maids and my fear of vexing you prevented me from saying so as passionately as I say it now. Dearest one, you are the light in my eyes, the blood in my veins, the breath in my lungs."

He put his strong arms about me, but I repelled him and showed that I meant it. "My name is not Melantho," I panted. "It is Nausicaa."

"At your orders."

"Then go up that staircase to the Tower room where Clytoneus is sleeping. Bring him here."

"Why?"

"Bring him here!"

Soon Clytoneus stumbled in, childishly rubbing his eyes and by no means pleased to be awakened after his hard day. Boys of his age need as much sleep as they can get.

"Brother," I said, "Aethon and I are marrying tonight. Will you give me away?"

Clytoneus seemed shocked. "In such haste, Sister?"

"In such haste. No, he has not already seduced me, if that is what you mean."

"But the betrothal, the bride gift?"

"Let him give you his wallet with the half-warm haggis. That is all he possesses; a suitor cannot give more than his all."

"And the wedding garment?"

"Let him wear the dead man's best clothes. They are of a size, and his ghost will be flattered. Now, Brother, enough of your objections. The only acceptable reason that I could give for not choosing one of the suitors is that I am married, and once I am married they have no excuse for staying."

"What do you expect our father to say?"

"If Aethon leads us to victory he will be received with joy. If he fails, none of us can be reproached for celebrating this marriage, because we shall all be dead: you and Aethon by the hands of my suitors, I by my own."

"And our mother? Are you sure of her consent? Though I should like nothing better than to see you Aethon's bride, I dare not oppose her."

"She cannot withhold her consent when Aethon proposes an immediate marriage as his price for saving the kingdom."

But our mother was standing silently in the doorway beside Eurycleia, and had overheard most of the conversation. "Clytoneus," she said, "rouse the men in the court of sacrifice. Order them to fetch the usual propitiatory offerings to Hera, Artemis and the Fates. They need not be told why the beasts

are required. Thornwood torches: we have a few somewhere
in the Tower. Flowers and flutes? No: respect for the dead
forbids their use until the third day. Candied quince; there
is still a box of that in the larder. I should have liked to draw
lustral water from the Fountain of the Nymphs. Never mind,
we can placate them later; our own fountain will do."

"And Ctimene?" asked Clytoneus.

Always Ctimene. Yes, she could scarcely be trusted with
the secret. But would she not be awakened by the coming
and going, the squealing of the pigs sacrificed to the Fates,
and the chorus of the Hymenaeus, however quietly we sang it?

In the end we decided to call her as a witness to the betrothal, and running upstairs, I knocked at the bedroom door.
She did not answer. I went in and called "Ctimene, Ctimene!"
Still no answer. I moved carefully towards her bed and
reached out a hand to touch her shoulder. The bedclothes
were still warm, the bed unoccupied; and when I came down
again, the only explanation that anyone could offer, shameful
though it might seem, was that she had gone into the garden
with the maids on the same errand as they. Yet we had no time
for speculation.

Our troth was plighted at the foot of my father's throne, in
the presence of my mother, Clytoneus and Eurycleia; and
Aethon solemnly handed Clytoneus, as his bride price, a bald
old wallet containing a haggis! The maids and menservants
stood wide-eyed about us, sworn to silence by oaths which
they would rather die than break. Aethon and I were cere-
monially washed by our attendants, each apart, in spring
water from the gateway fountain; then dressed in bridal
costume, and garlanded with leaves. What did I care if my

wedding dress wanted a deal of embroidery at the back? Clytoneus hastily slaughtered the beasts—the squealing of the
pigs would be interpreted by passers-by as the sound of
placatory sacrifices for Mentor—and I threw another lock of
my hair into the fire by way of farewell to Athene, whose
virgin priestess I could no longer be, though I adored her
none the less. Aethon and I then shared our slice of candied
quince, eaten for Aphrodite's sake, kindled the thornwood
torches at the braziers, and distributed sweetmeats, while our
attendants sang the Hymenaeus, but gently, gently, so that the
noise should not reach the garden. We also drank cups of
honeyed wine. At last the maids led me by torchlight into the
banqueting court, kissed me and tiptoed off.

Aethon followed, taper in hand, and found me trembling
beside a brazier. He unloosed my girdle and, lifting me up,
laid me naked on the white ox hide, covered with sheepskins,
which had been his bed.

Neither of us said a word, and never had I realized how
overpoweringly fierce is the Goddess Aphrodite. She maddens
her votaries, confounding pain and pleasure, love and hate,
joy and rage in a holocaust of passion, burning away all
shame, all memory of things past, all care for the future.
Yet I struggled against the Goddess, remembering poor foolish Ctimene: resolved upon keeping my woman's pride. I
must not let Aethon know that I loved him more than the
whole world, more than myself, more than anything in exist-
ence but the Goddess Athene, whom I invoked silently for
strength.

At grey dawn I left Aethon and went back into the house to
awake Eurycleia, who hurried down to remove Aethon's

wedding garment, the charred stumps of the thorn torches, and other relics of the festivities. When this was done she set the maids to whitewashing the cloisters, as had been agreed, while I slept again in my own narrow bed until high day, dreaming of the Golden Fleece. But Aethon remained in our nuptial couch dreaming of me.

CHAPTER
FIFTEEN
THE DAY
OF VENGEANCE

I T WAS A HEAVY MORNING. When Aethon awoke to
the swish of whitewash brushes—we use bunches of ass-grass
—and the low laughter of the women, he went into the court
of sacrifice and prayed softly to Cretan Zeus: "Lord, this is
the day of days, after a night of nights. Grant me two things:
lucky words from the first person I meet, and a lucky sign
from Heaven!"

Would you believe it? He had hardly spoken before a
distant roll of thunder sounded from a blue and cloudless
sky; and at the noise one of our Sicel slaves looked up from
the heavy quern in which she was grinding a mixture of wheat
and barley, and gave him his lucky word. I should explain
that, being weak in the chest, this woman was the last of a

team of six to complete the stint set her just before dawn; the others had already crept back to their straw pallets for a nap. All our maids must do an occasional spell at the quern; it is good exercise. As my father tells us: "A slave who does not eliminate the gross humours of his system, by daily sweats, is a sullen slave and soon will be a sick one." But, as the priests of Apollo say: "All things in measure," and the unusual consumption of bread, since my suitors had begun to plague us, made work at the quern ten times longer and more tedious than before.

The lucky words were these: "Father Zeus, for whom do you thunder assent like that? From a clear sky, too! Has some distressed nobleman prayed and found you in a good humour? Then, please, listen to a poor Siccl slave and fulfil her wish at the same time! Pitiful Zeus, let today see the end of impudent banquetry at the Palace! The quern is grinding away my life and breaking my back. May those greedy suitors never again eat the flour that falls from it!"

Aethon's heart leapt in his breast, and he prayed aloud to Apollo: "Archer Apollo, whose servitor I am, favour me on the festival of your vengeance!" For, this being the anniversary of the God's victory over the Python, we had chosen it to be the day of our vengeance also.

Meanwhile, Clytoneus had taken his spear from the spear stand and gone off to attend Apollo's public sacrifice, Argus following at his heels. Eurycleia kept the maids busily whitewashing, and when they had completed one wall, sent them to draw water, put purple covers on the settles, lay the tables with goblets, two-handled cups and trenchers, and strew freshly cut branches of juniper on the pavement. Before long

Eumaeus drove in three splendid hogs and, meeting Philoetius, who had brought a heifer and some fat goats ferried
across from Hiera, greeted him with: "Honest friend, the
Queen wishes to see you."

When Philoetius returned, he found Melantheus insulting
Aethon again. "Are you still about, troublemaker?" Melantheus stormed. "Didn't you collect enough food yesterday,
that you must beg for more? Where do you stow it all away?
Don't tell me you have eaten that entire haggis in a single
night as well as those scraps! Now, look here, fellow! Any
more of your mischief and you and I must come to blows. I
fancy that I can hit a trifle harder than Irus."

But Philoetius interposed. "This man is under the Queen's
protection," he said, "having cheered her with news of Prince
Laodamas. If it proves to be true, our troubles will soon be
over. The King and he will send those damned rogues pack-
ing, and give you your deserts, you traitor!"

Then he approached Aethon and pressed his hand, saying:
"My name is Philoetius, at your service."

Melantheus slunk out of the court. Philoetius was not a
man with whom he cared to quarrel.

About an hour later Clytoneus entered the Palace, followed
by the suitors, who threw their cloaks down on the settles and
lost no time in sacrificing the beasts provided by Eumaeus and
Philoetius. Being hungry, they set their servants to cook the
livers, kidneys, brains and suchlike in a huge mixed grill, resting them on the marrow bones, and called for wine and a great
deal of bread. Two big black cauldrons also bubbled at the
hearth fire, containing pigs' trotters, the heifer's heels and
tongue, sheeps' heads, and lengths of tripe, to which barley,

beans and vegetables had been added. The rest of the meat was roasted on spits of pomegranate wood and five-pronged toasting forks. Eumaeus, Melantheus and Philoetius acted as waiters, because the other servants were still working in the stables and the garden; it was not nearly dinnertime yet.

Clytoneus called to Aethon: "Beggar, come and sit at this table with me!" The table had been set on the threshold, just outside the front door, where the red stone dogs stood guard, and he filled a golden wine cup for Aethon, saying in a loud voice: "Cypriot, you may rely on me to protect you from any abuse or assault, though these uninvited guests often forget that they are banqueting in a palace, not a country tavern, and behave accordingly. My lords, are you listening?" He beckoned to Eumaeus, who thereupon helped Aethon, before anyone else, to a steaming bowl of stew.

A contemptuous murmur arose, which Antinous, who had arrived fairly drunk, interrupted. "Well," he said, "I suppose that we must put up with Prince Clytoneus's bragging a little longer; for I do not think that the Fates have measured him out a very extensive life."

Ctesippus guffawed. Then he shouted: "Comrades, our licenced beggar has already been served with food enough to satiate a smithy full of blacksmiths, and since Prince Clytoneus has shown courtesy to so distinguished a foreigner, I do not propose to be behindhand in following his example. Here is my contribution, and if he finds it too tough even for his ostrichlike stomach to digest, let him pass it on to Gorgo the goose woman or some other humble and deserving person."

Melantheus had brought him a dish of broth, and Ctesip-

pus, picking up one of the heifer's heels—but, because it was
very hot, using one of our best purple covers as a glove—
hurled it at Aethon. With one of those mirthless grins that
you see on the bronze figures of horned men imported from
Sardinia, Aethon moved his head aside; and the missile
struck the wall instead.

Clytoneus, grasping his spear, burst out: "It is fortunate
for you that the heel missed my guest, Ctesippus! If he had
not ducked in time, I should have spitted you like a sucking
pig. My patience has a certain breaking point and if you
stretch it any further, will snap. No doubt, you have decided
to kill me; but beware, for I will take one or two of you with
me to Hades first. My lord Agelaus, as the noblest born
Trojan present, next to myself, you must help me to keep
order here. When the Council chose you to act as Regent for
the King, did they authorize you to see his son publicly insulted?"

Agelaus answered, grinning: "Ctesippus is in merry mood.
Pay no attention to his practical jokes, which reflect a lively
and generous nature. You must remember, kinsman, that we
have absented ourselves from the town festivities in honour
of Apollo—after witnessing the introductory prayers and
sacrifices—at your personal invitation. You promised that
today the Princess Nausicaa will clearly name the man whom
she intends to marry, as she has been urged to do for a
couple of years at least. Once she does so, this series of
banquets will end, and there need be no recurrence of unpleasant scenes, which I deplore no less profoundly than yourself, but for which I hold you largely responsible."

Only one of my suitors, the Sican Theoclymenus, had

noticed that no arms were hanging in the cloisters; nor did
the whitewashing of the single wall deceive him. He cast a
keen glance of enquiry at Clytoneus, who raised the butt of
his spear a handsbreadth from the ground in warning, and
pointed to the side door.

Theoclymenus rose shivering from his stool. "My eyes are
darkened," he said. "The court is full of ghosts, and I hear a
sound of mourning in the air. Forgive me, comrades, if I
leave you and invoke the God Apollo in the market place." He
crossed the court at a run.

Everyone stared. But Antinous hiccuped: "Upon my word,
that was the neatest excuse I ever heard! To cover his confusion when he had been taken short at table and disgraced
himself . . ." A yell of laughter drowned the rest of his disgusting speech.

I paced up and down my bedroom for a while. Dolius
the gardener had stumbled on Ctimene's dead body hidden by
long grass in a corner of the orchard, by the melon patch. I
ordered him to say nothing to anyone and leave her where she
lay—explaining that we could not attend to the funeral rites
until I had announced my choice of a husband. I may say
at once that we never discovered who killed Ctimene, or why.
Her throat was cut from ear to ear and someone had evidently
dragged her to this place of concealment. My own view is
that, suspecting Melantho of a love affair with Eurymachus,
she had joined the party of maids, none of whom realized,
in the half-dark, who she was. She then followed Melantho, and
either cut her own throat when these suspicions proved to be
well founded; or perhaps Eurymachus (who never stuck at
murder) cut it for her. It does not matter. The curse of the

amber necklace had drawn Ctimene down to join my brother
Laodamas in loveless Hades.

The news animated me with a calm rage. I went into the
empty throne chamber and sat unobserved on a chair immediately behind the front door, from which I could hear
everything. When, by the sound of drunken laughter—at
my orders Philoetius and Eumaeus were assisting Pontonous
to keep the cups and goblets filled to the brim—it was at last
clear that the time had come for action, I slipped out again
and called Eurycleia.

"Eurycleia," I said, "the key of the storeroom, please!"

She accompanied me, and I remember that when, having
undone the thong attached to the knob, she unlocked the door
and pulled it open, the hinges gave a great vengeful groan,
as loud as a sacred bull who sees trespassers venturing across
his paddock. I read this as a good sign. On days of critical
importance one watches for every possible indication of the
Gods' will; but must be careful not to be deceived by the
ambiguity in which they love to cloak their designs.

I took up the fourteen well-stocked Sicel quivers that Clytoneus had secreted here, found a box of brass and iron quoits
used for our palace game of ringing the peg, and then with
trembling hands reached for the nail where hung a tall,
curved, glittering gold case engraved with ancient pictures.
My dear friend Procne had fortunately come to stay at the
Palace, now that her father had sailed for Elba. She and
Eurycleia between them managed to lift the long heavy box
of quoits, while I carried the golden case and the armful of
quivers. "Come," I said, and we filed through the silent
throne chamber and into the thronged banqueting court, very

slowly, not looking about us. I came to a halt beside the main
pillar that supported the cloister roof, and to my surprise
remained perfectly self-possessed.

The suitors, startled and pleased to see me wearing my
bridal robe and a garland of fresh flowers, beat on the tables
with their knife handles and raised a lusty cheer; which I
acknowledged with a slight nod before setting down my load
and addressing them. "My lords, the Prince Clytoneus decided to make no choice of husband for me that might prove
disagreeable to the King, and prudently left the decision to
myself. Finding this an invidious task, I appealed to the Goddess Athene, who appeared to me in a dream last night and
spoke as follows: 'Child, choose the man with the steadiest
hand and the keenest eye of all who sit at table in your inner
court; and since tomorrow is the feast of Apollo the Archer,
remember the bow of Philoctetes!' What could be plainer?
Homer describes how Isander and Hippolochus contended for
the kingdom of Lycia in an archery match; and though the
prize here is a smaller one, more than one hundred noblemen dispute it bitterly—passionate rivals for my love."

I let these words cut like a razor.

"Not only would it be tedious," I went on, "for so many
rivals to contend with the same bow, but I fear quarrels of
precedence. Therefore, to limit the entries, I have designed
a simple trial of manual skill. My brother Clytoneus will
set up twelve pegs in a row, one behind the other, across the
court: and no suitor may cast more than one quoit. Whichever
three men ring the most distant pegs are permitted to take
part in the archery match, which will consist of shooting
arrows through axe-heads. The bow I shall lend them is an

heirloom; this bow of Philoctetes, the most famous hero-relic in all Sicily. It belonged to Hercules himself, who bequeathed it to Philoctetes as he climbed upon his pyre on Mount Oeta. With this very weapon Philoctetes shot Paris first in the hand, and then in the right eye, thus virtually ending the Trojan War."

My speech provoked a deal of confusion, because they had expected me to choose one or other of the suitors whom my father had approved. Now, if the company as a whole accepted my means of deciding the issue, for which I claimed divine sanction, they too would have to stand by the result and change their plans. And the young men whose bride gifts had not been particularly handsome, thinking that here was a chance to improve their position, clamoured a full-throated assent. Clytoneus at once took a mattock and dug a long trench in the stamped earth of the court; then he fixed the pegs at three paces' interval along the trench, in accurate alignment, pressing the soil tightly around them with his shoe. Afterwards he drew a mark from behind which all competitors must cast their quoits. "You may begin, my lords," he said, as he strode back to his seat.

Antinous, drunk though he was, thought of a clever objection. Reminding us that Apollo had once accidentally killed the boy Hyacinth with a quoit, he suggested that it would be courting death to institute a public quoit game on Apollo's own feast day. "One of us would be bound to meet Hyacinth's fate. But I cannot agree that the archery match would be tedious; and, as for precedence, we can compete in a circle, beginning from this wine jar and continuing sunwise, as the wine is served. There seems to be a sufficiency of arrows. Let

the mark be a quoit suspended from the door yonder—the
one that leads into the court of sacrifice." This meant that he
and his friends would have the first shots and, to judge from
the previous day's funeral games, the contest would degenerate
into a farce.

Clytoneus, however, allowed him to have his way, despite
my bitter protests. He took the golden case from my hands
and, unfastening the clasps, pulled the bow reverently out.
I had never, as it happened, seen it before—a terrible-looking
weapon, standing as high as a man, and consisting of what
must have been the largest pair of Cretan wild-goat's horns
ever grown, fastened together with hammered bronze. Aethon
had already examined it when he visited the storeroom, and
provided a cord of twisted flax, four times stouter than an
ordinary bowstring, with a loop at either end, and of exactly
the right length.

The horns of a living goat have a certain suppleness, but
in the course of years they harden somewhat, and after
centuries set almost as hard as a stag's antlers.

Leodes came first. Being a junior priest of Zeus, he had
presided at all the recent sacrifices, which gave him the place
of honour next to the immense jar from which the wine circu-
lated. He accepted the unstrung bow and an arrow while
Eumaeus proceeded to nail up the quoit. Then Clytoneus
shouted: "Hey, there, Philoetius, bar that door from the outside; someone might enter unexpectedly and get hurt." Philoetius went round by the passage and did so.

Posted on the threshold, Leodes addressed himself to the
bow, which he struggled to string, using both hands and
knees; but succeeded only in ricking his back. "Friends," he

groaned, "I am defeated by this adamantine weapon, and lay odds of ten to one in wine or beef that nobody else can master it. The pull is enough to break the strongest heart. Princess Nausicaa has played another trick on us."

He leant the bow against the door, propped the arrow beside it and sat down again heavily. Antinous reproached him. "What nonsense! If Philoctetes could string it, his descendants can surely do the same? I never hold with the superstition that the men of old were stronger and more courageous than ourselves. The bow is a trifle stiff, that is all; it needs warming and greasing. Just because you were born on a moonless night—blame your mother—and are consequently slack-twisted, without strength in your wrists or shoulders, and take no exercise except backgammon and cottabus . . . Very well, I propose to take up your wager: two bullocks and two wine jars against twenty that I accomplish the task! Melantheus, put a panful of hog's lard to warm at the fire; when we have greased the bow, length by length, you will see how it recovers its spring. Age freezes, lard thaws."

Melantheus obeyed, after which two or three members of Antinous's party took turns in trying to string the bow, but without the least success. I should mention here that archery is not an Elyman accomplishment; most of my suitors had never handled a war bow in their lives. Meanwhile, at a prearranged signal, Eumaeus and Philoetius went out unobtrusively by the side door. Eumaeus ran to the main gateway, where his son was waiting with an expectant group of loyal grooms and gardeners. "When you hear the sound of fighting in the hall," he said, "attack the suitors' servants and

drive them from the court of sacrifice. Make a dash and
clatter as though you were an army, and yell threats in the
King's name." Philoetius hurried to tell Eurycleia: "Lock
the maids in their quarters, and keep them there." Eumaeus
then came back through the same door, which Philoetius
made fast outside with a bar and a yard or two of Byblus
cable, before regaining the hall by way of the throne chamber.

Eurymachus now snatched the bow from Noemon's hands,
but though he turned it slowly round in the heat of the fire,
and fairly smothered it with lard, succeeded no better than the
others. "Hades curse the thing!" he cried. "Leodes was right.
It will break any heart or back."

Antinous laughed. "When I come to consider the question,"
he drawled, "to string the bow on Apollo's feast day is even
more of a mistake than to cast quoits. Hercules used this bow
for numerous extraordinary feats during his Labours, but
Apollo and he, being rival archers, were always at loggerheads. Indeed, their hostility once degenerated into an open
brawl, when Hercules had pulled the tripod from under
Apollo's priestess Herophile and carried it off to found an
oracle of his own. Father Zeus was obliged to part them with
a thunderbolt. I believe that Apollo himself has stiffened the
bow—perhaps vexed at our abandonment of his public festivities. So let us adjourn the trial until tomorrow nad propitiate
the God by sacrificing certain fat goats which Philoetius has
driven in for us. Tomorrow will not be a day of such peculiar
sanctity, and may the best man win."

Antinous was applauded for this pious and ingenious suggestion. I suppose that he had planned to take away the bow,
which was now lying on a sheepskin by the fire at some dis-

tance from the front door, and replace it next morning with a large but more manageable one.

"Apollo, Apollo, favour us!" he cried. All the wine cups and goblets were hastily filled again to the brim, and each man poured a libation to the God before draining his vessel to the lees.

At this point Aethon bent down and, clasping Clytoneus's knees, said: "A boon, my Prince! When I return home to Cyprus (may it be soon!) my friends and kinsmen will ask me: 'What have you done? What have you seen?' And after recounting my adventures in Egypt and Palestine and Libya, I hope to add: 'Then I made a voyage to Drepanum, where is stored the famous bow of Philoctetes the Phocian, which settled the Trojan War. The King's son took this wonder from its curved golden case, engraved with the Labours of Hercules, and allowed me to handle it myself.' Let me, I beg, make good this hope, although to string it will doubtless prove beyond my power, since I am not of Phocian blood, like many of your gallant friends."

This was the cue for a pretended tiff between Clytoneus and myself. When he granted Aethon's boon, I was to round on him and say: "What, let a beggarman profane that holy relic with his foul fingers? Are you picking a quarrel? Replace the bow in its case at once and lock it up in the storeroom."

Clytoneus was to shout: "I have every right to entrust this bow to whomever I please, and I resent your interference. Go to your quarters now, attend to your own work and see that the maids attend to theirs. Your task is done for today, and I am master here. Eumaeus, bring me that bow!"

We must have spoken our parts convincingly enough, because a shout of laughter arose, which increased to a roar when Eumaeus hesitantly picked up the bow and brought it across the court to Clytoneus. Clytoneus handed it to Aethon with a look of pretended defiance.

I stamped my foot and flounced out, slamming the door behind me as if in a rage.

"Someone is going to have his face scratched tonight," Ctesippus taunted, "just to show who is mistress in this Palace."

Aethon held the bow lovingly in his hands, weighing it and turning it over as though admiring its ancient workmanship. He was addressing a secret prayer to Apollo and Hercules, begging them to compose their dispute and together guide his arrows. The suitors nudged each other and grinned: "He is an expert on bows, by the look of it—collects them, no doubt, the old vagabond. Or perhaps he thinks of setting up a bow factory." Aethon said gently: "My lords, what a marvellous bow this is, unstrung! But how much more marvellous when strung!" He took the flaxen cord and with a sudden commanding gesture grasped the horn and bent it slowly and effortlessly until the loop engaged in the notch; he might have been a musician fixing a new gut to his lyre, for all the trouble it gave him. Then he sat back, twanged the string with his thumb, making it twitter like a swallow, reached for the arrow and, almost without taking aim, sent it screaming across the court at the quoit nailed against the door. It struck the exact centre of the target and the arrow tip pierced the thick oaken plank.

Then, turning to Clytoneus with an easy laugh, he said:

"Prince, I stand on your sister's promise. I strung the bow, I hit the bull's eye, I am therefore her husband. Do you acknowledge my claim?"

"I acknowledge it publicly."

"That is well. Now I have another mark to hit. A certain man present treacherously killed my fellow clansman, the noble Mentor. I am come to avenge him: blood for blood. Antinous, prepare to meet black death."

Antinous was raising a two-handled cup to his lips, when the arrow passed clean through his Adam's apple and cut through the nape of his neck. He collapsed with a spasmodic thrashing of arms and legs, upset the table and spilt the bread and meat on the floor. Blood spouted from his mouth and nose all over the good food.

A shout of dismay echoed along the cloisters, but Aethon had fitted a second arrow to the bow and sat prepared to shoot anyone who opposed him. Eurymachus gazed wildly around the cloister walls and suddenly noticed that the weapons and shields were no longer there. He quickly made up his mind, and sang out: "Friends, this Cypriot is a master archer who will kill at least four or five of us before we can arrest him. And he was within his rights to shoot Antinous, in requital of blood; we cannot deny it. Moreover, if the Princess agrees to marry this stranger, let us not stand in her way but disperse to our homes; for the Goddess Athene herself has ordained the contest."

Mixed cries of assent and protest were heard. Then Clytoneus spoke: "My lords, listen to me. Antinous has died because he killed my uncle Mentor, whom the King appointed Regent in his absence. There are still two other plain mur-

derers among you. First, Eurymachus, who stabbed my
brother Laodamas—which was the beginning of all these
troubles—and drowned his body in the sea, as his ghost complained to the Queen. Next, Ctesippus, guilty of the murder
for which my brother Halius was wrongfully banished—the
barbarous disembowelling of a fisherman. Though each of
these criminals were to surrender his whole inheritance, it
would not be sufficient requital of the wrong he has done our
house. My lords, bind them without delay, haul them before
the Council, and you will thereby free yourselves from the
charge of blood guiltiness which overhangs every person in
these cloisters. Come Agelaus, come Leodes, come Amphinomus—I address you as the three most pacific of those who
have condoned the rebellion against my father—what do you
say?"

When they made no reply, Eurymachus shouted again:
"Very well then, friends! He refuses our offer and accuses
us of rebellion, which if proved would be a capital offence.
So let us kill him at all costs and have done with it! Out
swords; use tables for shields!"

He leaped at Aethon, sword in hand, but an arrow struck
him on the right nipple and down he went, knocking over the
table and a couple of stools in his fall.

"And now for Ctesippus," yelled Clytoneus. "With his
death, we can make an end of killing."

It was too late. Amphinomus, as Eurymachus's cousin-
german, could not refrain from vengeance. Keeping close to
the wall, he rushed at Aethon, who was looking around for
Ctesippus and had exposed his back. Clytoneus, however,
saw him coming and hurled his spear. Amphinomus fell trans-

fixed but Clytoneus, left weaponless, dared not run forward to retrieve the spear, for fear of being slashed with a sword. He cupped his hand and muttered in Aethon's ear: "Keep them off while I fetch spears, shields and helmets." He darted through the front door, dragging Eumaeus with him. Philoetius followed; he pushed his way through the tables where the fuddled suitors were all at loggerheads, some calling on the others to make a concerted rush on Aethon, some recommending surrender.

Aethon yelled above the din: "Any more for Tartarus? Any more for the Styx? Walk up, walk up, my lords! Here is a fool's chance for eternal extinction. But let those who love life keep twenty paces from the bow of Philoctetes. And avoid that side door!"

A general retreat across the court ensued, and the decision might well have been for surrender, had not Eumaeus's son, roused to action by the uproar, attacked the suitors' servants in the court of sacrifice and bawled: "Good news! The King's ship is sighted. Soon he will land and take vengeance."

Noemon, driven mad by jealousy when he saw Aethon string the bow and heard him acknowledged as my husband, rallied his comrades. "We are lost," he exclaimed. "The King will make no distinction between guilty and innocent but hang us all as rebels. Quick: we must overpower this single archer even if some of us fall to his shafts. We can then threaten to burn the Palace unless the King consents to pardon us. Seize your tables, and when I say 'One, two, three!' charge!"

Noemon had not counted as far as two before an arrow flew in at his open mouth and silenced him for ever. Then

Clytoneus and Eumaeus, hurrying back with spears and
shields, took up their positions on either side of Aethon;
while Philoetius, fully armed, ran to defend the side door.

Clytoneus made a gallant effort to avoid the odium of a
massacre. "This is your last opportunity to surrender, my
lords," he cried. "If you let it slip, here are fourteen quiver-
fuls of arrows, feathered with curses of my brother Halius, to
shoot you like dogs. Step towards me, one by one, with your
hands above your heads and submit to be bound. We promise
every man his liberty except Ctesippus."

"Never," shouted Ctesippus. But Leodes lifted his delicate
hands and said: "Friends, the battle is unequal and while
Ctesippus lives we are harbouring a murderer. I urge you to
surrender; for once we are dead, there is an end of love,
honour and the joys of this world."

Agelaus had been consulting with Melantheus, who volun-
teered to fetch the arms that were so desperately needed. He
entered the Tower, jumped from a first-storey window which
gave on the street, and ran to the kitchen entrance. Bursting
in, he worked his way along a series of passages, making for
the storeroom; from which his daughter and her foolish companions helped him to drag out armfuls of spears, javelins
and shields. They hurried these to the Tower, where Agelaus
pulled them up through the window for distribution among
his clansmen. Soon with a shout of "No surrender!" twelve
armed Trojans formed a line of battle, shield to shield.

Clytoneus beat his breast. "I left the storeroom key in the
lock," he cried. "Melantheus must have gone all the way
round. Quick, Eumaeus, prevent him from fetching more!
You too, Philoetius! Aethon and I can hold the doorway until
your return."

Philoetius and Eumaeus rushed indoors and caught Melantheus paying a second visit to the storeroom. They sprang on
him, felled him, pinioned his arms and legs with a length of
cable and, throwing the free end across a beam, hauled him
high up. Then, after belaying him to a pillar, they locked the
door, pocketed the key and regained the court, leaving
Melantheus dangling impotently.

Aethon grew anxious. He had counted on inflicting such
heavy losses on the enemy that they must surrender. But now
Agelaus was shouting: "Cypriot, lay aside your bow. If you
surrender to us, I swear to spare your life and send you back
to your island with golden gifts. If you fight on you are
doomed."

A strange thing happened. A swallow came flying into the
cloisters, circled around Aethon, and perched twittering on
the lintel above his head. Aethon, who is occasionally gifted
with the power to understand the language of birds, recognized the ghost of Mentor, promising him victory in Athene's
name.

The enemy advanced across the court and Aethon rapidly
shot three of them in the feet, so that they shrieked for pain
and let fall their weapons. Nevertheless, the mass of Phocaean
swordsmen sheltering behind the wall of Trojan shields swept
forward, and a ragged volley of spears flew at the defenders
of the door. All missed their mark, whereas Aethon's arrows,
and a return volley of spears carefully aimed, accounted for
three of the enemy, including Demoptolemus. Yet the charge
was not broken; on they came. Philoetius had the good fortune
to kill Ctesippus with a spear-thrust in the belly. "Payment
for the heifer's heel," he bawled.

In desperate fighting Aethon dealt Agelaus a blow of his naked fist which shattered his temple; and Clytoneus transfixed Leiocritus. The enemy wavered. Aethon raised a Cretan shout of triumph and they turned to flee. Leodes, who had behaved more correctly than most of my suitors, tried to surrender by clasping Aethon's knees. "Too late," said Aethon, striking off his head with the sword that Agelaus had dropped.

Had Procne not been beside me, I should scarcely have been able to bear the suspense; in emergencies no girl equals Procne. I swore to have her chosen as Athene's new priestess. All this while we were craning our heads out of my window. The cloister roof prevented us from seeing Aethon and Clytoneus, and we could not even be sure that they were still alive and unwounded. But when our champions went charging across the open court in full view, Procne and I gave thanks to Athene for the completeness of our victory. We watched them ruthlessly despatch the suitors, using swords now, drawn from the scabbards of the dead.

"No quarter!" cried Aethon. Suddenly my heart chilled, because among the twenty or thirty wretched, fuddled, helpless men I distinguished Phemius the minstrel, his lyre slung over his shoulder, distraught with fear and battering at the side door. He evidently wanted to escape and take sanctuary at the Great Altar. But finding no egress he cast his eyes wildly about him; and saw me.

"Save me, Princess," he shrieked. "The murder of a Son of Homer on Apollo's own feast day would curse this house until the seventh generation."

He was right. I screamed at Clytoneus and Aethon to pro-

tect Phemius; Clytoneus shook his head wilfully, Aethon did
not even look my way. Scrambling out of the window, I slid
down the cloister roof and dropped on all fours to the court
below. The corpse of Noemon broke my fall. Picking myself
up, I sprang in front of Phemius, and spread my arms wide.
Aethon came bounding towards us, drunk with blood lust.
"Aethon, beware!" This time my scream dispelled his trance.
He flung away sword and shield, fell at my feet, and worshipped me as though I were a goddess; while the other three
methodically continued their horrid task of hunting down
fugitives and cutting the throats of the wounded.

CHAPTER SIXTEEN HOMER'S DAUGHTER

I T WAS BY THE GREATEST GOOD FORTUNE that we not only saved the life of Phemius but also escaped the infamy of killing Medon the herald, which would, incidentally, have earned us the undying hatred of his patron, the God Hermes. Medon had rolled himself inside the ox skin that had served Aethon and me for our nuptial couch and was lying under the wreck of an inlaid settle. Clytoneus recognized the feathered shoes and extricated Medon, who had been his tutor and always treated him kindly. So he and Phemius were escorted to the court of sacrifice, where they sat cowering at the Great Altar, while we searched the cloisters and Tower for concealed fugitives but found none. The last survivor was one Elpenor, who had gone to sleep off his liquor at the top of the Tower.

Hearing the shouts of our men as they mounted the stairs, he started up in fright, toppled over the wall into the cobbled street and died instantly. It appeared, therefore, that we had accounted for every one of my hundred and twelve suitors, except the prudent Theoclymenus; and we checked this afterwards by counting the corpses. Pontonous had been killed too, for siding with the enemy. It was difficult to believe that our men had not been wounded in a score of places, so bloodspattered were they from helmet to shoe; but all proved to be quite uninjured—if one discounts Clytoneus's bruised wrist and Eumaeus's scratched shoulder. The dead lay in heaps, like fish emptied out of a net on the sand, no longer even gasping beneath the cruel rays of the sun.

"Well, they were warned," I said, protruding my Aegadean underlip in a grimace. "They were warned repeatedly." What else was there to say? Yet my mother had used the same words only the day before when little Telegonus and two of his playmates teased Argus once too often and got nipped in the legs. I laughed aloud at the inadequacy of language. Clytoneus laughed too, Aethon joined in, and we were soon giggling, as hysterical girls giggle, and saying with mock solemnity: "Well, they were warned—repeatedly."

I looked round the court at the broken stools, settles and tables, the spilt food, the stained purple cloths, the sprawled corpses.

"We must ask Eurycleia to send some maids along," I said. "The place needs tidying up,"—which set us off again roaring and wheezing and sobbing with laughter.

"Perhaps we ought to confess that we have broken a few things," Clytoneus added, between gasps. This seemed the best joke of all at the time, though it does not sound very funny now.

At last I pulled myself together and went to find my mother. For once she was not working and tears were rolling down her cheeks. "Poor, foolish boys," she said. "They never knew when to stop. And fully half of them were loyal to our house, there's the pity. The trouble was that they had no manners, but then hardly anyone has good manners these days. I blame their mothers more than anyone else."

"What are we to do with Melantho and the other maids who fetched those arms, Mother?"

"Get their names from Eurycleia, and when they have cleaned the cloisters and scrubbed the furniture, Clytoneus had better take them away somewhere and chop them to pieces. I see no reason why they should continue to live."

"Surely we could sell them in the Phoenician slave market?"

"That is just what your dear father would have said: disguising a soft heart behind mercantile interest. No, child: the men died to appease the ghosts of your brother and your uncle. The women must die to appease the ghost of Ctimene. We do royal justice here."

Eumaeus and Philoetius visited the storeroom to lower Melantheus and hack at him with sharp knives, lopping off first nose, then ears, then hands, then feet, until they had trimmed him like an apple tree in January. Meanwhile Aethon, Clytoneus, and the gardeners, led by Eumaeus's son, carried out the corpses. Being our own fellow countrymen, they were not despoiled, but propped in neat rows against the porch of the main gateway. A few, who proved to be still breathing, Eumaeus's son knocked on the head with his club. When Eurycleia ventured in to view the slaughter she raised a shrill shout of triumph. Aethon silenced her. "It is unlucky to exult over the dead, old woman, however infamous their behaviour may have been. Ghosts are thick about this court. When we have cleared away the blood, bring quantities of sulphur and burn it on the fire to drive them away."

The guilty maids had trooped in behind Eurycleia, terror-stricken because they read their fate in Clytoneus's eyes. He made them help the gardeners to carry out the dead, and afterwards wash down the tables, stools and settles with sponges, swab the cloister pavement and put the purple covers to soak in a trough. The blood, which coloured the stamped earth of the courts, was scraped off with spades, and the basketfuls of scrapings removed by the gardeners. Next, there was the court of sacrifice to clean: Eumaeus's son and his helpers had clubbed the servants to death there for fear they might escape and raise the alarm. Nothing is so fertile as blood—we always save the washings of the sacrificial altar—and the pailfuls of dark red water drunk that day by the quinces and pomegranates were acknowledged three months later in a bumper crop of fruit.

Clytoneus could not face the task of butchering the maids; being as yet a virgin he retained a natural awe of women's flesh, and ours were all very good-looking girls. Besides, he had been on joking terms with three or four of them. "Aethon, kill them for me!" he begged.

"The Queen ordered you to do so."

"I dare not disobey my mother; but neither can I shed a woman's blood."

"Then hang them and tell her that you considered death by the sword too honourable a fate for them."

"I prefer to plead a bruised wrist, which prevents me from further swordplay."

Clytoneus pinioned the maids, led them into the outer court, tied a noose at one end of a ship's cable, and forced each in turn to subject her head to it. The other end of the cable, rubbed with hog's lard, had been thrown across the roof ridge of my father's vaulted chamber. At a signal from Clytoneus, Philoetius and their comrades hauled the rope tight, digging their heels into the earth, until the victim was slowly raised off the ground. When her face grew black, she was allowed to drop and another woman suffered the same fate.

I lacked the curiosity or savagery to watch the scene, but saw Clytoneus coming out of the garden, where he had just vomited his dinner. He was still white-faced and retching.

"They kicked," he said, in a whisper, "but not for long."

"Are you unwell?"

"No, the fumes of sulphur as I passed through the banqueting court turned my stomach."

I gave him a drink of cordial wine, flavoured with pepperment, and some dry bread to munch, and after a good wash and a change of tunic he felt better. Aethon presently appeared, fresh from his bath, wearing his wedding garments with the air of an immortal god. He was himself again and took me affectionately by the arm.

"Let us consult the Queen," he suggested, "before carrying our war further. She will know what we must do next."

My mother smiled for joy to see us. "Well, children," she said, "now that our family ghosts have drunk enough blood to content them, we may as well complete the wedding. I notice that both of you are appropriately dressed, and we cannot afford to vex Aphrodite or flout public opinion by omitting the instrumental music and the dances. So fetch Phemius, and tell him to tune his lyre; and everyone must put on his holiday clothes."

Clytoneus protested: "No, no, Mother. By this time the news of the massacre must have reached the town and we shall have another battle to fight almost immediately."

But Eumaeus had posted men along the road and behind the orchard to prevent anybody from leaving the Palace or approaching it; even Theoclymenus had been detained.

We performed our wedding dance, men and women all together, in the court of sacrifice—I gave orders for the removal of the hanged maids—well content to find it our own once more. Eurymedusa and Procne played flutes and Phemius twanged the lyre as loudly as he could, and the noise of the Hymenaeus reached the market place and the docks. "Aha!" remarked sail patcher to net mender. "What is the betting that in the end she married Antinous? They say that he brought the best bride gift, and Princess Nausicaa thinks of nothing but treasure; just like her father."

When the dance was done and we had refreshed ourselves with wine and cakes, Clytoneus made a still more urgent protest: "Kinsmen and friends, if we stay here we shall be forced to stand a siege. Do not deceive yourselves: we fought at an advantage today, and the Gods assisted us. But their continued favour is not to be relied upon, nor can the Palace be defended by a dozen men against the entire town militia. They will soon set the main building alight with fire arrows and smoke us out. While there is yet time, let us escape to

Eumaeus's farm, where we can fend them off until the King marches to our relief."

"I remain where I am," said my mother sternly, "and forbid any of you to desert me. We have behaved most correctly ever since the King sailed, and need not apologize to our enemies for what has happened. Medon, hurry to the town and summon the Council. Say that Prince Clytoneus has an urgent message to deliver and is following close behind you. Clytoneus, accompany Aethon to the Temple of Poseidon, and allow Medon to speak on your behalf. He should announce briefly that because of the Council's refusal to take action you have been obliged to eject your sister's suitors from the Palace, and that large numbers of them have been seriously injured, and some killed, including the new Regent appointed by the Council. Let him add that your cousin Aethon the Cretan, now your brother-in-law, has landed unexpectedly and brought you armed help. They will conclude that Aethon was sent by your father at the head of a powerful force of Cretan mercenaries. If they are as cowardly as I suppose, you will be treated with unexceptionable politeness. Medon may then invite them to claim their dead, but without mentioning that there are no survivors."

She was obeyed. Medon's speech terrified and amazed every councillor present except Halitherses, who asked simply: "My lords, did I not warn you?" Aethon and Clytoneus returned unmolested to the Palace. They had no sooner gone, however, than Eupeithes, Antinous's father, voted that the town militia should arm themselves forthwith and muster in companies; he himself would lead them against the Cretan invaders.

The militia came marching up the road, nearly three hundred strong; but when they reached the main gateway and saw the extent of the slaughter, a universal groan arose and they halted in dismay. Our small force was marshalled just inside the court of sacrifice and by Aethon's orders stood silent and immobile, shield to shield, as if an outpost of a large army.

When Eupeithes recognized Antinous's corpse by its rich clothes, rage distorted his features. He brandished a sword and swore everlasting vengeance on our house. I was watching from the flat roof of the Tower beside my mother and my grandfather Phytalus, who, to be in fashion, had crammed a helmet on his bald head and taken a spear from the spear stand. Though over seventy years of age and plagued by rheumatism, he had been a fine soldier once. "Great Athene, guide my shaft," he prayed, and hurled it down with all the strength of his trembling right arm. The Tower is three storeys high and the spear gathered such momentum before it struck Eupeithes on the bronze cheek guard that the blade drove right through his head and killed him on the spot.

My mother, unfortunately, missed this glorious feat of her old father. She stood gazing out to sea, her eyes shining like stars. "Look, look, dearest child!" she cried, and grabbed my wrist. "Heaven is gracious: we are saved. Look, Elymans— two miles or less away! Do you not know the striped sail? It is your King come to restore order and approve our actions."

Yes: it was my father's ship; followed by an Elyman thirty-oarer and an Elyman fifty-oarer. The militia, on the advice of Medon, decided not to engage our supposedly enormous forces; but took up the dead and carried them in silence back to the town, using spears for stretchers.

My father's ship, under oars, had nearly threaded the
Straits of Motya on the homeward voyage when Antinous's
fifty-oarer ambushed her; and the fight was going against our
people until the thirty-oarer came bowling down the wind
and took the enemy in the rear. This was Noemon's ship, detained at Minoa by Halius, and Halius himself was in her with
the pick of his Sicel men-at-arms. I cannot recall the details
of the dingdong battle that ensued. My father had already
been knocked senseless and flung into the water. Halius dived
to his rescue. "May the Immortal Gods bless you, stranger,
whoever you may be," muttered my father, as soon as he recovered consciousness, grasping the hand of the Sicel chief-
tain who bent over him with solicitude. Thus he unwittingly
annulled the unjust curse that he had laid upon his eldest
son, and soon they disembarked and sacrificed side by side to
Athene the Uniter.

As the vessels drew alongside the quay, a crowd of working people ran to greet my father with cries of delight but no
single nobleman showed his face, which surprised him. Suddenly a huge wailing rose from beyond the town gates where
the dead had been carried for burning on a common pyre.
He reached the Palace in profound anxiety without in the
least knowing what to expect; but we had observed his approach from the Tower and sent Clytoneus and Aethon
forward to reassure him.

"Father," said Clytoneus, "we have preserved the honour
of the house."

"Well done, lad! And who is this?" asked my father, looking suspiciously at Aethon.

"Nausicaa's husband, Lord Aethon of Tarrha."

He flushed angrily. "Indeed, and who married her to him without my consent?"

"I did, for necessity's sake. The Queen and the Regent had given their warm approval."

"Ha! And the bride price?"

"A goat's haggis, Father. And several gallons of blood."

He lifted his hand to strike Clytoneus but, glancing at Halius, thought better of it and said in level tones: "I cannot solve that riddle, my son. Where is Mentor?"

"Dead."

"Dead, you say?"

"Dead, buried, bloodily avenged by your son-in-law."

My mother then came up, pressed Halius to her bosom and took my father and him for a walk along the road, explaining drily and carefully as they went all that had happened. Since the tale came from her, they believed it, thought it seemed incredible that one man, a boy and two grey-haired servants should between them have accounted for over nine dozen young Elyman swordsmen.

My father's greeting to me was brief and generous: "Daughter, you did well to delay your choice, having found a husband so acceptable to me."

Never before had my father acknowledged himself in the wrong; and I improved the occasion by saying: "Mother, have you told Halius that the honour of killing the rogue who falsely accused him of murder went to old Philoetius?"

My father kissed me. "Child," he sighed, "if you knew how cruelly I punished myself by banishing your brother in what I thought to be the interests of justice, you would not taunt me."

That night at supper he said: "My son Aethon, you and Clytoneus have raised a difficult point of law by this massacre of my rebellious subjects. When a man kills a fellow citizen, he is outlawed for a period of years and seldom ventures to return. For you two have together destroyed one hundred and eleven of your fellow citizens. Either outlawry is too light a punishment for the crime, and you therefore deserve to die like villains, or else you deserve olive crowns for having brought peace to this distracted kingdom and set an example of confidence in the Just Gods. I shall sleep on the problem, if you permit me, and deliver my verdict in the morning; as Alcinous of Drepane did in the song."

Aethon turned to my mother. "Queen Arete," he said smiling, "soften his heart towards us again!"

It proved to be the olive crown, not the hangman's noose; and at Halius's suggestion my father concluded a defensive alliance with the King of Minoa, which greatly strengthened his throne; and to give no cause for grumbling, he sent back the bride gifts to the families of the dead suitors. Nor did he exact the fourfold payment due on account of the beasts slaughtered and the wine drunk, but a simple fee of beast for beast, and pint for pint; with a return of the purloined cups, and of the treasures which Eurymachus had stolen from Laodamas's bundle. We found Laodamas's corpse when we dragged the harbour and, as his ghost had told my mother, the hilt of a dagger stood out between the shoulder blades. He was wrapped in the missing sails, wound about with the missing cordage, and weighted down with stones.

When our daily routine was something like normal again, I took Phemius aside. "Phemius," I asked, "what payment are you prepared to make for the new spell of life I gave you?"

"I had been wondering when I should have to answer that question," he said. "The answer is: I accept the price you name, though I fear it will be a high one."

"For so valuable a life it must be exceptionally high. Besides, I might have been killed myself in saving you. Come then, it is as follows. Since you are a Son of Homer and your guild alone is privileged to perform in the courts of Greece, I demand that you shall approve, sing and circulate an epic poem of my own composition on which I am already working and which, if Athene continues to inspire me, I shall finish within two or three years. It begins with the opening verses of *The Return of Odysseus,* as far as his visit to the Lotus-eaters. After that the story will be different. Probably it will include the adventures of Ulysses (whom some believe to have been Odysseus) and end with the massacre of Penelope's lovers. I have a fair notion now how Odysseus managed it singlehanded. The *Iliad,* which I admire, is devised by a man for men; this epic, *The Odyssey,* will be devised by a woman for women. Understand that I am Homer's latest born child, a daughter; and listen attentively. When I have finished the poem, and written it out in cuttlefish ink on sheepskin, you must memorize it, and (if necessary) improve the language where it halts or flags. One day I shall send you back to Delos and you will carry my poem to all the courts of Asia. When princes and princesses—but especially princesses—praise it and heap gifts on you, asking: 'Phemius, golden-mouthed minstrel, where did you learn that glorious story?' you must answer: 'My ancestor's songs are highly esteemed by the

Elymans, who live at the far western fringe of the civilized world; and it was at the Elyman court that I learned this *Odyssey*.' I shall be careful to include nothing that might betray the land of its origin, though immortalizing my own name and Aethon's and yours in the course of the story."

"But if I refuse, Princess?"

"Then you may expect a worse fate than Melantheus. Be wise: take your oath by Athene and by Apollo."

Eventually he swore: perhaps because he thought me incapable of completing the immense labour which I had set myself. As though I ever fail in any of my undertakings!

I must confess that Phemius behaved very well when, a couple of years later, I presented him with a manuscript of more than twelve thousand lines—not written on sheepskin but on scrolls of Egyptian papyrus which Aethon won in his glorious sack of Canopus. After all, Phemius is a professional bard and I am a mere interloper and a woman; and we had several serious tiffs while I was composing it. However, I let him have his way sometimes when he protested that this verse or that was faulty. But not always.

He hated me to borrow passages from the *Iliad* for what he considered improper contexts, and he grew furious to find that Homer's lines about the water being heated to wash Patroclus's dead body were now used to describe the warm bath prepared for Odysseus, and that I had put part of Hector's farewell speech to Andromache into Telemachus's mouth, when he forbids his mother to meddle in men's affairs. Phemius called me heartless to treat any passage so tragic as the first, or so moving as the second, with such disrespect.

"I am heartless, eh?" I countered, my eyes blazing. "In that case you had better behave a little more subserviently or you will find yourself sold to an upland farmer. Do you like gruel and skim milk and rags?" He drew in his horns, which are tender, and tears ran down his plump cheeks. It was a ridiculous threat, of course, and if I had made it to a man like Demodocus he would have laughed in my face.

Yet I admire Phemius, who helped me to smooth out incidents in which the Goddess Athene had not been particularly helpful.

For safety's sake, on his advice, I have consigned to oblivion all the names of my living characters, giving them pseudonyms—as I also do here, with only four exceptions. I retain my own as a personal signature; Phemius retains his as a reward for the collaboration; I allow Odysseus to call himself "Aethon son of Castor" and tell Aethon's life story in one of his many fictions; and (as I decided halfway through the poem) Eurycleia deserves to be immortalized for urging Aethon and me to marry. Our most heated argument concerned the preponderance of women in my epic and Athene's ubiquity, and the precedence given to famous women when Odysseus meets the ghosts of the departed. I had mentioned only Tyro, Antiope, Alcmene, Jocasta, Chloris, Leda, Iphimedeia, Phaedra, Procris, Ariadne, Maera, Clymene and, naturally, Eriphyle, and let Odysseus describe them to Alcinous. "My dear Princess," said Phemius, "if you really think that you can pass off this poem as the work of a man, you deceive yourself. A man would give pride of place to the ghosts of Agamemnon, Achilles, Ajax, Odysseus's old comrades, and other more ancient heroes such as Minos,

Orion, Tityus, Salmoneus, Tantalus, Sisyphus and Hercules; and mention their wives and mothers incidentally, if at all; and make at least one god help Odysseus at some stage or other."

I admitted the force of his argument, which explains why, now, Odysseus first meets a comrade who has fallen off a roof at Circe's house—I call him Elpenor—and cracks a mild joke about Elpenor's having come more quickly to the Grove of Persephone by land than he by sea. I also allow Alcinous to ask after Agamemnon, Achilles and the rest, and Odysseus to satisfy his curiosity. For Phemius's sake I have even let Hermes supply the moly in passages adapted from my uncle Mentor's story of Ulysses. In my original version I had given all the credit to Athene.

While altering the saga of *Odysseus's Return* to make my Elyman suitors serve as Penelope's lovers, I had to protect myself against scandal. What if someone recognized the story and supposed that I, Nausicaa the irreproachable, had played the promiscuous harlot in my father's absence? So, according to my poem, Penelope must have remained faithful to Odysseus throughout those twenty years. And because this change meant that Aphrodite had failed to take her traditional revenge, I must make Poseidon, not her, the enemy who delayed him on his homeward voyage after the Fall of Troy. I should therefore have to omit the stories of Penelope's banishment and the oar mistaken for a flail, and Odysseus's death from Telemachus's sting-ray spear. When I told Phemius of these decisions, he pointed out, rather nastily, that since Poseidon had fought for the Greeks against the Trojans, and since Odysseus had never failed to honour him, I must

justify this enmity by some anecdote. "Very well," I answered. "Odysseus blinded a Cyclops who, happening to be
Poseidon's son, prayed to him for vengeance."

"My dear Princess, every Cyclops in the smithies of Etna
was born to Uranus, Poseidon's grandfather, by Mother
Earth."

"Mine was an exceptional Cyclops," I snapped. "He
claimed Poseidon as his father and kept sheep in a Sican cave,
like Conturanus. I shall call him Polyphemus—that is,
'famous'—to make my hearers think him a more important
character than he really was."

"Such deceptions tangle the web of poetry."

"But if I offer Penelope as a shining example for wives to
follow when their husbands are absent on long journeys, that
will excuse the deception."

Admittedly, I made several stupid mistakes which I wish
could be amended: for instance, when I composed the story of
Odysseus's escape from Polyphemus the Cyclops, I put a
rudder at the prow of his ship as well as at the stern. This
was because, misled by the equestrian metaphor "turning her
head about," frequently used by our sailors, I presumed a
prow-rudder, which I had never noticed. And I have since
discovered that one cannot cut seasoned timber from a growing tree as Odysseus does in Ogygia, and that hawks do not
eat their prey on the wing, even in prodigies, and that it
takes more than two or three men to hang a dozen women
simultaneously from the same rope. Alas, a verse once sent on
its travels can never be overtaken or recalled; nor can I
fairly blame Phemius for not pointing out these mistakes to
me. They all occur in passages which he criticized on other

grounds, and I had threatened him with a diet of bread and water if he changed a single word of them.

I also got into difficulties by first calling Eurycleia "Eurynome" and then forgetting and using her real name; so that later on I had to pretend that there were two of her. And I forgot, in my account of the massacre, that Penelope's lovers—whom I make her suitors because the legend, as Phemius used to tell it, disgusts any decent audience—could have armed themselves with the twelve long axes through which Odysseus shot, and used them as maces to hack him and his men in little pieces. But Homer, I am sure, went equally wrong at times, and I flatter myself that my story is interesting enough to blind Phemius's listeners to its faults, even if he has a cold, or the banquet is badly cooked, or the good dark wine runs short.